GRAND MASTER

Demons, book 3

By Marina Simcoe

To My Captain

Grand Master

Chapter 1

CLUTCHING THE CURTAIN in my sweaty hand, I stared out at the dark street. The streetlight in front of my apartment building was broken. Again. And the only illumination came from some distant storefronts and the lit windows of our complex.

All the lights in my apartment were off on purpose—standing in a brightly lit window made me feel too exposed and somehow more vulnerable.

Nobody is forcing you to go ahead with this.

I inhaled, attempting to calm the nerves that tied my stomach into a quivering mess.

It was true. No one made me stand here, wearing a tight black dress and a pair of 'hooker' boots, waiting for a vehicle to arrive and take me some place unknown, to entertain a group of men I'd never met.

No one was forcing me except for my insatiable appetite for adventure that my mum lamented would be the cause of my untimely demise one day.

Maybe this was the day she always worried about?

As the youngest of five children and the only girl, I was definitely spoilt growing up. But having four older brothers made me want to keep up with them in everything or die trying. Whatever sport any one of them played, I had to play too. And I needed to excel at it, no matter what it took.

Always chasing another adrenaline rush, I'd tried every extreme activity I could—skydiving, bungee jumping, swimming with sharks, and surfing in the potentially neck-breaking waves in the ocean.

I grew up fearless.

Dreaming of one day becoming a spy, I begged my parents for a Russian tutor when I was seven and diligently learned it along with other languages taught in school.

The spying dream had disappeared by university, but not the hope for international adventure. Believing that learning languages would help when traveling, I kept taking French and Russian classes in addition to earning my degree in international business. Never in a million years would I have guessed that by the age of thirty, I'd end up in an ordinary office job.

Well, my job was with an international communications company, in their subsidiary in Minsk, Belarus, and my job as manager of public relations included organizing events and socializing. I did get to meet a variety of people, from pop stars to government officials and business moguls. Still fun and fairly exotic for someone born and raised on the east coast of Australia.

During one such event—a late night party in a restaurant with a number of clients and local politicians—I stepped outside to get some fresh air.

The opinion of Belorussian officials on sexual harassment was not quite on the same level as that of the West. I often found myself educating many of them on proper workplace etiquette. It became even more necessary at parties like this one, where alcohol was involved.

After having fought off the advances of yet another middle-aged bastard in power with grabby hands and a trophy wife sitting forlornly at home, I needed a break and stepped outside. Sucking in the crisp night air, I leaned against the restaurant's wall, a few feet away from a young woman smoking a cigarette.

Everyone seemed to smoke in this country—that wasn't what brought my attention to her. Neither was it her short skirt and mile-high heels or the way she glanced up and down the street, scanning every single passing car. She looked and acted very much like a prostitute waiting for a client, which wasn't unusual for this place or time of the night.

What made me watch her with more than simple curiosity were the obvious signs of extreme nervousness. Her trembling fingers all but crushed the cigarette with every long inhale she took. She rubbed her upper arms through her cheap pleather jacket as if chasing the chills away.

I didn't think she was drunk or stoned, but she swayed in her stiletto boots, as if she would pass out any minute.

"*S vami vse v poryadke?—Is everything okay with you?*" I did not speak Belorussian, but people mostly spoke Russian here anyway so I threw it out there.

To be honest, I didn't expect a response beyond maybe a suspicious glare from her. The girl didn't appear to be in the mood for a friendly chat. Besides, I'd learned early on that people preferred to keep to themselves in this part of the world, not being particularly keen on conversations with strangers on the street.

She swore under her breath and indeed threw me a glare. Then, as if having reconsidered, she turned my way.

"Listen. I'm really not sure what I'm getting myself into." She tossed the unfinished cigarette on the pavement and crushed it under her foot, only to get another one from her purse immediately after. "I'm scared."

"What do you mean? I can get you a taxi," I offered. "Do you need a ride home?"

She shook her head so energetically it appeared to be in danger of falling off.

"No fucking way. I could never say 'no' to the kind of money they're paying."

"Is it enough to risk your life?" I didn't need to know the details to guess that whatever she was up to might be dangerous.

She attempted to light the cigarette and failed—her fingers shook too much. Her body vibrated with a choked laugh.

"My life isn't worth much."

Without thinking, I reached over to move a strand of blond hair away from the lighter, lest she set herself on fire. She jerked her head away from my touch, her eyes narrowed at me.

"Who are you? Are you a tourist? You speak with an accent."

"My name's Jade. I'm here with the party." I tipped my head towards the restaurant door behind us.

"Are you from England?"

"No, Australia." Not prepared to reveal more about myself, I changed the subject back to the issue at hand. "I mean it, I'll pay for a taxi to take you home."

She shook her head again and tossed the unlit cigarette back in her clutch then took a mobile phone out instead.

"Can I get your phone number?" She asked out of the blue.

"What for?" I took a step back.

"Here." She shoved the phone with the picture of a sombre teenager in my face. "This is my sister. Her name is Sveta." She gave me one long, assessing look then exhaled sharply as if having made a decision. "I'll give you my home number. Can you call tomorrow morning? If she picks it up instead of me, can you tell her that I won't be coming home? Ever."

The harsh reality of life was often more brutal in some parts of the world than in others. The grim determination with which this girl seemed to have accepted the fact that she might not make it through the night was soul-crushing. Yet I knew that if I were able to talk her into going home right now, she'd most likely be out here again the very next night.

"Should I call the *Militsya* instead, maybe?" I asked softly.

"What's the point? They'd do nothing."

Sadly, there was a good chance she was correct on that one. The local law enforcement seemed to be rather selective in their response. Besides, she sounded like someone who spoke from experience.

"So, you didn't tell your sister where you're going?"

"No. She is thirteen. The less she knows the better. Besides, she wouldn't have let me go if she knew." She moved from foot to foot and anxiously glanced down the street again. Her eyes widened at the sight of the black car turning around the corner. "They're here. Quickly! Copy her number."

Hurriedly, she shoved her phone my way again, and I promptly copied the numbers from her screen to my phone as the car approached.

"So, you'll call her then?" Her eyes flickered to my face, the glimmer of desperation made my heart ache.

"I'll talk to *you* in the morning."

"Promise you'll call," she demanded.

"I will."

With a nod, she stuffed her phone back inside her shiny clutch.

The car pulled up in front of us and the back door opened, as if on its own.

She took a few hesitant steps towards it. Her shoulders hunched as she ventured a nervous peek into the darkness of the interior, then threw a quick glance over her shoulder at me.

"My name is Tanya," she said quietly before getting into the car.

The door closed almost immediately, and the vehicle drove off into the night.

My phone still in my hand, I quickly took a picture of its licence plate. If something happened to her, I vowed Tanya would get justice, even if she didn't believe that her life was worth it.

Chapter 2

THE PARTY LASTED LONGER than usual, and I didn't make it back to my apartment until the early hours of the morning.

Showered and changed into my lacy nightshirt, I climbed under the covers. However, sleep didn't come easily. The image of Tanya's haunted eyes wouldn't leave my mind.

Tossing and turning for what felt like an eternity, I finally got out of bed.

What time would a working girl normally come home? I had no idea of the exact hours they kept, but now I really wished I knew.

Finally at sunrise, I couldn't wait any longer. If something bad really happened to Tanya, it was best to wake her sister now, when there might still be hope of doing something about it.

"Allo," a girly voice I didn't recognize right away answered my call.

"Sveta?"

"No, it's Tanya. Jade? Is that you?"

A feeling of overwhelming relief flooded me. "Tanya? You're home? Please tell me you're okay."

"I'm okay," she said with a little laugh, her voice hushed. "My sister's still asleep. I don't want to wake her up, but Jade, I made a ton of money last night."

I sighed. *No money is worth risking your safety.* But who was I to tell her that? I knew nothing about her life or about what this money might represent to her. Another month of rent for a place for her and her sister? A few weeks' worth of groceries?

"How are you?" I asked instead. "What happened?"

"I'm fine. Honestly." She giggled. The happy sound made her seem much younger than her age, whatever it was. "They didn't do much. I didn't even get to see their faces—they blindfolded me. I don't know how many there were, but I'm fairly sure it was only one who touched me."

"He touched you?" It was to be expected, considering the nature of the business Tanya was in. Still, her words caused a response in me I couldn't name. Unease? Curiosity? "And you have no idea who he was?"

"No."

Personally, I was no prude and considered myself to be in touch with my sexuality. Granted, I'd never done it for money, but I'd had a number of partners during my life. Some of them happened to be more adventurous than others. And a few even agreed to fulfil a number of wild fantasies with me. The problem was that nothing ever seemed to be enough for me. My satisfaction never lasted for long.

Over the years, I had tried every possible position under the sun, used a multitude of toys, and even had a threesome. On the suggestion of my boyfriend at the time, I allowed another woman into our bed. It turned out to be a disaster, as it quickly became apparent the boyfriend was more interested in her than me at that point.

Maybe I should have invited an extra man instead, or even better—two completely different men instead of my arsehole ex.

"How was it?" I heard myself asking. The question surprised me. Did I really need to hear the details of a night in the life of a call girl? However, something about her cheerful voice—along with the images of several men and a blindfold—made my heart speed up and my curiosity spike.

"Honestly? Wonderful!" she replied, obviously eager to share her excitement with anyone, even a complete stranger like myself. "You wouldn't believe it, Jade, but I actually came. Twice! That has never happened before."

"You never had an orgasm before?"

"Well, not on the job. Are you kidding me? Most clients are complete asses, one way or another. But guess what? I don't need to keep any of my old clients. These guys offered me a contract. I'll come to see them once a week, and they pay me as much as they did today. Every time. Can you believe it?" She giggled again. "I won't have to worry about rent or food ever again. Hell, I may even save enough for that computer course for Svetka. She is a smart kid, you know."

"Why are they paying you so much?" I hated to rain on her parade, but some questions needed to be asked.

For some reason, I cared about this girl and her wellbeing from the get-go, and now I was afraid she might be getting herself into something treacherous without even realising the threat.

"Fuck if I know." She chuckled softly. "There really isn't anything special about me. But I'm not going to worry about it, Jade, as long as they pay my bills."

OVER THE NEXT FEW WEEKS, I talked to Tanya often. I even had her sister Sveta, whom she called 'Svetka' or 'malaya,' meaning *the kid*, over at my place a few times overnight when Tanya went to work for the mysterious men.

Over time, she told me more about them. She claimed she only got to see one of them. But even *his* face was always obscured by the hood of the grey robe he wore. He sat in the back of the car with her on the way there, but never touched her, never so much as leaned her way, unless it was to put the blindfold on her.

Each night Tanya had a chance to set the rules before anything started, choosing how it all would go. Then, naked and restrained, she was brought to orgasm, sometimes multiple times through the night.

There was definitely something dangerous about being whisked away in a car by a stranger. However, as Tanya assured me, there was no actual threat. The man was always polite to a fault with her, and she was never hurt in any way.

Even after multiple visits, she couldn't explain the ultimate purpose of the proceedings. Blindfolded, she never saw a thing.

"For all I know, a whole bunch of them may be sitting there jerking off," she replied with a shrug when I had asked her. "Except that I never hear anything either. Maybe they're behind soundproof glass?"

The mystery shrouding her weekly visits, only made my curiosity burn brighter.

Chapter 3

"BUT WHAT IF THEY CANCEL my contract over this?" Tanya's voice was panicked through bouts of raspy coughing. "What if they end up getting someone else for Thursday nights? I'm sure a thousand girls would die to have this gig!"

The sad part was that Tanya was probably right, there'd be plenty of girls willing to fill her shoes.

"But, sweetie, you said you're running a fever close to forty. You simply can't do it in your condition. Maybe they can move it by a few days until you get better?"

Tanya's employers seemed to be rather punctual about having her there weekly. But I didn't need to see Tanya to know from her cough and the sound of her voice that she needed to stay in bed tonight.

"Ugh!" She groaned. "Why did this have to happen to me?"

"Everyone gets sick once in a while. Call them, they should be understanding about this."

"But what if they fire me?" she whined. "Replace me with someone else? Wait!" She blew her nose loudly. "What if I had my own replacement for tonight?"

"What do you mean?"

"Jade, I have to do *something* to make sure I keep my time slot with them. What if I found a girl to fill in for me, just for tonight? Someone who wouldn't be after my job in the long run?"

"Okay, that might work."

"Jade?" Something in her voice made me snap to attention. "Any chance you could do it?"

"Me?" I nearly choked on the air in my apartment.

"Listen," she continued hurriedly. "These guys are really nice."

"You can't be absolutely sure—you've never even seen their faces."

"That's the best part. *You* won't have to see them. No one even needs to know your name. You'd be wearing a blindfold, so even if they videotape you—"

"Videotape?"

"I'm not saying that's what they do," she backtracked quickly. "Actually, I'm sure that's not what it's about. Otherwise, why would they do the same thing to me over and over again? Wouldn't they go for some variety if they recorded porn or something?"

"That's not the point, Tanya." I steered away from the argument about how *nice* these men were or how varied their possible video-tape collection might be. "I have a job—"

"Well, if taking money makes you all weirded out," she replied, her tone flat, "you can do it for free."

"Again, this is not the point. I just can't do it."

"Sure you can, Jade. There is nothing you *can't* do. There're just things you haven't done yet."

Obviously, she had learned enough about me by now to know exactly what buttons to push.

"I've seen your face when I tell you about them," Tanya went on. "You're curious. Here is your chance to find out for yourself what it's like."

I sighed and said nothing, her words swirling through my mind. Not that I was going to agree, of course not, but . . .

"It's not dangerous," Tanya added. "Trust me, they won't hurt you."

No, I'd heard enough from her to know that her bosses weren't into causing pain. She had taken the burden of proof onto her slender shoulders, seized the risk of going there first, and paved the way for my curiosity—*if* I chose to act on it by following in her tracks.

"Why don't you call them first, see what they say?" I suggested, feeling too scattered in my thoughts and emotions to make a decision at that moment.

"About you taking my place?"

"No, you turkey," I said with an exasperated huff. "About you calling in sick."

PHONE IN HAND, I LAY on top of the covers of my bed, still in my bathrobe. Going to sleep was the furthest thing from my mind. Eyes wide open, I watched stripes of light move across the ceiling from the passing vehicles outside.

If Tanya called again, should I go in her place? And if I went, would it be hitting a new low in my life-long chase of a new high?

Of all the wild adventures during my younger years, playing a prostitute in real life—outside of the safety of my own bedroom as a part of role-playing with my boyfriend—was something I had never done.

Would it be something I wanted to do, though?

The excitement of a new adventure rushed through me at the thought of surrendering my body to the hands of Tanya's mystery men—the feeling of a thrill I had experienced less and less lately.

The older I got, the more distant my wild teenage years had become. Working in international business and travelling the world to do my job seemed exciting at first. But in reality, it had turned out to be rather boring and predictable. I worked long hours and came back to my company-rented apartment just to sleep and shower.

Ever since coming to Belarus nearly a year ago, I'd had only two sexual encounters. Both were one-night stands. And both turned out rather lacklustre.

The last one was over two months ago. Since then, the most action I'd been getting had been the wandering hands of some government official or a businessman at a work party.

My personal life had been considerably more vibrant before coming here. But even then, it always felt like something was missing.

What if it was my destiny to always crave more than I got? Maybe I was born with a glitch—unable to be satisfied by just one man? But how could I find out for sure if I didn't try?

The phone buzzed in my hand, startling me. The screen lit up with the message from Tanya.

'Called them. Best bosses in the world! I can take tonight off, they're keeping Thursdays for me.'

Another message came in moments later, while I still stared at the first.

'He said to take the time to rest and even asked if I have someone to take care of me. Can you believe this?'

Yes, actually, I could. Harry, my boss at the office, would have done the same. But, obviously, Tanya and I had different labour standards. As messed up as her situation was, I was glad she'd found some peace and stability in her current 'employment.'

'You don't have to go tonight,' popped up with another buzz, bringing a shocking pinch of disappointment.

'Unless you want to.'

Tanya texted a phone number next.

'His name is Andras,' came immediately after.

'Go to bed. You need to rest, remember?' I punched in quickly, hit the 'send' button, and collapsed back in bed.

Eyes closed, I prayed for sleep, but my imagination had been stirred. I pretended I couldn't open my eyes because of a blindfold. Tossing the phone aside, I untied the belt of my bathrobe and let it slide open, baring my breasts. My nipples tingled, hardening before I even touched them. I imagined those weren't my hands, but the hands of a stranger—no, several strangers—massaging my breasts, pinching my nipples, sliding between my thighs . . .

It'd been so long since I'd allowed someone's hands on me. Why did I let it go for this long? I wondered if the subconscious fear of another disappointment kept me celibate all this time. Whatever the case, it only made the craving for a man's touch stronger now.

I patted the sheets, searching for my phone. I had a way to bring my fantasy to life. And all I had to lose was potentially getting disappointed in the process.

In the semi-darkness of my bedroom anything seemed possible, and taking on this daring experience felt exciting.

I dialled the number.

"Allo," came after a mere second. Said in a deep, low rumble, the word made my breath hitch.

"Hi. I . . . um," I mumbled, my ability to speak Russian completely deserted me all of a sudden. "Andras?"

"Yes."

I might have imagined the warm note in his voice. Still, it gave me the courage to continue. "I got your number from Tanya. She can't come tonight, and I was wondering if . . ." I inhaled, closed my eyes, and blurted out at once, as if ripping off a band-aid, "if I could take her place."

"Where would you like to be picked up?"

That simple?

"Um . . ." I knew that Tanya met them in front of the restaurant and made them drop her off at a Metro station. She chose not to give them her home address, protecting her sister.

I had no one to protect, and I would rather avoid taking a train at night.

"My place." I gave him the address of my building.

"We'll be there in an hour. I'll have the money for you—"

"I don't want to be paid," I spoke quickly.

"No?" There was a genuine puzzlement in his voice.

"No. Instead, can I have the option to stop . . . um, whatever it is? If I want to, I mean."

"To stop?" He seemed unable to comprehend what I was asking from him.

"Yes. If at any point of the . . . proceedings, I get uncomfortable and want to go home, would you let me?"

He didn't answer right away, possibly considering his reply. Or maybe wondering what kind of a prostitute I was and if he should even bother with me.

"Alright," he finally said. "You will have to wear a blindfold at all times, and you can't speak of this to anyone besides your colleagues who might be interested in working with us. Other than that, you will have full control over everything."

His voice sounded sincere and his words straightforward, putting my mind at ease a little.

"Okay." I nodded, even though he couldn't see me. "I'll meet you outside my building in an hour."

Chapter 4

SO, IT WAS HAPPENING. I was getting a chance to live out my fantasy.

Watching the black car pull over, I wrinkled the curtain in my sweaty hands.

I could only imagine how Tanya must have felt getting into the car that first night. She did all the hard work for me. Now, I could expect to be reasonably safe.

Still, my hands shook as I took the lift downstairs.

The back door of the car opened as soon as I approached, and with another bracing inhale, I got into the back seat.

"Andras?" I asked the man sitting there.

"Hello." He inclined his head in greeting.

"Hi," I croaked in reply, closing the door behind me. The vehicle took off immediately.

Now there was no way back.

I swept the dark interior with my gaze, stopping on the man by my side.

Dressed in a dark robe, with the hood pulled low over his face, he appeared no more than a shadow. The light from the street, muted by the tinted windows, faintly illuminated the hard edge of a jaw covered with dark stubble. The rest of his face remained securely hidden in the shadows.

I swallowed hard, noticing the strip of black velvet in his leather-clad hands.

"Blindfold," he said simply, making a move in my direction.

I took a deep breath and nodded, closing my eyes.

The movement of air around me along with a faint whiff of spicy male scent alerted me to his proximity. Then the soft velvet touched my face, as he tied the blindfold around my head.

"No need to be nervous," he said, moving away again. "We will let no harm come to you. You don't have to worry."

"I'm not worried." I made an effort to keep the edge out of my voice.

"Yes, you are," he replied confidently, as if he could read the scrambled mess of my thoughts. "But you don't need to be. From this moment on, you have full control over everything that happens."

"Everything?"

"Yes."

The absolute certainty in his reply gave me hope that I didn't just make the biggest mistake of my life.

"Good."

THE REST OF THE DRIVE was silent, interrupted only by my occasional deep breaths as I tried to calm my nerves. Excitement and anticipation led an unceasing battle with anxiety inside me.

My companion remained silent, which was just as well. I didn't think I would be able to carry on a conversation, consumed as I was by my inner turmoil.

Finally, the car stopped and the door next to me opened almost immediately.

"Welcome," another male voice greeted me from outside.

Then I felt a leather-clad hand take mine.

Completely blinded by the velvet over my eyes, I leaned heavily on the offered support as I got out of the vehicle.

"Please follow me," the same voice coolly invited.

The man seemed to have given me all of his attention as he carefully led me down a flight of stairs then along something that felt like a set of long corridors.

The air inside smelled clean, with the artificial quality of air-conditioning and purifying. The heels of my boots clicked against the hard surface of the floor—the sound echoed off the walls around us.

"Please have a seat." The man carefully manoeuvred me onto something cushioned like a couch. The dusty smell of old furniture joined the sterile air of the room he appeared to have brought me to.

"Keep your blindfold on at all times. Andras will be here shortly."

"Okay," I exhaled, even as my fingers itched to rip the blindfold off. Without having a visual of the room, I felt utterly confused and disoriented.

The sound of soft footsteps came as someone entered.

"Thank you for joining us this evening." I heard the voice of the man who had travelled in the car with me.

Andras.

All I had was his name. No one else had introduced themselves to me, and no one had asked my name either.

Good.

This was supposed to be a nameless, faceless fantasy after all.

"What would you wish for tonight?" Andras asked, catching me unprepared.

All I had was the desire for something new and exciting but no clear scenarios in my head, just a series of vague, alluring, and passionate images.

"Um." I inhaled. "I don't know."

Worry and doubt stirred inside me again.

Should I have planned this better?

"You don't have to give me any details unless you want to," Andras replied, as if hearing my thoughts. "We can do it all. In this case, I'll only need your permission for us to take control."

Take control.

The two words alone shouldn't have been so arousing. I squirmed in my seat, as sudden anticipation quivered through my lower stomach.

"Will I be safe?" I asked the most important question once again.

"Absolutely."

I loved the unwavering sincerity in his voice.

"Can I stop at any time?" I reiterated.

"Promise." The same firmness in his tone.

"Is there something like a safe word?"

"No. Your wish to stop would be enough."

"You mean my *voicing* my wish to stop?" I clarified.

"Yes. Sure."

"Okay." I nodded.

"Our only requirement is that you keep the blindfold on at all times."

"Deal," I agreed, with more confidence in my voice than I felt. "Oh! Sorry." I remembered. "I do have one request."

"Anything." His voice held the true promise of fulfilling my every wish.

"Can there be more than one man, please? I mean, touching me."

Voicing my innermost fantasy out loud immediately set my face ablaze. My cheeks burned so hot, I was afraid they'd set the blindfold on fire.

"How many?" Andras's voice didn't change. There was no mocking, no judgment, not even surprise in his tone.

"Um . . . well, two?"

Let's start slow, Jade.

"Done," he easily agreed.

I took a deep breath and rubbed my palms on my dress where it stretched over my thighs.

"Well then, you have my permission to take control over the rest." I nodded again and asked, "Now what?"

"Would you need help to undress?" Andras inquired politely, as if asking me if I wanted him to pour me a glass of water.

"Yes. Um, no. I mean, I should be able to manage it on my own. How much do you need me to take off?"

"As much or as little as suits you."

Weird, so weird.

Wouldn't they have at least some kind of preferences if they ordered a prostitute and paid her good money for this?

You're not a prostitute, and they're paying you nothing.

"Okay," I said again and got up to my feet, struggling to remain steady in my high heels.

Falling off my feet while blindfolded would not be sexy at all. These would have to go. I sat down again, unzipped and took off my boots. Next went my leather jacket, the dress, and the strapless bra.

In one resolute movement, I yanked down my lace panties, unsure if Andras was watching me. Without hearing a sound from his direction, I wasn't even certain he had remained in the room at all.

I contemplated for a second whether or not to leave my thigh-high stockings on. Since there was nothing but my fantasy to guide me, I decided to take everything off, because in my sexy dreams I had always been naked.

Rolling the stockings down and off my legs, I straightened up to my full height—completely nude, save for the blindfold.

"I'm ready," I announced into the room, not knowing which direction to face.

"Please take my hand," Andras's voice came immediately.

I guessed he might have stood nearby all this time after all, watching me take my clothes off. Was that supposed to be his thrill in all of this? I thought back to the rather quick and efficient way I had disrobed, wondering if he would have preferred me taking my clothes off in a more slow and sensual way.

Well, if I was here to fulfil any of *his* fantasies in exchange for them fulfilling mine, then Andras should have voiced his preferences earlier.

Stretching an arm out, I searched around for his offered hand.

"Let's do this."

Chapter 5

WITH THE BLINDFOLD still firmly over my eyes, I couldn't see the room Andras took me to. But the echo of someone's boots hitting the hard floor on their way to me had a longer way to travel before it bounced off the walls, indicating that the space was fairly large.

With a belt around my waist and a set of padded handcuffs on my wrists, I had been strapped to some sort of vertical surface, a wall or a contraption that held my hands up, arms stretched over my head.

I had no idea where Andras went and no clue who else might be in the room with me. Two sets of footsteps stopped in front of me. Someone then softly brushed my hair away from my face.

It was unexpected.

This might have been *my* fantasy, but surely the people who were giving it to me had their own kinks to satisfy? Somehow, I half-expected tonight to be rather rough, with my body being used under the control of strangers for someone else's pleasure. That was the reason I had made it abundantly clear that I wanted the power to stop if it went too far for me.

This gesture of his felt out of place, even as it was . . . nice.

The soft caress moved down the side of my face, skimmed along my neck then traced the length of my collarbone.

Nothing I would ever consider as overtly sexual, yet the tenderness of it stirred something inside me—sweet and powerful.

Unable to resist the promise of his touch, I leaned into it, wishing for more.

So much more.

As if having guessed my wish, the velvet-clad hand was joined by others in a sensual dance along my body.

Sometimes barely there, like the flutter of butterfly wings against the sensitive skin inside my arms and thighs, sometimes with a gentle squeeze of my breast or my hip, the two pairs of hands fanned the flame of desire coursing deep inside me.

A throaty moan reached my ears, and I realised it came from me.

Lost deep in the rhythm of the strangers' hands on me, I rolled my head. The side of my face brushed by something cold and hard.

Helmets?

Did the ones who touched me wear masks?

Nameless and faceless.

Just like I wanted.

A fierce wave of arousal, unleashed by the caress of their hands, flooded me.

VADIM

He watched the Source writhe on the cross, just as he had watched them every single night for close to a year now, sitting in this very armchair. Before that, as one of the Council members, he sat just a few chairs down to the right. For centuries.

Tonight, something was different.

From the first delicate filament of her energy that reached him, he realised she was not from the Base.

This Source must be one of those that Andras had hired. Although, her energy was something that none of the others had produced.

Another wave of her arousal reached him, and he sucked it in greedily.

Blinded by the undiluted potency of her passion, he struggled to collect his thoughts to figure out what made this woman so different from anything he had experienced before.

There was no fear in her—no darkness of panic or any trace of the muddy fog of insanity. The small cloud of initial worry had cleared quickly from her, and the hint of nervous anticipation that lingered for a while added a heady spice and effervescence to the taste of her emotions.

Never, in the centuries of his existence, could he recall sampling anything like this. Neither could he remember seeing anything similar to the vortex of light and colours that burst out of her with every touch of the Handlers.

Every shade of pink. The glowing warmth of orange. A bright, magnificent red.

All churning in an ever-growing whirlwind, filling the room wall-to-wall and curling through the beams under the ceiling.

Spectacular!

Needing to get more of her intoxicating taste, he shifted from his usual reclining position in the chair. His hands pressed into the armrests, he leaned forward, ready to lose himself in her lust.

More.

The essence of his very being focused entirely on the delicious energy bursting out of her in fountains of exploding stars.

Take all of it—the very last whiff, spark, and strand. Reach deep inside her and consume her whole . . .

Until none of it was left.

He blinked, forcing himself out of the trance she had put him under.

With a jolt of surprise, he found himself mere feet away from the Source, writhing through the shudders of her first climax. He had no memory of getting up from his chair, led by the all-consuming hunger for her enticing emotions.

His attention still on her, he sensed a movement in the room, which alerted him. All members of his Council had abandoned their seats and now circled the Source like a pack of starving wolves ready to pounce.

None of the thirteen wore gloves, him included. If they touched her—she'd be no more. Then all of this spectacular energy would be lost forever.

No!

Without a word of command, he threw his arms out to the side, spreading them wide to halt the demons.

They didn't all stop at once. Struggling to obey their Grand Master, some still made a few halting steps, lured to the Source by the power of her desire.

Their bodies vibrated with strain, as they fought to control themselves. They closed their blazing red eyes, to sever the visual contact with the delicious hurricane of temptation, and froze in place, absorbing what they could from their distance and savouring each and every drop of it—the same way Vadim did.

Feet planted firmly on the concrete floor, hands fisted at his sides, he waited until the magnificent lightshow of her orgasm had subsided.

With a small throaty moan, she slumped in her restraints. And the eyes of all the demons opened again.

Silently, he gestured for the Council to return to their seats. This time, they obeyed without a moment of hesitation. Mentally, he gave himself the same order and increased the distance between her body and his avaricious hunger.

Only when he was back in his chair, did he allow an exhale of relief from his chest.

He knew that Andras had promised absolute safety to the women he had sourced.

As the Grand Master, it was his responsibility to ensure this promise was fulfilled. Yet he realised how close the Source had come to being drained tonight.

Centuries ago, he vowed to do everything in his power to make sure no Source was ever drained in this room again. Eventually, he understood that the only way to fulfil his vow was to attain the title of Grand Master, and he had spent the rest of that time working to become one.

In the past eleven months since he took this seat, he had been able to keep his promise—no Source was drained. However, he'd known it was unsustainable—if he continued to run the Base following the old rules, sooner or later the women would start dying again.

Human beings were fragile creatures, their physical and mental health deteriorated quickly if they were held in the captivity and isolation required by the rules.

Vadim had spent every spare minute, trying to find a way to ease their sufferings without jeopardizing the wellbeing of the Incubi who were his main responsibility.

Andras had piqued his interest with some promising ideas, and Vadim let the demon work in peace.

He knew that Andras had to be feeding outside of the Base, since he refused to participate in the Feedings when invited. However, Vadim chose not to prosecute him for breaking the rules, never even ordering an investigation.

He'd worried that his lack of punishment in this case might create a precedent for others to follow. Giving leniency to one meant closing his eyes to the misdeeds of others, letting them slip from under the Council's control one by one.

On the other hand, during his short time as Grand Master, he'd also realised it was not truly the Incubi Councils who were in control here.

The real power lay with the Priory—people were the ones enforcing the rules against humanity.

The Source stirred on the cross, snapping his attention back to her. She stretched through the entire length of her body, forcing his gaze to slide along it—from the thick waves of her long, auburn hair with rich terracotta highlights to the toes she braced against the wood of the platform.

"*Esche ras? —One more time?*" she begged. The sweet, hesitant plea in her throaty voice resonated through his body in ripples of pleasure of another kind.

Blood rushed through his veins, pooling in his groin with a long-forgotten, throbbing ache. The physical response was so unexpected, he had to glance down to see the bulge of his straining cock push against the fabric of his pants, just to reassure himself that it indeed was happening.

With those two short words, she woke up more in him than just the hunger for her energy.

"Can I ask you for a favour, please?" With her eyes covered by the blindfold, she addressed the centre of the room. "Could you get me out of the handcuffs? It's uncomfortable staying in them for so long," she explained with a short little laugh that stroked his skin like the caress of silk.

Tonight, she was in charge. All he could do was obey her wishes.

He gestured to the Handlers. One of them immediately unlocked the handcuffs from around her wrists. The other stepped aside only to return moments later, rolling in a padded table draped in red silk.

The first Handler carefully placed the Source on top of the silk where she stretched again—languidly slow.

Every curve and valley of hers had been on display all this time. Yet only now did he become fully aware of her body, paying attention to her every move, just as much as he did to each curl and churn of the glowing desire in her.

Shifting in his seat to ease the pressure in his pants, he gave another signal. Already, the anticipation of *more* lit his insides with a delight he'd never known.

Chapter 6

AFTER A WHILE, I LOST track of my orgasms.

"I can't," I had to whisper eventually, my body still trembling with the last ripples, my inner muscles quivering. "I'm so tired . . ."

I had no idea to whom I was talking. Without a way for me to know who was in the room, how many of them were there or who was in charge, I spoke into the void. As soon as I had voiced my desires, however—or even before that—all of them had been fulfilled.

So, it didn't surprise me that the gloved hands did not resume their dance on my body with my last sentence. Instead, two strong arms lifted me from the padded surface where they had put me.

Boneless, I leaned against the cool, hard plates on the chest of the one holding me.

Not just helmets. They seemed to be wearing full body armour, too.

Even weirder, but that much more exciting.

Everything about this night was exciting, even if it seemed strange. And most of it was unexpected. Listening to Tanya's recounts of her sessions did not fully prepare me for this experience. I knew I'd be pleasured, and I could reasonably expect to be brought to orgasm. However, I had no idea it could be done with so much care and attention.

It seemed they anticipated my every need before even I was aware of it. These men seemed to know what I wanted better than I knew it myself.

Here I was, heading out into the unknown, thinking I could use some intense, head-against-the-headboard fucking. And what I got was an incredibly sensual night of mind-blowing sex.

There hadn't even been any actual fucking involved—no intercourse, not even penetration with a vibrator. Just the caress of dexterous hands and the expert use of toys.

Yet I had enjoyed it so much more than any of my previous sexual experiences. I had no idea how many times I'd orgasmed. After the first time, it all seemed like one endless ocean of ecstasy, with waves of various length and intensity, from sweet ripples to crushing swells of bliss.

Afterwards, the armoured man carried me somewhere that sounded like another corridor, then placed me on yet another padded surface. Someone tucked a soft blanket around my naked body.

"You can stay here as long as you need," Andras's voice came from a distance.

I was fairly certain he was not one of those whose hands had just brought my fantasy to life, just as he was not the one tucking me in right now.

His voice, always polite and even friendly, otherwise sounded detached and impassive, making it hard to believe he was personally involved in anything that happened around here, beyond coordinating the logistics. In fact, if I didn't see the man with my own eyes in the car, I would have easily believed he was not a man at all but just a disembodied voice.

"You can sleep if you wish. We'll take you back in the morning."

"No." As tired as I was, staying the night in this place had never been my intention. Despite the pleasant experience, I did not feel comfortable enough here to have a relaxing snooze. "I'd like to go home now."

Clutching the blanket to my chest, I made a move to get up, but it wasn't easy. I didn't feel dizzy or incapacitated, only deliciously tired in every bone and muscle. Sleep tugged at me, and the blanket seemed to weigh me down, luring me back to the mattress.

With an effort, I sat up. "I need to go home."

"As you wish," Andras agreed. "We'll help you get dressed."

By *we*, I now understood, he always seemed to mean all of them as a group, for there was no way the hands that reached for my blanket and then started putting my clothes on me could have belonged to him, judging by the distance from which his voice came.

For me, unable to see anything from behind the blindfold, there was just his voice in the room and a pair of someone else's hands that followed his orders.

Before I knew it, my stockings were rolled up my legs, my underwear was pulled up my hips, and the hooks of my bra closed at my back.

All of this was done in a quick and efficient way. The occasional brush of the gloved fingers on my skin felt nothing like it did earlier. Whoever was dressing me, obviously had no intention of causing further arousal.

Once my jacket was on, zipped up to my chin, the armoured man lifted me up again and carried me outside, then placed me inside a vehicle.

I must have dozed off as soon as the car began to move, because when someone's hand lightly shook my shoulder and Andras's voice softly called out to me, I had no recollection of the actual drive back to the city.

"We're here."

"Already?" I mumbled, trying to get my bearings with the blindfold still around my head.

Andras untied it, and I blinked, squinting in the faint light from the street outside the car windows.

He sank back into shadows before I had a chance to take a good look at his face, remaining but a backlit silhouette in the dark interior of the car.

"Thank you for coming tonight."

'Thank you for making me come.' The thought made me smile inside.

"Do you still insist on forfeiting your payment?"

"Absolutely."

"Can we hope to see you again?"

Again?

Flutters of anticipation took flight in my stomach at the opportunity to repeat tonight's experience.

"I—I'd like that," I replied.

"Next week then?"

"A week? No," I protested, in an attempt to curb my cravings. Even though I felt like I could do it all over again just after a few more hours of sleep, I reasoned I needed to space the sessions out, lest they take over my mind and my life completely, like a bad addiction. "Next month?" I asked instead.

"Very well. We'll see you in a month."

The door on my side magically opened on its own, and I got out. My legs felt like cotton. Stumbling up the few steps leading to the door to my stairwell, I punched in the code and stepped inside. Through the narrow strip of glass in the door, I watched the car leave then leaned with my back against the wall.

Everything that happened tonight was surreal to the point that it would have been easy for me to believe it was all just a dream—if it weren't for the sweet ache of thorough satisfaction in my body and the lingering sensation of the gentle touch of strangers' hands.

Chapter 7

THE FOLLOWING MONTH, the date fell on a Sunday, not Thursday as it was the previous time. I was unsure if my visit to that place still stood as agreed, never having called Andras to confirm in the weeks prior to it. This way it felt more like leaving it up to fate rather than making a conscious decision on my own.

Yet the anticipation that had been building up inside me as the day approached had reached its apogee. I once again stood by the window with the curtain in my hand, watching the dark street in front of my building for the signs of an approaching car.

This time, instead of a miniskirt and high heels, I wore biker boots and jeans, which were warmer and more comfortable.

A pent-up desire warred with apprehension inside me again. As wonderful as my first night with the strangers was, not everything about continuing to go there seemed right. Following my kinky desires felt very much like allowing an addiction to take over.

There was still no way of telling what the strangers got out of this.

Was Tanya right when she mentioned videotaping? Could it be some porn production? In which case I was really grateful for the blindfold concealing my face. Still, it didn't make much sense for them to ask me for *my* preferences instead of them having a script for me to follow.

The headlights of the approaching car brought me out of my thoughts.

Andras did not forget after all.

The same dark vehicle with tinted windows pulled over to the entrance to my stairwell and stopped, its headlights went off. For a moment, I wondered how long it would remain there if I didn't come down tonight. Then, I grabbed my leather jacket from the bed and headed out.

"HI," I SAID THE MOMENT my ass hit the cushioned backseat of the car.

"Good evening," came the reply, and I realised it was not Andras next to me. The voice was deep and pleasant but clearly different from Andras's low drawl.

"Who are you?" My back tense, I gripped the door handle, ready to bolt even as the vehicle had been brought into motion already. "Where is Andras?"

"He had to leave the country for a little while. Sorry for not having warned you. I hope you don't find me taking over his duties detrimental to your experience in any way."

Polite to a fault.

Who expressed themselves this way nowadays?

"Any other changes I should know about?" I asked warily, my hand still firmly on the door handle.

"None. Unless you wish for any." The even cadence of his voice had a somewhat calming effect on me.

"No." I shook my head. "No changes, please."

The sudden appearance of another man unnerved me, so it was best to stick to the known for now. Besides, why change what wasn't broken? I saw no problems with experiencing the same orgasmic bliss tonight as I had last month.

The stranger silently inclined his head in agreement, and I slid an exploring gaze along his tall form folded into the seat next to me.

Unlike Andras, he was dressed in modern clothes—a pair of dark pants and an asphalt-grey sweatshirt, with the hood low over his face. Shadows skimmed his smooth-shaved jaw, obscuring most of his face and leaving visible only his strong chin and his full lower lip.

The way he crushed the black blindfold in his gloved hands reminded me how I had clutched the curtain just a few minutes earlier.

Could he be nervous too?

Why?

Finally, he lifted the blindfold from his lap.

"I have to put this on you."

Was there a hint of hesitation in his voice?

"Sure." I nodded, with a tinge of regret myself.

As much as being blindfolded was a necessary part of the game, I still wished he would delay putting it on me tonight.

All talking had stopped when Andras blindfolded me the last time, and I still had some questions for tonight's companion. I bit back the urge to ask his name, but only because I feared he would ask mine in return when I preferred a complete anonymity.

His scent reached me as he leaned in to tie the blindfold. Unlike the exotic spice of Andras, his smell reminded me of a warm ocean breeze with a hint of salt. I stilled for a moment, taking a breath just a little deeper than necessary.

Mmmm. Did all of the guys at that place smell delicious?

I stole another quick sniff, before he finished tying the knot and moved away.

"You're not from here, are you?" he suddenly asked, proving wrong my assumption of no talking after the blindfold was on.

"No, I'm not." I've been told my accent wasn't strong. However, I knew it was there.

"What is your mother tongue?"

I hesitated. Was there any harm in admitting the truth?

"English."

"Would it be more comfortable for you to speak it then?" He asked this in perfect English, with no accent whatsoever.

"Um, sure."

Actually, talking Russian felt more like doing business to me—mostly because it was the language I used at work. Speaking English felt more intimate in that moment, making our conversation less of a business transaction and more like an intimate chat.

Unsure of what I wanted it to be, I decided to go with the flow.

"Where did you learn to speak English so well?" I asked.

"I didn't need to learn. I've always spoken it."

"So, you weren't born in Belarus either?" I strained my ear, trying to figure out from his speech where he came from.

The problem was, he really had no accent. His pronunciation sounded academically perfect but fell somewhere in the middle, without placing him anywhere in particular.

"I wasn't born here," he replied, without elaborating. "Why are you in Minsk?"

"For work. You?"

He took a moment to answer. "I work here too."

A sharp sting of curiosity urged me to ask more, but I stopped the questions that dangled on the tip of my tongue.

Any honesty from him might result in me having to reciprocate, and I wasn't ready to reveal the details about my life or my identity. I had a job and a reputation to maintain. He was a part of what made up my fantasy life, with no place in my everyday one.

The smooth road must have been replaced by a bumpier dirt one, judging by the movement of the car. We must have been farther from the city now, getting closer to wherever they were taking me.

My heart sped up again.

I had every reason to believe that tonight would be exactly like the last time. However, I still couldn't hold back a little apprehension seeping into my excitement.

"You will be safe." His voice was firm and reassuring. "I give you my word."

Something in his tone made me believe he was personally accepting the responsibility for my safety. And that put my mind at ease.

Chapter 8

"WHAT IS YOUR WISH TONIGHT?"

I sat in the same chair, most likely in the same room as last time. Yet, everything felt slightly different somehow.

Perhaps because, unlike Andras's friendly, impassive tone, the voice of this stranger vibrated with some sort of emotion. The low raspy note he hit when asking the question sent a rush of goose-bumps down my arms.

The way he asked, made me imagine it'd be *he* who'd be fulfilling my wishes tonight—his hands touching me in places where his voice had already made me tingle with anticipation.

"The same." I cleared my throat. "Like the last time."

"Would you need assistance with getting undressed?"

Would you *be the one providing the assistance?*

Where did this flirtiness come from? He was simply here to deliver me my fantasy. Nothing more.

I shook my head, kicking my boots off. "I'm good."

Standing up, I threw my jacket on the chair behind me then began to unbutton my blouse. The tiny pearl buttons kept slipping through my fingers, and I realised that the reason for my fumbling was the feeling of being watched.

By him.

I didn't need to see him to know he was observing me as I undressed. I could almost feel his gaze on my skin, ripples of sensation running down my back and chest.

He kept incredibly quiet. I didn't believe I heard so much as the sound of breathing from his direction. Yet I was positive he remained here, in the room with me.

I forced myself to slow down, then shrugged the blouse off my shoulders in a nonchalant gesture, even as my heart felt like it was about to jump out of my throat. My nipples grew hard when I took my bra off, the tingling sensation spreading through my breasts as I imagined his stare gliding over my half-naked body.

Taking off my tight jeans in any sensual way proved nearly impossible, making me wish I'd worn a dress after all. I shimmied my hips out of the jeans but nearly lost my balance, attempting to yank my foot out of the narrow leg.

"Careful," came right above my ear.

Strong hands gripped my arms, and a whiff of ocean breeze curled around me, making my head spin a little.

What was he doing to me?

I'd never been this aware of any man in my life.

He lowered me into the chair behind me then tugged at my jeans, releasing one leg at a time.

A moment later, I felt his gloved fingers at my hips as he hooked them under the elastic of my underwear, and I lifted my backside off the chair to help him slide my panties off me.

All without saying a word.

"Thank you." My voice had a husky rasp to it.

He cleared his throat. "I'll get them to take you to the meeting room."

Meeting room?

Was that what they called it?

"Wait." I rose from my seat. "Will you be there, too?"

This was something I definitely shouldn't have asked. Tonight was supposed to be all about a faceless, nameless fantasy with full and utter anonymity. The people who touched me were supposed to remain strangers, without so much as a voice or a scent attached to them.

Still, my excitement grew when I heard him say, "Yes."

I fired off another question before I could stop myself. "Will you be the one touching me?"

"No," the response was firm in tone.

Unexpectedly, my heart dropped, but I brushed away the disappointment.

This was for the best.

Anonymity.

It was supposed to be just a fantasy—a game I could finish any time I liked, with no strings attached.

I heard footsteps—heavy boots on the concrete floor—and someone lifted me up in the air. Instinctively, I threw my arms around the person's shoulders and leaned in as the armoured man carried me.

His smell reached my nostrils—leather, metal, the warm smell of another male . . . Nice, but not quite the same.

I LAY ON A LONG TABLE. With my hands cuffed high above my head and my ankles chained at the opposite end, my body stretched like a string, singing with passion caused by the two pairs of hands on me.

Two men filling me with pleasure head to toe—my long-time fantasy turned into an even more mind-blowing reality.

Heat coursed through me, building between my legs, and I attempted to press my thighs together, desperate for release.

Someone squeezed my breasts and plucked my nipples, sending another electric charge down through my core.

A hand glided up my thigh, and I twisted on the table towards this touch. Something hard slid between my legs. The toy felt cool against my heated folds when someone pressed it against me, promising relief in every sense.

With a moan, I arched my back as much as the restraints would allow and tried to squeeze my legs together, to trap the vibrator between my thighs.

All-consuming need took over my senses. At that moment nothing else existed for me—just those hands, building up the pleasure that coursed through me with their every touch, the achy pressure between my legs driving me mad with the need to come.

My head thrown back, I inhaled deeply, suddenly catching a trace of freshness and salt of the ocean in the air.

He *was* here.

Right there, at the head of the table.

What was going through his head as he watched me? Did he want me? Was he touching himself?

Unthinking, I flexed my arms, shifting my body up the table, towards him. The orgasm exploded through me at that very moment, rippling through me in blissful spasms. Completely oblivious to everything around me for a few second, I rode the waves of intense pleasure as the hands of strangers reaped more and more wonderful shudders out of my body.

Finally, as my climax ebbed, I was able to draw in another lungful of air.

His scent was gone.

He must have stepped back, but now I knew in which direction he stood.

I threw my head back again.

"More," I begged him and him alone.

VADIM

Her energy churning inside him, he closed his eyes for a moment, steadying himself on his feet before retreating another step.

Yes, he was out of his chair once again. And this time, he made it closer than any other members of the Council. Tonight, they all knew what to expect from her and were better prepared to stay in control.

Except for him, it seemed.

Caught off guard by the faint strand of a highly alluring aroma in her emotions, he couldn't resist getting closer again. The taste of her arousal was even more tantalizing than the last time, for it seemed to be flavoured with something even more special, *just for him.*

Her skin flushed glowing pink, her body arched in ecstasy. He slid his gaze along the Source stretched on the table, taking in every single detail he never noticed in the others. And everything about her caused his own body to respond.

The way her chest heaved as she panted coming down from the crest of passion. Her breasts rose and fell, trembling with her heavy breathing. Her nipples swollen and red, almost the same colour as the swirls of her arousal curling through the air.

He wondered how warm each breast would feel if he sucked the tips into his mouth, one after another. How hard the tight bud of her nipple would be if he rolled it with his tongue.

The idea of tasting her skin along with her emotions rushed through him in a swell of heat, sending another charge to his crotch. His already painfully hard erection throbbed with a renewed wave of arousal.

Fisting his hands at his sides, he forced himself to take one last step back before his legs hit the edge of his chair and he collapsed back into it.

"More," she moaned. And he made a gesture to her Handlers to continue.

Who was he to deny her anything?

He was but a hungry demon, quickly and hopelessly becoming addicted to her every emotion.

Chapter 9

"YOU CAN STAY HERE AS long as you like."

There was so much in his voice when he offered—warmth, concern, kindness. Hope?

Surely I was reading too much into his tone. The whole experience of this place seemed to alter my perceptions of reality for as long as I remained here.

"No." I shook my head, sitting on the bed where they had placed me. "I should go."

"I'll help you dress." It wasn't a question.

The air around me moved, mixing in with his scent, as he shifted closer and took the blanket off me. His hands circled my ankles as he turned me in bed to face him then eased my feet to the floor.

He started putting my clothes on me with calm efficiency. Yet I caught slight differences from the way the armoured men did it last time.

The way his hands lingered at my hips after he had pulled up my panties. The way his fingers brushed down my back after closing the small hooks of my bra. I felt him lean my way as he buttoned my blouse.

With my eyes closed, all my other senses tuned in to him, catching details I might have missed if I could see. His slightly uneven breathing, the tremble in his fingers. The strength of his arms as he helped me off the bed in order to tug my jeans up my legs and close the button at my waist.

Awash in his scent, I basked in his attention. It felt so unexpectedly pleasant to be taken care of by him.

Still unsteady on my feet, I swayed and braced myself against his arm. My fingers landed on the stone-hard bulk of muscle covered by thin fabric.

He must have taken off the sweatshirt he wore in the car because the material of his shirt felt much finer under my fingers. The warmth of his skin underneath seeped into me.

For one brief moment his breath hitched and I froze, afraid to move, lest I scare away this sudden sense of intimacy between us—something I couldn't recall ever sharing with anyone before. The feeling descended like a warm, fuzzy cloud, isolating us from the rest of the world.

Then his bicep rolled under my hand as he let go of my waistband and the sensation disappeared.

"They'll take you to the car." Rougher than before, his voice distanced as he moved away.

THE DRIVE BACK WAS quiet.

Not that I didn't have any questions to ask or topics to talk about, but I held back. My sudden attraction to this complete stranger was puzzling enough. I wanted to know more about him but was afraid he would no longer be a stranger to me if I did. And I wasn't ready for that.

"Will I see you next month?" he asked as the car came to a halt outside my building.

It was then I realised what else made this man different. Andras always used *we*, which distanced him personally from what was happening. Tonight's companion, however, used *I* and *they*, setting himself apart from the rest, making me consider him as an individual.

"Will it be you or Andras next time?" I asked in return.

"Me."

I couldn't even begin to explain the warm feeling that rose inside me at this answer.

"I'll see you next month then," I replied, unable to hold back my smile.

It almost sounded like a date.

WHAT IS GOING ON WITH me? I wondered lying in bed that night.

I stared at the ceiling, going through everything that had happened earlier. The thing was, I never got to see his face. I hardly even got to touch him. We had only exchanged a handful of sentences. Yet he seemed to have filled tonight's whole experience with his presence.

No man had ever affected me so much with so little.

Could it be that not having a boyfriend for this long made me hungry for any kind of intimacy?

There was still a whole month until I got to 'see' him again, and I could only hope that the unsettling feeling for him would calm down over the weeks until then.

Chapter 10

DURING THE MONTH THAT followed I kept waiting for the memories of him to fade away. And every day the elation of seeing him again overshadowed any sexual excitement I felt about the approaching date.

My sudden draw to this one man confused me. Then, as the time passed, and I still failed to get the feeling under control, it began to anger me.

This was *my* fantasy, dammit. It was supposed to be just a notch above the images and sensations that would go through my head on the nights when I made myself come with my vibrator. Whatever happened during my visits with the strangers was supposed to disappear with the sunrise the very next morning.

None of it was meant to follow me into everyday life. Not the memory of his scent—which wouldn't leave me, no matter what I did. Or the sound of his deep voice. Not the sensation of his dexterous hands on me as he dressed me with care and efficiency, leaving me anxious for more . . . so much more.

Less than a week before the date of my next rendezvous with the strangers, I couldn't take it anymore. I couldn't get in that car again, having this stampede of butterflies in my stomach.

Finally, I gave up and dialled the only contact number I had for them, Andras's number.

For a moment as it rang, I caught myself wishing to hear *his* voice, but then Andras's deep drawl answered.

"I'm calling to cancel my visit this Monday," I blurted out without a greeting or introduction. "I can't make it."

"Are you well? Is everything all right? Do you need any assistance?"

I did not expect this type of concern.

"No . . . I mean yes. I'm fine. I just can't make it."

"We'll see you the month after that, then."

I'd called with the intention of cancelling indefinitely. No more visits, no more getting into that car. My fantasy had turned into something unexpected, and I knew I shouldn't continue with this when the focus of my mind and my body seemed to have whirred off course, narrowing onto one man.

Yet right at that moment, I couldn't bring myself to burn all my bridges.

"The month after," I repeated after him and added, "Will it be you then? Picking me up?"

"No. Vadim demanded to be the one picking you up from now on. I'll let him know about your cancellation."

My heart thundered in my chest as I hung up the phone.

Vadim.

Now, *he* had a name.

ON MONDAY NIGHT, THE night of my cancelled visit, I had a late dinner at home while watching the news on my laptop, then showered.

Passing by my bedroom window, I caught myself casting glances outside every time I went by.

Ridiculous.

Anger stirred inside me, at myself and my inability to get a grip on my emotions. Here I was, scanning the street for the headlights of the car even after I had cancelled, hoping for what?

Pathetic.

With a huff, I stomped to the window to draw the curtains closed when the headlights of an approaching vehicle made me pause.

A black car with tinted windows pulled up in front of the entrance.

It couldn't be them, could it? I had cancelled.

Still, the car stopped. Its lights went off. Someone inside was waiting.

For me?

Did Andras forget to pass on the message?

How long would he sit there like that?

Should I even care?

Determined to ignore the car, I yanked the curtains closed.

Not my business. I'd called. I'd cancelled. It wasn't my fault that the line of communications between them seemed to have broken down.

I brushed my teeth and took my bathrobe off to change into a camisole for the night.

Something strong and powerful—and absolutely beyond my control—made me go to the window again.

The car was still there. No lights. No motion in or around it that I could see.

How long was he intending to stay there? And how was I supposed to go to bed and fall asleep, knowing that he was out there? I didn't plan on him taking over my thoughts or highjacking my fantasies, and now, here he was, intruding into my everyday life, too.

Anger seethed inside me.

I threw on a t-shirt and a pair of jeans then shoved my feet into a pair of ballet flats.

A recent thunderstorm had left large puddles outside, and the May evening still called for a jacket, or at least a jumper. But I wasn't going for a walk or anything. All I wanted to do was to give that man a piece of my mind. I didn't intend for it to take long.

Storming out of my apartment, I dashed downstairs without bothering to wait for the lift.

The back door of the car opened the moment I ran out of the front entrance.

"I cancelled!" I snapped before I even came close to the vehicle. "I'm not coming with you tonight."

I stopped in front of the open door, unable to see into the dark interior.

"You have to leave." I crossed my arms on my chest.

"Get in." His familiar voice was low but held a hard edge.

The note of command caused a conflicting reaction in me, stopping me in my tracks. On one hand, I wanted to scream in protest and rebel against the order. On the other hand, the urge to obey made me weak at the knees.

I did neither.

Instead, I took a small step closer to the open door and just stood there, my hands rubbing the chill out of my arms.

"Please," he added. And the sudden, almost desperate plea in his voice proved to be impossible to resist.

"I cancelled," I mumbled, sitting gingerly on the seat.

"I know." His voice was soft, luring me in. "It made me worried—"

"Don't." I held my hand up, as if shielding myself from his allure. "Not another word."

He shouldn't worry about me in any way, and I shouldn't care whatsoever.

I couldn't allow myself to start feeling something about one of these people, without having any clear idea of what was going on.

For me, it was just a fantasy, but I hadn't figured out what it was for them. I actually preferred not knowing. However, it didn't mean I didn't have questions.

Why would a group of people hire prostitutes for regular visits if none of them actually had sex with them? What was the purpose of making women come? What did they get out of it? If I started to care about him—if I allowed us to get closer in any way—I would need some answers, and I might not like them.

The best I could do was to stay out of it, to detach myself from it.

If I could simply continue to live out my fantasy for as long as it might last, the novelty and excitement of it would eventually wear out—then I would stop and leave it all behind.

Unless I allowed myself to get attached.

I lifted my head, making out the outline of his massive shape in the darkness.

The same dark clothes. Hood low over his face.

He bit his lower lip, and it glistened in the streetlight when he released it. A sudden image of me running my thumb along it flashed through my mind.

I blinked and cleared my throat.

"I can only continue with all of this," I waved my hand, encompassing him and the interior of the car with my gesture, "if you don't talk to me. Ever. At all."

He didn't immediately reply, and I kept staring at his gloved hands as they twisted the blindfold in his lap.

"I will need to know if there are any changes in your requests," he finally said. His voice even, if maybe a little lower than usual.

I continued to stare at his fingers as he anxiously tugged at the velvet.

This nervous awkwardness around me that I sensed in him was oddly endearing. It made me want to set him at ease by talking, laughing, and getting to know each other better. Combined with the confident authority he often displayed in his behaviour, it created an irresistible mix in a man for me, drawing me to him. And not just physically, I realised.

I fought my own desire to deepen this relationship in any way.

"No. No changes," I bit out and yanked the blindfold out of his hands.

Leaning all the way against the window, as far away from him as possible, I tied the wide strip of velvet around my head, blindfolding myself.

The visual of him was gone.

However, during the long, silent ride in the car, I could not avoid breathing in his alluring scent or hearing his slight movements.

And I could do nothing about the overwhelming awareness of him being this close to me.

Chapter 11

VADIM

He didn't need to be a demon to sense the dark cloud of anger and frustration hanging over her. It pulsed wildly, shrouding her from him and making the darkness inside the car near absolute.

It unnerved him, increasing his own anxiety.

However, no amount of irritation inside her could completely obscure the delicate tendril of her attraction to him. Warm and bright, it weaved its way through the treacherous mists swirling around her—fragile, like a kite lost in a thunderstorm.

He forced his back to remain flush with the seat of the car but couldn't help snatching the delicious emotion as soon as it stretched his way.

Intoxicating.

His head swam with joy the moment her light entered him.

He had waited for this moment.

Normally only partially aware of the time passing by—years and decades morphing into centuries with little difference to him—he spent the past month counting days and even hours, waiting to see her again.

He didn't expect Andras's message about her cancellation a few days ago to upset him as much as it had. For the first time ever, he had taken a car and left the Base for a completely personal reason—to make sure she was okay on the day he got the message.

That morning, he hid in the shadows and watched her leave for work. Only when he had seen she was alive and healthy had he returned to the Base, determined to wait patiently for her visit the following month.

However, waiting had become more difficult as the night of her cancelled visit approached. The disappointment of not seeing her became outright unbearable when the time came.

Unable to deal with it, he gave up, called the car, and drove all the way to her place, against all hopes of seeing her.

No amount or concern or anxiety could suppress the overwhelming relief and joy he felt from her being in the car next to him now.

Excitement bubbled in him. He wanted to talk to her, ask the many questions that had been barraging his mind, learn everything there was to know about her.

Yet she ordered him to be quiet. So he held back his excitement, which wasn't easy despite the centuries spent in almost complete silence before now. Or, maybe because he spent most of his existence either silently complying with the orders of others or giving brief orders himself, that he actually craved a real conversation now.

Afraid that one word from him might plunge her mood deeper into anger or that she'd order him to turn the car around there and then, he said nothing all the way to the Base.

Chapter 12

FOR THE NEXT SEVERAL months, my life followed the same pattern—a month-long wait for that one night, only to begin waiting again as soon as the morning came.

Despite all my determination not to let those nights take over the rest of my life, somehow it had happened anyway. No matter how satisfying the orgasms were, they didn't take care of my cravings for the rest of the month.

Afraid that no one would measure up to the strangers and their expertise, I avoided the potential mess of living out my fantasies in real life and didn't pursue any relationships, not even quick one-night stands. Instead, lying in bed on my own, with no one else but my vibrator for company, I re-lived the sensations of those nights over and over again.

However, the images shifted in my imagination. Slowly, my fantasy had evolved from having two strangers touching me, to the hands of just one man. He was still faceless, but more real than a fantasy should be. He had a voice that made me weak in my knees and a scent that drew me in like a magnet.

The image of the black velvet of the blindfold crushed in his hands would surface in my mind whenever I touched myself. I imagined what it would be like to have him touch me. Would he restrain that hidden power that I had sensed inside him? Or would he let it all go, taking me greedily, with abandon?

The desire to find out what it would feel like to be with him grew stronger with every visit and with each day in between.

I forbade him to talk. Yet I couldn't stop the tension and my pent-up attraction from charging the air between us during the long ride in the car each month.

Craving his touch, I had no willpower to refuse him dressing me after the sessions, savouring every brush of his fingers against my skin, every stolen touch of his hands, and every moment of being close to him.

Vadim.

I hadn't called him by name to his face. Following my order of silence, our verbal interactions had been reduced to a handful of brief questions and answers.

However, I used it in my mind whenever I thought about him, which I did almost constantly now.

Vadim was a fairly common name in Belarus, but I thought it suited him specifically, and I loved the sound of it.

In just four months, by the time of my September visit, there was no way to deny it—Vadim had taken over my fantasy completely.

Standing by the window, waiting for the car to turn into the street in front of my building, I felt no apprehension. The fear of the unknown was long gone.

The anticipation that fluttered though me had nothing to do with the strangers who were about to lock me into restraints and touch my naked body. But it had everything to do with the man who took me to them.

Chapter 13

"THE MARKET CONDITIONS in this country are not the best for us, Jade." Harry, my boss, leaned back in his chair, folding his arms across his barrel chest. "We took the risk by moving in, but the experiment hasn't worked out the way we've hoped."

He had called me to his office the moment I got in on a rainy October morning. I knew something was up when he had greeted me in English. Harry and I were the only native English speakers in our office in Minsk, and we rarely interacted in our mother tongue, preferring to use Russian for the benefit of the rest of the staff.

Harry grew up bilingual, with a Russian mother, and his language skills were even better than mine. His speaking English to me now signalled the importance of our conversation and an obvious attempt to bring it to a more casual, friendly level.

"When are we closing?"

"The management wants to let it go until the end of the fiscal year."

"So, the end of March then?"

The closing of any operation usually came with a certain feeling of sadness—we had all put a lot of time and energy into getting this subsidiary off the ground. However, it wasn't the first time I'd had to pack up and change cities, countries or even continents, and the upcoming move itself wouldn't normally bother me. With my restless nature, I actually tended to welcome the change.

But this move meant I'd be saying goodbye to people I'd met here. Tanya had become a good friend by now, and I would really miss her and her little sister. The reason for the achy tightness in my chest, I realised, was not just Sveta and her, though.

Leaving the country would also mean the end to my monthly excursions to the mysterious place outside of the city . . . and to my meetings with Vadim, the man whose face I hadn't even seen.

"You won't be left without a job," Harry rushed to reassure me, obviously catching the shift in my mood but missing the real reason for it. "Our Moscow office is thriving. I've already contacted them. They are dying to have you. With your experience and expertise—"

"Thank you, Harry." I leaned my hip against his desk to steady myself. Even the prospect of working in the Russian capital, the city that had always fascinated me, felt less than thrilling at the moment. "How about yourself?"

"Apparently, they need me in London." Harry shrugged then added, animatedly, "You know, I'm looking forward to moving back to my home country for a while. It'll be nice to see the family more often. And food!" he exclaimed. "I didn't even realise how much I've missed the good old British food."

He laughed, and I smiled too.

"Well, I'm really happy for you then, Harry."

WAITING BY THE WINDOW for the dark car to appear the night of my November visit, I calculated that tonight would be one of my four remaining nights with the strangers—five if I managed to squeeze one into March, before I left.

This filled me with an inexplicable sadness. Now there was a firm deadline to this adventure. Just over four months from now, I'd have to leave this fantasy behind.

I'll have to say goodbye to him.

That was the true source of this heavy feeling inside me—having to part with Vadim, a man I hardly knew, whose face I'd never seen, but who intrigued me more than I'd ever thought was possible.

I had made a conscious effort not to learn anything about him. But now that there was the end in sight of whatever time we could have together, I wondered if I should get to know him a little better after all. If only just to figure out the source of this inexplicable physical attraction to him on my part.

I grabbed my leather jacket and left the apartment before the car had even arrived that night.

LESS THAN A MINUTE after I exited the stairwell, the car turned into the courtyard from the street and pulled over in front of me. The door opened and I slid in the back seat.

Vadim silently handed me the blindfold, but I didn't take it.

"Listen," I exhaled, unsure what I was going to say, but my mood was different tonight. The news of the upcoming move to Moscow loomed over me like a storm cloud. "If I promise not to pay attention where you're taking me—not even to look out of the window—would you let me *not* wear this tonight?"

After months of enforcing silence between us, I wanted to talk now.

"Can I put this on later?" I gestured at the blindfold.

"No." His firm answer made me raise an eyebrow in surprise—I'd been too spoilt by their *as-you-wish* attitude to accept a rejection without questioning it.

"Why not?"

"It's for your safety," he explained. "For the safety and anonymity of others, too."

Others?

I reckoned there must be more women coming to their place, besides Tanya and I. Or was he talking about the safety of the men who touched and watched me?

He lifted the blindfold, and I scooted closer then inclined my head for him to tie it around my eyes.

His fresh scent enveloped me, making my heart skip a beat in the now familiar way. Except that the feeling was tainted with sadness this time—I was going to leave here soon.

"My name is Jade," I whispered on impulse.

"I know." He finished the knot and leaned back.

"You do?" I turned more his way. My knee touched his, but I didn't shift back in the seat. "How?"

"We do a thorough background check of all the Sour—um . . . women."

"You do?" I gaped in shock—so much for my perceived anonymity.

"We'd never share your information with anyone, but it's necessary for us to know whom we invite," he explained. "For the safety of everyone involved."

"So you knew all about me from the very first time we met?"

"Yes. The facts that is. There are still many things I wish to know."

"Like what?"

"You want to talk tonight," he stated, then asked, "Why?"

"Would you rather I be quiet?"

"No. But something is different about you tonight. And I wish to know the reason." The tone of his voice was a bit too intense for a casual small talk. As if the answer really mattered to him.

I took a moment before replying, not feeling like talking about the upcoming move or generally bringing anything about my work into tonight's experience.

"I simply feel like talking right now, Vadim. That's your name, isn't it?"

"Yes, but I don't believe I've ever introduced myself."

"You haven't. Andras mentioned it over the phone once. Did he break any rules by doing so? I don't want to get him in trouble or anything."

"No, it's fine. In fact, I should have introduced myself to you earlier. Please forgive my poor manners—I don't get to interact with humans often."

Humans?

"Why not?"

"There is no need."

"Does that mean you live out of town, too?" I asked, because being in the city would make interacting with people pretty much unavoidable, in my opinion. "Anywhere near where you're taking me?"

"I live *where* I'm taking you."

"The same building?"

I never had a chance to actually *see* the place, but to me it felt almost like it could be located somewhere in another dimension, a different reality. Finding out that it was actually someone's home seemed odd.

"Yes," he confirmed calmly.

His answers only bred more questions.

"How long have you been in Belarus?" I asked.

"Just over half of my life."

"And where were you before?"

"In the Islamic Empire."

"Where?"

"Er . . ." He paused for a moment. "The Middle East it's called now."

"Is that where you were born?"

"No."

I was happy he replied at all, but the more I asked the less I knew. His answers didn't give me much, and our small talk was beginning to feel more like an interrogation on my part.

As if sensing my frustration, he heaved a long sigh.

"You have to excuse me, Jade." His deep voice sounded apologetic. "I truly enjoy your interest in me—more than you may realise. Unfortunately, I'm not able to answer your questions properly, for various reasons. I wouldn't be able to give you honest answers, and I don't think you would appreciate me lying."

"No, I wouldn't," I agreed with a sigh of my own. "Well, that may make any small talk difficult for us—I can't ask you questions, and you already know everything about me . . ."

"No, not everything," he replied quickly. "Not even close."

"Well, you did an 'extensive background check,' didn't you?"

"Yes. So, I know the facts. Nothing more."

"What else is there to know? Do you still have questions for me?"

"Many," he said softly.

"Like what?"

"Why did your start visiting us in the first place?"

"Isn't it obvious?" I exhaled a short laugh. "I had a fantasy I wanted fulfilled."

"Why are you not afraid?" The question was somewhat unexpected and made me pause. "Even that first time, you had no fear, just some apprehension."

I noted with surprise that not only did he correctly identify my emotions back then, he also remembered what I felt that night after all this time.

"I don't have any reason to be afraid," I replied after a few moments. "I've never been harmed by any of you."

"You took a risk coming in the first place."

"Not as much as you may think," I disagreed. "I knew someone who did it before me, and she wasn't harmed either. So there wasn't that much risk."

"The danger is always there," he argued. The certainty in his voice prickled along my spine with unease. "Sometimes more than you can know. Why do it at all? Why not stay home, where you're safe? What makes you get in this car month after month?"

More like *who*.

By now, Vadim had become my main reason for these visits. I had been looking forward to spending a couple of hours in his proximity in this car even more than to the orgasms delivered by others.

There was no way I would confess anything like that to him, though. And I chose to speak to my initial reasons, instead.

"It's a fantasy I have. What you, I mean *they*, are going to do to me tonight is something that I find exciting. Don't you have some fantasies too? If, let's say, Wonder Woman knocked on your door in real life, begging you to have a night of hot sex with her, wouldn't you jump at the chance?"

"No," he replied coolly. "She's not my fantasy."

"Well, you may be the only straight man in the Universe then." I huffed a laugh, then a sudden thought doused me like a bucket of ice-cold water.

Straight?

What if he wasn't? What if I had imagined the response to me that I sensed from him? After all, he'd confessed he'd never touched me in that room and he had never voiced any desires for anything more between us.

"Vadim." I cleared my suddenly dry throat. "You said you're in that room with me on the nights of my visits."

"Always," he replied slowly.

"Do you . . . watch me?"

"Yes." His voice descended lower, thick and soft, like the velvet around my eyes.

For once, I was actually grateful for the blindfold—it gave me the courage to be direct.

"What do you feel while you watch me?"

"Everything you feel, Jade." His voice caressed my skin, more titillating than the hands of the strangers.

"Everything?" I repeated, feeling a little lightheaded now.

"Your anticipation," he continued, "Your desire, your lust—I feel them all."

"Do you . . . touch yourself?" It came out rather throaty, and I pressed my knee more firmly to his—the only physical contact between us.

"No."

"Do you touch . . . um, anyone else?"

"No."

"Then why? What's the purpose of tonight?"

He inhaled deeply and moved his knee away.

"This is another one of those questions that I can't answer, Jade."

Chapter 14

THE CAR STOPPED, BUT the door didn't immediately open like it usually did. Instead, I heard Vadim exit first. Then the door at my side opened and his hand found mine.

"Careful," he warned, helping me out of the vehicle.

The fact that it was he who led me inside the building and down the stairs this time did not escape me. Little by little, he seemed to be taking over the functions that used to be performed by others—first, helping me dress and demanding to be the one picking me up, and now walking me through the building himself.

"Do you need help?" he asked when we stopped at the chair in the room where I usually took my clothes off.

His hand was still in mine, and I couldn't bring myself to let go. I didn't want him to step back either, afraid I'd miss his scent and his touch—even through the leather of his glove—as soon as he moved away.

"Yes," I replied, and then specified, lest there be any misunderstanding, "I need *your* help to undress."

His squeezed my hand gently.

"If it's your wish—"

"Yes. My wish." My voice was even firmer this time.

He cleared his throat again and stepped closer, letting go of my hand.

I swayed forward, leaning into his scent and the warmth emanating from his large body.

He brushed his hands down my shoulders, taking off my jacket, then slowly unwrapped my scarf.

Instead of turning me to get to the long zipper of my dress, he circled his arms around me, bringing me closer to him than I'd ever been.

He tugged the zipper down. Then the soft leather of his gloves skimmed along my spine, eliciting a web of tiny shivers across my skin, as he snapped my bra open and let it fall to the floor along with the dress.

My breathing grew fast and shallow. With his hands pressed to my bare back, I was surrounded by him. It wasn't quite an embrace—he strained his muscles to keep from actually hugging, simply enclosing me into the circle of his arms, instead. His proximity was enough to make my head spin, though.

Suddenly unsteady on my feet, I rocked forward and pressed my forehead to his chest—his muscles flexed under the thin material of his shirt, but he held still. So still, I hardly felt his breathing.

Emboldened by the fact that he wasn't moving away, I slid my hands up his stomach—feeling the hard ridges of his abs tense under my touch—then up his chest, to his shoulders and neck.

The tips of my fingers barely skimmed the skin over the collar of his shirt when his whole body shuddered and he withdrew from me so suddenly, I nearly lost my balance.

He grabbed my wrists, yanking my hands away from his neck.

"Jade . . ." His voice was choked. His reaction enough to make it clear—my touch was not welcome. Still—vibrating head to toe, shocked by my body's reaction to his—I couldn't let go.

I needed more of him. And now that there was a definite end to whatever time we could have together, I had no strength left in me to fight this need.

"Can it be you?" I begged. "Please, can you be the one to touch me tonight?" Afraid to hear another cool '*no*' from him, I added quickly, "This is my *wish* for tonight. I want it to be you."

"Jade," he exhaled, his hands squeezing my wrists harder, deep regret unmistakable in his voice. "That is impossible."

"Why?" I wouldn't give up, even as I realised I was begging a man for intimacy that he'd made clear he wouldn't or couldn't give to me.

"They will take you in," he said softly, letting go of my arms, and severing the only contact between us.

I couldn't see him, the sound of two pairs of boots from those entering the room drowned out his footsteps, but I *felt* him move away. The warm fragrant cloud of his presence around me disappeared, taking along the light, heady feeling I always experienced near him.

Quickly and efficiently, the hands of the strangers took off the rest of my clothes for me. Then someone—not Vadim—lifted me up, pressing me to the cool chest plates of their armour, and carried me to the other room.

They lowered me on the table, the silky sensation of the padding underneath me familiar. The click of cuffs around my wrists and ankles, the expert glide of leather-clad hands on my body, even the rising arousal under their touch—had become a routine.

All I had to do was to surrender and let them give me what I'd come here for. Over and over again. For as long as I could take it.

With a deep inhale, I stretched my back, trying to get into the moment, to enjoy what I thought I craved.

Frustratingly, it wasn't that easy this time.

The bitterness from his rejection still lingered, bringing a feeling of disappointment and loss.

The hands of strangers, no matter how dexterous, couldn't substitute for what I wanted—*his* touch.

Suddenly, the glide of their hands on me felt more intrusive than exciting. The arousal fizzled to nothing. I yanked at the chains holding me, needing to be free from all of this . . .

"Stop!" Vadim's voice came from right above me, closer than I expected. With his order, the strangers ceased immediately, as if by magic. "Release her."

The tone of authority in his command resonated through me, renewing the rush of excitement. Still, I was glad when the cuffs were taken off. It was obvious that my fantasy had changed irreversibly and my body now craved someone I couldn't have.

I sat up on the table and wrapped my arms around myself, suddenly extremely aware of my nudity in a room that might be filled with strangers.

Someone threw a sheet of silk over my shoulders, and I tucked it around me to cover up.

"Can I . . . take this off?" I lifted my hand to the blindfold.

The fantasy was over. This was reality, and I felt vulnerable—naked, blindfolded, and alone.

No one responded to my question. So I tugged at the knot at the back of my head, untying the strip of black velvet from around my head.

I expected semi-darkness—red silk, black leather, chandeliers. Instead, glaring white light greeted me, making me blink and squint for a few moments until my eyes adjusted to it.

As soon as I could see again, I swept the room with my gaze. It was big, as I had expected—glaring white walls, thick beams under the ceiling, balconies along two opposite walls.

The sight of the two dark figures standing at the table where I sat made me gasp. They were dressed in a sort of modern armour suits—a combination of charcoal-grey fabric and pewter—their heads completely covered by helmets that hid their faces.

Their size alone made them seem imposing and menacing, contributing to their appearance of robot-soldiers from some surreal army, ready to attack.

Unnerved by their silent presence, I pulled my legs up to my chest and twisted around, looking for *him*.

"Vadim?"

"I'm here."

The familiar voice came from behind me. Standing at the head of the table, he took a step closer until his thighs hit the silk-covered edge.

Slowly, I slid my gaze up his tall frame. Dark jeans, army-green shirt with long sleeves rolled up to his elbows.

Speechless, I took in his strong neck, the collarbone in the triangle made by the two top buttons of his shirt left open. Vadim wasn't wearing his hoodie, and my jaw dropped at the sight of his face—he was incredibly handsome, in a strong, powerful way.

His dark-chestnut hair had copper highlights and just enough length to sink my fingers in.

His frown hardened his features, but it didn't make him any less good-looking. In fact, the intensity in his gaze made him even more stunning, in my opinion. The deep line between his thick, dark eyebrows spoke of concern, not anger, to me.

With his eyes narrowed at me like that, I couldn't quite make out their colour, but I believed I caught a hint of green.

"Vadim?" I asked again, just to make sure.

"I'll take you out of here." He rolled his sleeves down.

Besides him and the two silent 'robots', there was no one else in the room.

"Where is everyone?"

"I dismissed them all."

"You did? When?"

"Two months ago."

"Why? And how about these two?" I tipped my chin at the two figures at the table.

"They were your wish."

Well, that was true. I wished for the hands of faceless strangers on me. And these two were as faceless as could be.

"Why did you dismiss everyone else?" I asked quietly, shifting under the red silk wrapped around me.

"That was *my* wish," he said firmly. "I didn't want anyone in here but me."

Was that a possessive note in his tone that made my heart skip and my stomach flop?

He buttoned his shirt all the way and even lifted the collar up, too.

In preparation against my touch? I remembered his recoiling from my fingers barely touching his neck.

He stretched his hand towards one of the males at my side.

"Your gloves," Vadim bit out.

It seemed to take the man in armour a moment to process the request. Then he silently pulled his gloves off and handed them to Vadim.

With both hands now covered, Vadim scooped me up from the table along with my sheet. I hooked my arm around his shoulder, leaning in as he carried me, but mindful to keep my hands away from his skin this time.

Chapter 15

EVEN THOUGH NOTHING had happened tonight, and I didn't feel boneless or out of control as I usually did, Vadim insisted on dressing me.

Watching him slide my black lacy underwear over my hips then carefully roll my stockings up my legs, I desperately tried to read him.

He didn't seem to mind being close to me. Why did he appear to loathe my touch?

I made a conscious effort to keep my body away from any unnecessary contact with his when he circled me with his arms to zip up my dress. But I couldn't help a long inhale of air rich with his warm scent when his chest came close to my face.

Kneeling in front of me, he helped me put on my boots then got my scarf and jacket for me.

The lingering silence between us quickly grew uncomfortable. And by the time we both got in the car, I couldn't stand it anymore.

"Say something," I demanded. "Or I'll think you're angry with me."

"Me? Angry?" He sounded genuinely surprised.

"You're not talking." After months of enforcing silence between us, I now desperately needed him to speak.

"I am not much of a talker," he replied with a small shake of his head. "And right now, I am actually terrified that if I say the wrong thing, I risk never seeing you again."

"Why would you care either way?" I challenged.

"The way you felt tonight . . . Will you still come next month?"

I twisted the silver ring on my finger for a few seconds, thinking about my answer before honestly replying, "I don't think so, Vadim."

His large body slumped in the seat as if deflated.

"I can't go through with it anymore," I rushed to explain. "The fantasy . . . it seems to have worn itself out for me. I don't want them touching me again. I can stop at any time," I reminded. "That was the deal."

He remained quiet.

"Are you upset that I don't want other men touching me anymore?"

"No," he shook his head. "Of course not. But I want to see you again."

"Why?"

He rubbed his forehead.

"Because I simply cannot accept *not* seeing you anymore."

"Why?" I repeated, feeling confused by his mixed signals. "Vadim, I don't understand you. What is it that you want with me?"

"All of you, Jade." He lifted his head to face me. His eyes glistened in the moonlight filtering through the car windows, his burning gaze inescapable. "Never in a thousand years could I have hoped to meet someone like you. My body responds to you and my mind craves you. I'm afraid if I let you go, I'll spend the next thousand years, waiting for someone like you to come my way again."

"And you say you're not much of a talker . . ." I breathed out, my chest tight.

"I mean every word." He covered my hand with his on the seat between us. "I *need* to see you again."

Just a few months.

That's all we had. With no chance for anything long-term, there couldn't be any harm now in spending some of this time together. Could there?

I'd better use every moment of it then.

"Are you hungry?" I asked, tilting my head to the side.

"Hungry?" he gritted through his teeth. Something dark flashed through his gaze, but the squeeze of his hand remained gentle on mine.

"Will you have dinner with me tonight?" I asked softly and added with a smile, "Since I just happen to have the night free."

"I FORGOT TO BLINDFOLD you," Vadim said with a frown as we took our seats at the restaurant where I brought him when we got back to the city. "This is the first time I've neglected my responsibilities."

His expression—a mix of regret, puzzlement, and a dash of wonder—prompted me to pat his gloved hand in comfort.

"No worries. I was rather taken by our conversation to pay any attention to where we were driving."

"If you knew the location, would you tell anyone?"

I searched his face for any signs of suspicion or accusation but found none.

"No," I replied honestly. "I would not. If you want me to keep it a secret, all you have to do is ask."

He nodded, apparently content with my answer, but I couldn't take my gaze away from his face.

Physically, I was attracted to Vadim way before I saw his face. I loved his large body, the way he held himself with innate dignity. His deep voice. His scent. At this point, I didn't believe his face would matter that much to the way I felt about him. And it didn't.

Still, as I stared at him, I couldn't help but admire the absolute perfection of his features and the stunning combined effect of them together.

The sharp angles of his jawline and high cheekbones under his tanned skin conveyed strength.

The firm set of his mouth, strong chin, and thick, dark eyebrows that seemed to be permanently drawn into a solemn expression spoke of dominance and power to me.

Impossibly long eyelashes softened his stern face, giving him a dash of true beauty that only intensified his handsomeness to the level of almost unbearable.

"I can't figure out the colour of your eyes." I squinted, fully aware that my staring at this point was borderline rude.

Not my fault, he is so easy on the eye.

"There is a lot of green in them," I continued. "But not quite emerald . . ."

"Jade," he said, and I blinked, feeling my cheeks warm up with pleasure that trickled through to every part of my body. The way he said my name, with that deep velvet in his voice, sounded so incredibly sensual.

He meant 'jade' as his eye colour, you dummy!

For that was exactly what they were—the shade of green was warmer than emerald, with yellow specks.

"True. They are jade." I shifted under his gaze.

The waiter brought my plate of cold cuts and filled our glasses with sparkling water. Vadim hadn't ordered any food, claiming he was not hungry. I wasn't either—to be honest, I couldn't even think about food right now—but I felt I had to order something since the dinner was my idea after all.

"What is this?" He pointed with his chin at my plate.

"Oh, it's sliced beef tongue, a local delicacy." I tilted my head. "You've been in this country long enough to know that. Have you tried it?"

"No. May I?" He lifted his fork with the question.

"Sure." I slid the plate his way. "It's not bad, once you get past what it is. I like the texture—very tender."

He lifted a slice on his fork and inspected it carefully.

"Humans have a wide variety of ways in which they prepare their food," he said slowly, as if speaking to himself.

"This one is just boiled, I believe, with some spices, but you can have it marinated as well."

Vadim took a tiniest bite of the slice on his fork. "And?"

"Interesting." He placed the fork with the remaining meat on the side plate. "I don't believe I've tasted anything like this before."

"You don't eat meat?"

"No."

He reached for his glass of sparkling water and took a sip then quickly grabbed his napkin before sneezing in it.

"Bless you." I smiled.

"Sorry." He stared at the bubbles rising to the top in his glass, in clear bewilderment. "I did not expect this."

"What do you mean?" I leaned back in my chair. "Don't tell me you've never had carbonated water before."

"No. I don't believe I have," he replied, his expression completely serious. "Gas bubbles in water must be fairly new."

"New? Well, I'm not sure when it came to Belarus, but water was first carbonated sometime in the seventeen hundreds."

He nodded, as if it made a perfect sense to him now.

"That would explain it. I was long on the Council by then, with almost no contact with humans outside of the Base," he muttered, only confusing me further.

"What?" I asked, hoping I didn't hear him right—he was speaking rather softly—because otherwise I'd have to worry about how sound his mind actually was.

"Nothing." He blinked, his attention fully on me again. "I don't go out much, as you might have guessed by now." The sudden, wide smile he gave me almost made me forget any concerns.

"Do you mean you spend most of your time in that building out there?"

"I spend *all* of my time there, with very rare exceptions."

"What do you do in that place?"

"Work. Live."

I waited for him to elaborate, but he asked me a question instead, "What happened tonight, Jade?"

His avoidance of talking about himself was becoming harder to ignore. My curiosity was tinted with worry now. What were the reasons for his evasiveness? What was he hiding?

Still, I resolved to be as honest as possible with him. I had nothing to hide. Maybe if he saw how open I was, he would grow more comfortable with opening up, too.

"Tonight? I'm not sure I can explain it properly. It just stopped being fun," I said, pushing the slices of meat on my plate. "With me, it happens often. Things I find exciting stop being that after a while."

"What other things have you liked?"

"Oh, many." I laughed. "I guess for me it's always about doing something new, thrilling, and a little dangerous. Have you gone sky-diving?"

"No."

"Bungee jumping? Surfing? Rock-climbing? Skiing? Mountain-biking?"

He kept shaking his head to every question.

"Nothing at all? Is there anything that would get your blood pumping with adrenaline and start your heart going?"

"Yes. You."

I snapped my gaze to his. His calm way of delivering compliments caught me off guard every time. My face heating with a blush, I blinked, gaping at him for a moment.

"I meant an activity, Vadim. Something you'd do for fun, like sports?"

"For fun? All of what you've mentioned comes with risk to your life," he pointed out.

"Hence the thrill," I agreed.

"Human life is short and fragile as is. Why would you deliberately risk it?"

I'd heard the same question from people before. However, from him, it didn't sound like judgment. Vadim seemed to be genuinely puzzled by my choices.

"Well, some things do carry more risk than others. To tell you the truth, I'm glad I've done skydiving and bungee jumping, but I don't think I'd ever do it again. I believe, however, that there is always at least one thing for everyone that stays with you. Something you'd do over and over again. And instead of wearing off, your enjoyment from doing it only grows."

"Do you have a thing like that?"

I nodded.

"For me, it's surfing. I've been doing it since I was a kid, and the more I surf the more I love it. In fact, that's one of the things I miss the most from back home—next to my family—the ocean."

"What do you like about surfing?"

"Oh God, so much!" I exclaimed, trying to think of everything I felt when on my surfboard. "The way your mind and body work in a perfect harmony. When you get every muscle in you to do exactly what you want it to do." I paused for a moment, searching for words to describe the feeling of pure joy and awe swelling inside me at the memories. "Then everything aligns perfectly, and there is this one moment when you, the board, and the wave become one, gliding together through time and space. Nothing else exists. You can feel the power of the ocean, the Earth, and the Universe—and you truly become a part of it all. It's incredible . . . magical." I exhaled and added with some frustration, "I'm sorry, I can't explain it better. I wish you could feel it . . ."

"I do."

The flickering light of the candle on the table between us must have reflected in his eyes, as sparks of blue flashed from under his long eyelashes.

A little too bright and too blue for the candlelight . . .

But the expression of wonder on his face stopped my concerns. Suddenly, I felt so close to him, as if we shared a true understanding that could only be possible between people who knew each other inside and out.

I wanted to share more with him—my joy, my thrill, my passion.

"I wish I could take you surfing one day, Vadim."

"I'd love that." He smiled, and to me his words sounded like a promise.

Chapter 16

OUR DINNER TOOK MUCH longer than expected, although neither of us ate much. Vadim continued to avoid answering personal questions, but we still found many topics to discuss. Mostly about me.

As few answers as he had for me about his own life, he seemed to be filled with questions about mine. His desire to know more about me and his attention to everything I said appeared genuine. I told him about my family back home, my childhood growing up with four brothers, studying in the United States, and working all over the globe afterwards.

I hardly noticed how the time flew by. The night sky above us was already edged with grey as I stepped out of the car.

"I'll walk you to the door," Vadim told me as soon as he opened my car door, taking my hand to help me out of the vehicle.

Suddenly, I wasn't ready to part with him yet.

"Thank you, Vadim. For the ride and the dinner." Despite the invitation being mine, Vadim had insisted on paying the bill. "I really enjoyed it."

Suddenly, uncharacteristically shy, I stopped at the door. My gaze down, I felt his stare on me but couldn't bring myself to meet his eyes.

"Me, too." His voice dropped a notch as he stepped closer. His breath stroked the side of my face. "I enjoy being with you."

He didn't touch me, yet him being this close, his voice flowing around me, his scent washing over me—made it impossible to part with him.

"Would you—" I swallowed hard, my dry throat making my voice husky. "Would you like to come up?"

"Yes," he replied immediately.

With my gaze somewhere on his belt buckle, I fumbled in my purse for my key, then realizing I didn't need one for the building entrance, punched the code in the lockpad.

My stomach fluttered with butterflies, and my chest expanded with something light and shimmering.

Excitement and maybe a little danger...

Was Vadim my next thrill? Would this feeling for him fade too? The possibility of that brought in a shadow of sadness, and I chased it away immediately, unwilling to spoil this night.

"Come," I said resolutely, grabbing his hand and dragging him through the door with me.

"WOULD YOU LIKE A GLASS of wine?" I asked the moment we entered my apartment. Not waiting for his answer, I walked swiftly through the tiny hallway to my not much larger kitchen.

"No, thank you." His voice sounded close behind me. Very close.

"Well." I exhaled sharply, hating the onslaught of nerves. "I'm going to have one."

Saying this, I opened the cabinet and took out a glass and the bottle of red wine I had there.

I couldn't remember the last time I felt this nervous, and the reasons for me feeling this way were puzzling. Was it because I really cared about how tonight would go? Or maybe because I already hoped there could be more than just this one night?

"Are you sure you don't want any?" I asked, draining most of the glass in three gulps.

"No. But would you happen to have some sparkling water?" he asked unexpectedly.

"You liked it, huh?" I smiled. " Sorry, I don't have any here. But I'll make sure to get some next time—" I cut myself short.

Next time?

Nothing had happened between us yet. I couldn't possibly be thinking about spending more time with him already.

With my thoughts all over the place, I grabbed the bottle and poured another glass for myself.

"You're extremely nervous," he stated.

"No shit!" I half-emptied my second glass of wine before setting it on the table.

What was going on with me?

Where did this anxiety come from? Like one needed to get drunk to have sex with someone like him. If anything, getting pissed would be a perfect way to make a fool of myself.

"Why, Jade?" He gazed inquisitively at me. "Why are you feeling this way?"

I inhaled deeply, shoving the glass away, and stepped closer to him.

"I–I'm not really sure why, to be honest, but having you in my place tonight . . . It feels . . . special."

"It is special," he agreed, his deep voice soft and caressing.

My body flush with his now, I raised my arms and splayed my hands on his chest. He tensed under my touch.

Maybe because of the wine or because of him, but my head swam as a wave of heat spread through me. I slid my hands to his shoulders and lifted my face up to his, yearning for a kiss.

"Jade," he groaned, circling my wrists to stop my hands in their journey up to his face.

"Kiss me," I rasped.

Never had I ever had to beg a man for anything before. Never had a kiss felt as vitally important as it did right now. I needed it more than anything in the world at that moment.

"No." He took a step back. "I can't."

His words were more sobering that an ice-cold shower.

"Sorry?" I dropped my hands, confused. "I—"

The proper thing to do here—the only thing to do, really—was to retreat, to preserve whatever dignity I had left after his rejection. But the wine lent me the liquid courage. And the built-up frustration at the dissonance between his words and his actions fuelled my anger.

"What is going on, Vadim?" I met his gaze, determined to get an answer from him, even if it meant destroying what was left of my dignity. "You said you want it all." I stepped back and leaned my hip against the kitchen table. "Yet you shrink away any time I get close, as if I carry the plague."

Even his body language was confusing. He leaned forward—towards me—hands fisted at his sides, the hunger in his stare fierce and hot. Yet, he took another step back.

"Things I want to do to you . . ." He closed his eyes for a moment, drawing in a deep inhale. "I haven't felt like that for a woman in . . . ever. But I'm scared. Terrified that if I touch you, I would harm you."

The pain in his voice triggered compassion in me. His words, however, put me on guard.

"What do you mean? How?"

"Until a couple of months ago, the smart thing—the only honourable thing for me to do—would be to walk away. I should have resisted picking you up in the car in the first place, getting someone else to do it when Andras left. But I had already tasted your energy and needed more of it, in whatever form I could get it. Besides, something happened about two months ago. A human woman proved to the world that it is possible to love one of us. I saw the fierce, magnificent love in her eyes, and I hoped . . ." His voice trailed off and he shook his head, breaking eye contact. "Hope made me do irresponsible things," he muttered.

"I don't understand, Vadim." Hardly anything he'd just said made sense to me.

"I don't want to lie to you, Jade." He met my gaze again. "But I have no idea how to tell you the truth."

"What truth?" I searched his face for answers, finding none. "Just tell me, please. Whatever it is . . ."

"I'm not human," he said gravely, his eyes firmly on mine. His grim expression left no doubt it was not a joke.

Slowly, I took a step back.

"What are you then?" A chilly suspicion that this beautiful body may hold a fractured mind dawned on me. I clasped my hands tight. "Vadim . . ."

"I want you to know, Jade, I'd rather burn in hell for eternity than see any harm come to you."

"Why would there be any harm?"

He exhaled heavily then swayed my way before taking another step back.

"I have . . ." he rasped, avoiding eye contact with me now. "I have killed before."

"What?" I shook my head in disbelief. Vadim might not be well, but I refused to accept he was a murderer.

His gaze slid to somewhere past my shoulder.

"I killed a woman . . . With my bare hands. When all I wanted was to make love to her . . ."

As he spoke, sombre and completely serious, cold dread settled inside me, turning from a chilly trickle of suspicion to a solid brick of icy fear.

Sobering up at once, I shifted closer to the knife drawer.

"Why did you do it, Vadim?"

His gaze snapped back to me, making me regret speaking aloud—drawing his attention.

"I couldn't stop myself in time."

His answer turned my dread to horror.

Just because he hadn't hurt me during the months that I knew him didn't mean he wouldn't do it now. After all, this was the first time we were truly and absolutely alone, with no armoured men outside the door and no car driver nearby.

One on one with a murderer...

My curiosity and thirst for adventure got me in trouble after all, even if not exactly in the way I would have predicted it.

Blindly, I reached into the drawer behind me and grabbed the first knife my hand landed on.

"Jade..." he exhaled at the sight of my weapon. "You don't need that. I would never hurt—"

"But you *have* hurt before," I cut him off, my voice hard and sharp like the knife I held in front of me. "You said so yourself."

He dropped his shoulders, without denying a thing.

"Leave," I ordered.

"Please."

"You need to leave." I raised the knife higher, my heart thundering with fear. "Now."

Vadim gave me one last glance then inclined his head, as if conceding, and turned to the exit.

Holding the knife in my outstretched hand, I followed him to the hallway, to make sure he left.

He stopped suddenly at the front door.

"It's been centuries since I've spoken to a human—a woman— before you, Jade. I may fail to accurately express myself. But I've seen what a woman can feel for a demon like me. And hope is a stubborn emotion." A corner of his mouth lifted in a bitter smile as he took a card from his pocket and placed it on the hallway stand. "Now, I will spend the rest of eternity waiting for your call."

The longing in his voice and his expression made my heart squeeze with compassion, but I only tightened the grip on my knife.

"Go," I croaked, my own voice breaking.

Shoulders slumped, he nodded mechanically, as if lost in thought, then took a step to my apartment door and then . . . kept on walking, right through the door, without opening it.

With a strangled noise, I watched him disappear through the hard surface, as if it had absorbed him. Nearly dropping the knife from my shaking fingers, I leaped to the door and splayed my free hand on it.

Solid, firm, and unyielding under my palm, the wood didn't seem to change in any way and had no signs of a man having just passed through it.

A man?

I shrank away from the door in shock, understanding dawned on me.

'I'm not human.'

'A demon like me.'

And a self-confessed murderer.

I picked up the card he left. A plain light-grey rectangle with a phone number typed on it—all twelve digits of a local cell phone number, including the country code, but no name.

'I'll spend the rest of the eternity waiting for your call.'

His words echoed in my mind, scrambling any coherent thought I could muster.

Chapter 17

I TRIED TO GO ON ABOUT my life as usual for a few days. However, going through the motions of my day-to-day routine, my thoughts never strayed far from Vadim, making *the usual* impossible.

Nothing was the same anymore.

Every time I looked at my door, the image of his back disappearing through it rose in my mind, making me question my own sanity. I was certain he did not open that door when he left. What he did was impossible for a man.

However, Vadim didn't claim to be a man.

'A demon like me.'

I also recalled him referring to people as 'humans' on several occasions, as if talking about a separate species.

'I will spend the rest of eternity waiting...'

Grave and wistful, he sounded as if he knew exactly what an eternity of solitude felt like.

Did he?

Unless I was out of my mind myself, there could only be two explanations to all of this.

Either Vadim was delusional or he really was not a human.

Was he unwell? Was that why he seemed to spend most of his time in that house, isolated from the society?

I thought back to the building in the woods. His behaviour there was far from that of a mentally disturbed patient. On the contrary, he emitted an air of undisputed authority that had others obeying him wordlessly.

A demon?

Could something like that even be possible?

A demon . . . who had killed.

His words rang through my mind over and over. *'When all I wanted to do was to make love to her.'*

Was it an accident, then? Or was I searching for reasons to excuse a murder, somehow trying to justify it?

It might be easier for me to forget him if I could dismiss my attraction to him as purely physical. However, thinking back to our dinner together, I couldn't ignore the connection I felt to him. Whoever or whatever Vadim was, that evening he seemed to be the closest being on the planet to me—someone who understood me without words.

It scared me and made me miss him, all at once.

After tormenting myself with questions for days, I realised I couldn't leave the country without at least getting some answers.

One evening a few days later, I found myself rummaging through my hallway stand for his card.

I took out the plain rectangle of paper. Staring at the phone number again, I slid to the floor, my back to the wall. I knew the last thing I should do was call him, but there was someone else who might be able to answer my questions about Vadim.

Crumpling the card in my hand, I dialled another number.

"Hello," Andras's pleasant drawl greeted me.

"Hi, it's Jade." I'd never told him my name, but if they'd done the background check on me, it was reasonable to expect Andras would know who I was.

"Hello, Jade." His voice remained calm and even, as always.

"Would you be able to answer a few questions for me, please? It's about Vadim."

"Curiosity is a sin not a virtue, Jade." His tone had turned guarded now. "It can be dangerous."

"I *need* to know how he is doing, Andras."

"He is fine," he replied flatly. "Would you like me to let him know you called?"

"No. Please, don't."

"Well then—"

"Wait!" The fear that he would hang up urged me to rush in getting my words out. "Please. Just a couple of questions."

"Why?"

"I . . ." I closed my eyes, gathering my thoughts. "I need to know, Andras. He said some things to me, odd and disturbing things. He walked through the freaking door . . ."

"He did?" The note of disbelief in his tone made me wonder if Andras hadn't known what Vadim was. "It's not like him to be that careless," Andras muttered. "What made him forget himself like that? How did it happen?"

It seemed Andras didn't question Vadim's ability, just him displaying it to me.

"Well, we were at my apartment. He confessed he'd murdered someone, a woman. And I told him to leave. He did. Without opening the fucking door, Andras. I need some answers here. It's driving me insane."

I heard him take a deep breath.

"Would you like to talk to him?"

"No. I called *you*." The way my heart jumped at the thought of talking to Vadim only proved that any contact with him was not a good idea at this point—I needed to listen to my brain right now, not my heart. "Just a couple of questions, please. And I promise I'll never bother you again."

A long pause stretched through the line between us once again. My hand began to cramp from the tight grip I had on my mobile phone.

"For me to answer any questions at all, we'll have to talk in person, Jade," Andras finally replied. "I'll need to see your emotions."

"My emotions? Facial expressions, you mean."

"I said what I mean. When and where do you want to meet? Unless you would like me to send a car for you."

"No." I did not want to go to that building again. "Let's meet here in the city." I dug in my brain for a suitable public location not too far from my office. "*Prospect Nezavisimosti*," I named the main street in Minsk. "I'll wait for you outside the Metro station, Victory Square, at noon tomorrow."

"I'll see you then."

The line went dead.

HANDS IN THE POCKETS of my leather coat, I paced the pavement just outside Victory Square, scanning the pedestrians in search of Andras.

The day had turned out to be rather pleasant for November. The sun shone bright in the cloudless sky, and there was just a slight breeze in the fresh, autumn air.

I spotted his tall figure almost a block away.

Out of his grey robe and dressed in a leather jacket and jeans, Andras wouldn't be easy to recognize, if not for his above average height and build.

"Hello, Jade." He approached me, his face partially obscured by the shadows from the hood of the grey sweatshirt he wore under the jacket. "I hope I'm not late."

I shook his gloved hand.

"No, you're not. I came too early."

In fact, I'd had a hard time concentrating at work today, leaving the office a half-hour before my lunch break.

"Have you eaten yet?" he inquired politely. "There is a café on the corner—"

"No, I haven't, but I'm not hungry. Are you?"

"No," he replied simply, a corner of his mouth curling up slightly. "Not at all."

"Good." I wasn't sure I'd be able to sit still in a café anyway. The anxiety eating me from the inside urged me to move. "Would you mind if we just went for a walk? To the next Metro station maybe?"

"As you wish," he replied in the same tone he used to discuss my desires during my visits to the building in the woods.

"How long have you known Vadim?" I asked as we strolled within the pedestrian flow along *Prospect Nezavisimosti*.

"All his life."

I shot a glance his way.

"I should say 'all my life', too." He shrugged a broad shoulder, his hands in his jacket pockets.

"You're the same age?"

Andras nodded.

"You grew up together then?"

"I did not say that."

"Wouldn't knowing someone all your life imply that you had some contact in childhood?"

"Not necessarily."

I caught him watching me—dark eyes glistening from the shadows of his hood.

"That would be true only if both of us had a childhood," he explained.

"Doesn't everyone?"

"Humans, yes. But not us."

I stopped in my tracks, holding his gaze.

"Are you going to tell me you're a demon, too?"

Or was that building in the woods an institution for the insane, after all?

"Would you believe me if I said *yes*, I am?"

The earnest note in his voice made me pause.

I searched his face for any indications he might be joking, finding none. "I don't really know what to believe at this point." I shook my head, muttering under my breath, "Although the fact that I'm even considering the existence of demons may mean I belong in an institution myself."

To my surprise, a wide smile spread on Andras's face, open and sincere.

"Natasha said something along those lines, too, when I told her what I was."

"Who is Natasha?" I began walking again, and he followed, catching up to my pace.

"She is my Mistress. My woman. My *girlfriend*, you would say. When I first told her, she tried to talk me into seeing a psychologist at the hospital where she works."

My head felt like it was about to explode, and I rubbed my forehead.

"Did she believe you at the end? Does she really think she is dating a demon?"

"Yes." His smile grew wider.

"What convinced her?"

"I'd love to say something profound like 'her faith in me' or 'her love for me,' but it was my showing her a few things that would be impossible for humans to do."

The image of Vadim's body disappearing through the door rose in my head again.

"Did you walk through a locked door, too?" I asked.

"A wall. Between our apartments. I've bought a place in her building, just to be closer to her. I also broke a cast-iron frying pan in half with my bare hands to show her our strength. These two abilities would probably be the most obvious differences between you and us, visually. However, Jade, the similarities are far greater."

My thoughts went back to my last conversation with Vadim.

"Did you know that Vadim killed someone?" I asked, my throat tightening.

It felt like the world had stilled around us at that moment.

"We all have." Andras's voice went grave and low, any smile gone from it completely.

"What do you mean?" I stepped in front of him, forcing him to face me, despite the cold trickle of fear down my spine. Being in the middle of a crowded street made me feel much braver.

"Jade, it's been nearly a millennium since we came to Earth." He gazed at me calmly. "The world was very different back then. Most humans killed or were killed in never-ending wars and battles that they constantly led against each other."

"Is that an everyone-is-doing-it-so-it's-acceptable excuse?" I squinted at him.

"Not an excuse but a way of life for most of human history. Had any one of you lived as long as we have, you all would have had blood on your hands, too." The conviction in his voice was unshakable and his gaze on me was sombre and cold. "It's not about whether we killed or not at this point. Our past is long and dark, and we can't change it. It's about what we've learned over the centuries. Just like humans have evolved, we've evolved too. Our process has been slower, stilted by inside and outside forces, but we have changed as well."

"How on earth am I supposed to believe and accept all of this?" I exhaled, speaking mostly to myself here, trying to wrap my mind around the existence of demons in our world.

"I think you're already there." Andras lifted an eyebrow. "Or at least well on the way."

Breaking eye contact, I glanced around us, the people rushing past were completely unaware of the centuries-old secrets I was learning.

"Why are you telling me all of this?"

"I see you care about Vadim, Jade. And I want you to know the truth. A woman once told me that lies are not a good start for any relationship."

"I—I'm not looking for a relationship with Vadim . . ."

He gave me another one of his deep, penetrating stares, as if verifying something inside me.

"If that's what you choose to believe." He inclined his head, obviously avoiding an argument. "You had questions," he reminded. "I can help you answer some of them."

"Right." I paused, gathering my thoughts once again. There were so many questions. One topic, however, was still at the front of my mind. "Did all the murders happen a millennium ago?"

"It's different for each of us."

A crime was a crime, regardless of when it happened. I never believed that time alone would give a murderer absolution.

However, I could see Andras's point, too.

We distance ourselves from the past crimes of humanity because 'those were different times and other people.' But what if we lived through those times ourselves? What if I committed something as horrible as murder long ago? Would I be able to forgive myself centuries later? Would I *deserve* forgiveness?

"What have *you* done, Andras?"

He rolled his shoulders back with a slight frown. Whether or not he had forgiven himself, the memories obviously still bothered him, and I couldn't see an escape from that.

"My last victim was a vampire hunter in the middle of the nineteenth century," he began. "He was a part of a group who cornered me, spraying me with holy water and chanting prayers. Someone shot me with a silver bullet as he drove a wooden spike into my chest, crushing my ribs. I shoved him aside, inadvertently snapping his neck."

"What happened to the rest of them?" What he described could have been a scene in a movie, except that for Andras, it was real. He lived through it and had to deal with the consequences ever since.

"The rest chased me through the city, shooting at my back, until I hid from sight under a dock in the port. Murder is not our first instinct, Jade, but it has happened."

"Vadim told me it was a woman." I said slowly. "Do you know anything about her?"

"No. We all have our dark memories, which we don't particularly like bringing into the light. Even if I knew, I would advise you to talk to Vadim himself to get the answers you seek."

"I don't believe I should see him again." I inhaled the late-autumn air, wishing it would clear the mess in my chest and straighten the chaos of thoughts in my head.

He gave me a penetrating stare. "Are you afraid of him?"

"Wouldn't you be?" I snapped my gaze to his hidden in the shadows of his hood. "I mean if you were in my position?"

"Jade, you have been coming to our Base, a place where the danger is still very real. Vadim kept you safe every time. Harming you is definitely not what he wants to do."

"Apparently, his good intentions didn't help the woman he killed," I insisted.

"Just talk to him," Andras suggested, his voice pacifying. "I can see how you feel about him—"

"Is it that obvious?" I frowned, even as something tugged at my heart again at the thought of Vadim.

"Not for everyone. But we see human emotions plainly. I can tell you are not indifferent to him. You are also confused and worried. Would an honest conversation ease your mind?"

I bit my lip, unable to deny what he had said about my feelings but still unsure about what he'd suggested.

"I went through something similar before opening up to Natasha," he continued. "I told her about myself following the advice I got from a human woman. Alyssa was the first one I met personally who fell in love with one of us, giving hope to all of us."

Hope, *the stubborn emotion* Vadim had called it before he left that day.

Could I leave the country without seeing Vadim again? If I ran, could I hide from wondering what could have been for the rest of my life?

"Where is Alyssa now?"

"In Canada. Lending her expertise to our brand-new project of repairing, well, *building* a bridge between humans and Incubi."

"Incubi?"

"That's what our kind are, Jade. I am an Incubus. Vadim is, too."

Chapter 18

WALKING SLOWLY ALONG the main street in Minsk for the next hour, Andras explained to me what it meant to be an Incubus—a sex demon. Something I had thought was only a myth.

As he talked, the pieces began to fall into place. The purpose of my nightly visits became clear, explaining some of Vadim's behaviour, too. A picture of the Incubi world emerged, along with Vadim's life in it.

"When do you have to return to work?" Andras asked after a while, glancing at his phone.

"I, um, I don't think I'll be going back to work today." I took my own phone out of my purse, with the intention of calling Harry. My mind was too scattered by everything I'd heard right now to have any hope of a productive afternoon at the office.

"Would you like to meet Natasha? I'll have to pick her up from the hospital in twenty minutes or so."

Natasha. The woman who managed to have a relationship with a demon, to become his girlfriend—his *Mistress* as he called her.

"I'd like that."

"HI, *zaichik*." A tall, young woman with a strawberry-blonde ponytail hopped into the backseat of our car shortly after we pulled over at the hospital. With a quick kiss on Andras's cheek, she settled next to him.

Zaichik—a bunny-rabbit in Russian. There was nothing cute and cuddly that I could see in the tall, imposing Andras, but Natasha's view of her demon clearly differed from mine.

"Jade, meet Natasha. Natasha, this is Jade, Vadim's woman," Andras introduced us matter-of-factly.

"No. Not *his*, not at all," I protested.

The idea of being someone's *woman* rubbed me the wrong way the very first time Andras referred to Natasha like that. When applied to me it sounded even worse, as if he were talking about me as Vadim's property, like his wallet or a pair of pants.

Besides, at this point, technically, we really were *nothing* to each other, nothing at all.

"A 'casual acquaintance' would be a much more accurate term," I corrected him. "We hardly know each other."

"He told me you had a date."

"Dinner," I corrected. "We had dinner. Once. As *casual acquaintances*."

Seemingly unconcerned about the importance of definitions, Natasha cheerfully offered me her hand. "Nice to meet you, Jade. Are you American? Your Russian is amazing. I don't think I've ever met a foreigner with a better command of the language."

"Thank you. I'm Australian, actually."

"Really?" Her light-grey eyes grew wider. "This is like on the opposite end of the Earth! It must be hard to be this far away from home."

"Well." I paused, side-tracked by her questions. Here was a woman, who apparently was dating a demon, yet thought my being born on a different continent was something extraordinary. "I'm used to it now."

"I've never been to Australia. With all the unique animals over there, it really seems like an alien planet to me."

"I'll take you there, whenever you want." Andras wrapped his arm around Natasha's shoulders, drawing her for a kiss to her temple.

"Look at you." She smiled at him, playfully. "My wish is your command—my own personal genie."

Watching them getting all warm and cozy with each other, I was beginning to feel like I had landed in some alternative reality where it was perfectly normal to have a demon for a boyfriend.

"How long have you been together?"

"Well, we've known each other for close to two years now," Natasha replied. "We were neighbours at first."

"Natasha helped me one night, on her way from work," Andras chimed in. "That was how we first met. Then I moved into her building because I realised I needed to be where she was."

Natasha took his hand, a warm expression on her face.

The driver, a man in the uniform grey hoodie, turned around to ask for the destination address over his shoulder.

No, not a man. *A* demon.

"Would you like to come over, Jade?" Natasha offered. "We can have some tea at my place."

"Thank you. But maybe some other time? I think I'd like to go home now." I truly felt dazed and confused at the moment. All the information from Andras, coupled with the visual of their obviously deep and happy connection with each other, created a buzzing unrest in my head that needed some time to settle down.

"I'll give you my phone number." Natasha reached into her purse. "All of this can be rather overwhelming at the beginning. Please, call me any time you feel like talking to, you know, a human female." She smiled as she wrote her number on a piece of paper.

"Alyssa and Sytrius, her partner, are coming to Germany for Christmas if you'd like to meet them," Andras added casually, as if I had already become a part of this peculiar group comprised of demons and humans—close enough with them all to celebrate Christmas together.

"Thanks," I mumbled as the car pulled over at my apartment building. "I'll think about it." Before opening the door, I turned to Natasha, unable to stop myself from asking. "What is it like, to date a demon?"

Her expression grew serious.

"It's a big responsibility, first and foremost." Her reply was unexpected.

"In what way?"

"When an Incubus loves, he gives you his heart and his soul. You have to be careful not to damage the gift. For it would ruin him forever."

Chapter 19

NATASHA'S WORDS STILL rang in my head as I walked to the entrance of my stairwell.

"Jade." A tall figure moved my way from the wall by the door, a white plastic bag in his hand, with something hard and cylindrical weighing it down.

"Vadim?" I took a step back. Despite the shock of surprise, a wave of familiar tingles ran over me at the sound of his deep voice. "What are you doing here?"

"We need to talk."

My heart raced as warm effervescence spread through me—the pleasure at seeing him again.

God, I really had missed him.

"Do we?" I couldn't muster enough determination to send him on his way.

"Yes. Can I come inside?"

Except for a different style of leather jacket, his clothes were nearly identical to those worn by Andras. His hood was also drawn low over his head, leaving only that tantalizing bottom lip on display.

"I don't think that's a good idea," I protested, although it didn't come out very convincingly.

Talking to Andras and seeing him with Natasha had put my mind at rest a little. I no longer feared for my life when being one on one with Vadim. However, judging by the way my emotions swirled in a twister at the mere sight of him, being one on one with him still held another kind of danger for me.

"I'm not sure I want to talk."

"You called Andras." There was a clear note of reproach in his quick reply. "Why would you talk to him, but not to me?"

Dammit.

I hadn't asked Andras to keep our meeting a secret, but I certainly didn't expect him to spill the beans this quickly. Apparently, demons chatted like schoolgirls behind people's backs.

"Here." He stepped forward, taking something out of his pocket.

"What is this?" I leaned back but stood my ground as he held out what looked like a polished disk on a string.

"An amulet. It will force me to keep my distance. Put it on."

"How does it work?" I asked cautiously, but took the pendant from him.

He gestured at the entrance door. "Come, I'll show you."

"I—" Holding the string in my hand, I took a closer look at the pendant. Even in the daylight, I could see bright swirls of orange and yellow light moving inside. It was both eerie and pretty at the same time. "What is it made from?"

"I'll tell you inside." Obviously short on patience, he grabbed the pendant out of my hand and slid it over my head. "Come," he said, as if I had already agreed to have a conversation with him.

Something inside me protested at the tone of command in his voice, yet the plea in his eyes prompted me to unlock the door after all.

Vadim held it open for me, letting me enter before him.

"Listen." I turned around as soon as I was inside. "Let's go talk elsewhere. I know a bar that would be open already. There aren't that many people there at this hour. Quiet enough to have a talk, whatever it is you want to tell me—"

It was a weak attempt on my part to avoid being one on one with him, but not one out of fear. I simply didn't trust myself to make sound decisions around him.

Vadim dismissed my suggestion, as if he hadn't even heard it. "Invite me in, please," he said grimly, firm concentration on his face.

"What?"

With force, he punched the space in front of his face, his fist bouncing off something that appeared to separate us. Carefully, I swept the air around his fist with my hand, encountering no barrier whatsoever.

"What is happening?"

"I guess Andras didn't get this far in his little talk." The bitter note was still there in his tone. Vadim really seemed offended by my choosing Andras over him for that conversation. "The amulet." He gestured at the disk around my neck. "It's made from *soros* stone which came from our world. It recognizes us."

One hand on the disk at my chest, I was still touching the space all around his fist with the other, in search of the undetectable-to-me barrier.

"You brought a necklace with you?"

My sarcasm bounced off him.

"Those were our urns," he replied gravely. "Coffin-like enclosures for our physical bodies made from *soros* stone, to give us some protection for the journey between the dimensions. The urns disintegrated on impact with this world. The pieces can still be found all over. Some have been carved into pendants by humans who used them to detect us among them. I've had this one since first coming to this area in the fourteenth century."

"Do you remember things that happened that far back?"

"Much further than that."

"How about the day you came into this world? Do you remember that, too?" I had a hard time comprehending the expanse of time stretching over a millennium. The idea of someone walking the Earth for that long boggled my mind.

"Vaguely, but I wish I didn't."

"A millennium ago?" I had just a general knowledge of what the world was like back then—simply what I'd learned from history lessons in school and some books I'd read.

Vadim was someone, who'd actually lived through it all.

"We survived the journey," he continued. "Barely. With the *soros* stone urns smashed to pieces, our physical bodies, just as fragile as those of humans, ended up being broken and injured too." He paused, his forehead wrinkled, with a deep crease forming between his thick eyebrows. "Those were our first days on earth. Scattered all over the world, immobile and in pain, waiting for the broken bones to heal."

"For how long? How fast do you heal?"

"Not faster than you, but unfailingly and completely. Eventually, we all healed, found each other, and have been *plaguing* the earth ever since."

"Plaguing?"

"Isn't that how you would view our presence in your world? A swarm of parasites who are always taking, corrupting the minds and bodies of innocents with sin, giving nothing but death in return? At least that seemed to be the opinion of people who learned about our existence over the centuries."

"No wonder you're striving to keep your being here a secret." I exhaled a sigh, taking a step towards the lift. "Come in, Vadim," I invited, thinking at the very least I could listen to whatever else he had to say. I had no reason to doubt he would respect my wishes if I asked him to leave anytime later again.

Vadim slipped through the invisible barrier and entered the building.

"Come." Taking my hand, he urged me into the lift with him.

With the same resolve, he headed to my apartment door, tugging me behind. As soon as I unlocked the door, he entered first—so the amulet around my neck wouldn't stop him, I guessed.

He let go of my hand only in the hallway, marching to my kitchen in long determined strides. There he produced a bottle of red wine from the plastic bag he'd brought with him, setting it on the table.

Confidently, as if he lived here, he got a wine glass from the cabinet and a bottle opener from the kitchen drawer then poured some wine into the glass.

"Here." He handed it to me. "I want you to be able to listen to me, calmly. Wine seems to relax you somewhat."

He took me by my shoulders and spun me around to face my bedroom, giving me a gentle shove towards it. "Now go inside that room, please. Don't let me in until I'm finished."

"Are you saying I'm in danger from you, Vadim?" I stared at him over my shoulder, searching for his eyes in the shadows of his hood.

"Jade." His voice softened. "Please. For my peace of mind, stay in the room."

Holding the glass of wine in one hand and clutching the pendant in the other, I stepped into the bedroom. "Okay, I'm ready."

Hands fisted over his head, he leaned with his arms against the barrier created by the amulet. His stern concentration wavered with something raw and fragile in his eyes.

"You're safe here, Jade. Just let me say to you what I came here to say, please. Ask me anything you want. If after all that you still want me to leave, I won't bother you again."

I took a step back and plopped on the bed.

"Tell me about the woman you killed. When did it happen?" Releasing a breath, I took a huge swig from my wine glass, hoping it'd calm me, just like he said.

"Sixteen seventy-three," he replied without hesitation. "April. I was away from the Base on Council business. One of the very few times I've ever left the place. This also happened to be my only time among humans on my own. Usually, we go everywhere in pairs to keep an eye on each other, but my partner had been hurt and stayed behind, waiting to heal enough before making the journey back. I had to return to the Base on my own to deliver the information we had collected for the Grand Master at the time. I stopped at a guest-house to water my horse."

He paused for a moment, his gaze glossing over as if he no longer looked at me but into his past.

"She worked in the kitchen. I didn't even go inside, just found a stable-hand to get feed and water for my horse, but she came out with some errand and spotted me. We chatted. Well, she was the one talking. I was just watching her, marvelling at the happy colours of her emotions swirling around us. She said she made money on the side by providing sexual favours to travellers but that she liked me enough to do it for free."

"I can't believe that wouldn't happen more often," I muttered. "As far as all of you are concerned."

"Any direct contact with humans was strictly forbidden. I knew I was breaking the rules even by listening to her saying things like that to me."

"Is that why you cover your faces?" I found odd their apparent need to stay in the shadows. Even during our walk, I noted the way Andras tended to keep to the buildings along the sidewalk, as if hiding from the attention his athletic figure commanded from passers-by.

"Yes, when we're in public." Vadim shoved his hood back now. His short, tousled hair made my fingers itch with the urge to smooth it out. "Sexual energy is hard for us to stay away from. It is nearly impossible to resist when offered freely."

"She took me to her small room at the back. Undressed me." He rubbed his neck, leaning with his shoulder against the invisible wall separating us. "She did things to my body that no one had ever done before or after that night. Her energy was sweet, light, and simple. She giggled . . . Happy."

He slid down the barrier to sit on the floor, getting lost in his memories.

The images created by his words in my mind tugged at my heart with a new emotion, and it took me a moment to recognize it for what it was.

Jealousy.

It wasn't easy to hear about him being with another woman, even if it happened hundreds of years ago, before any of my known ancestors ever walked the earth. Yet I understood his need to tell this to me. It was his past, and he wanted to tell me all, so I could get to know him, completely.

"I had never touched a woman before. The whole experience was indescribable. I lost myself in her energy, which was all mine to take. I lost my head, and I took it all. Once I was inside her, I couldn't stop, greedily taking it all as it came off her, wave after delicious wave—lust, attraction, passion. I never noticed when I dipped into her life force, and stopped only when she slumped in my arms, but by then it was already too late. She was dead, a smile of utter bliss frozen on her face."

Sitting on the floor, with his back to me, forearms on his raised knees, he wouldn't face me, choosing to talk into the darkness of the hallway instead.

"A kitchen hand found me at her dead body and raised the alarm. Their justice was quick They swarmed me, using anything they could get their hands on for a weapon, and I didn't fight them. I needed the punishment—I wished they could kill me then and there. But you see, my sweet, innocent Jade, this is part of our existence—we cannot die, no matter how much we may want to. There never was a choice for me but to keep going. Beaten and broken inside and out, I had to go on."

"How did you? Go on, I mean."

"What I had done could not be reversed—there could never be atonement for me. All I could do was to make sure it didn't happen again. Yet it was continuing to happen. Women were killed every year routinely, right there at the Incubi Base."

"They were?" My hand cramped from the firm hold I had on the wine glass, yet I barely noticed it.

"Before you, we had to kidnap women to feed."

"You did *what*?"

He continued, without any indication he heard me, "I've served on the Incubi Council for centuries and knew how it was done. We would get an approved list of names and addresses from The Priory of Grimien—the human organization that has been governing our existence in this world for the past six hundred years. Then the retrieval teams would kidnap the Sources and deliver them to the Base. Every night, the Sources would then feed the Council members."

"The same way the demons fed off my fantasies?"

"Yes."

"No one kidnapped me, though. I came on my own."

Again, he didn't seem to acknowledge my statement, continuing with his story, instead. "The process of Source acquisition was set up by the Priory at the time we signed the treaty with them six centuries ago, and had been executed with little change ever since. Taken from their lives and everyone they knew, human women were held at the Base with no contact with the outside world, their mental health slowly deteriorating. Sooner or later all of them had to be drained, one by one."

"Oh God, Vadim. What are you saying . . .?" My hands shook so much, I placed my glass down, lest I spill wine everywhere.

The aura of danger and mystery surrounding that concrete building I had visited to live out my fantasy, turned out to be more real than I could have ever imagined. People had been kept in captivity there. And murdered.

"Are women still held there?" The very memory of my entering that place was forever tainted by this discovery now.

"No." His voice was hard as steel. "Haven't been for months."

"But there were? When I first came . . ."

"Yes. However, we were already working on the process of changing that, searching for other ways."

"Like hiring prostitutes?"

"At first. Yes. And inviting women like yourself, who came for the thrill of the mysterious and exciting—"

"There are more like me?" That was surprising. All my life I felt different from the norm. Apparently, not as much as I had thought.

"Ever since the night I killed her," Vadim went on, "I have been searching for ways to stop the murder of our Sources. The enforcement of these rules fell on the Council, and I spent centuries on the campaign to become the Grand Master of the Eastern Council. I finally earned this position a year ago, and none of the women held at the Base were killed after that." His voice held grave determination. "I delayed many new acquisitions, too. We needed to feed in order to function, but I refused to keep following the murderous path laid out by the Priory for us. I knew some of the Incubi started to furtively skim emotions off humans in public places, coming closer than the treaty allowed, but I let it happen as long as there was no physical contact—for our touch kills."

"Does it always, though?"

My mind strayed to the kisses I witnessed between Andras and Natasha. He might have worn gloves during our whole conversation, but their lips definitely touched when she greeted him in the car, and he kissed her face again a little later. I did not recall sensing any fear on her part or any restraint on his. It happened easily, casually, as if it had occurred many times before.

"In my case, I believe it does." The grim certainty in Vadim's voice made my heart ache. "The others also had to work to control their hunger enough for a human to sustain their intimate touch. I didn't know it was possible to achieve at all until a woman proved me wrong."

"Alyssa?"

"Yes."

"Not only her, though. Natasha, too. Andras's girlfriend. I met her today."

"There are a few more now, I've heard. Having a permanent source of energy at his side sates a demon's hunger, eliminating the need for further kidnappings. This was exactly the solution I hoped for. Only it turned out to be so much more than that. The union between a human and a demon enriches the lives of them both."

"Why has it taken this long for Incubi to realise this?"

He glanced at me over his shoulder.

"You have to know, Jade, that all of the changes I've been allowing to happen here are done without the prior approval of the Priory."

"The organization that allowed all this cruelty to happen in the first place? They've basically legalized kidnappings."

"Don't ever forget that *we* are the real source of the cruelty, Jade. The chaotic feedings were stopped by the treaty, allowing humans to control what we took. Back then, the rules were considered to be a progressive solution to the situation."

"Why haven't the Priory been looking for a better solution since? What are they saying about all of this now?" It was a no-brainer for me—Alyssa and Sytrius had found the perfect way to end it all.

"Until the events of this year, the only consequence of people and demons coming together was devastation and death. No one knew for sure that loving relationships were even possible between us. For centuries, Incubi have been kept at limited mental capacity.

"As a member of the Council, I have been better fed than most. That was meant to ensure that the thirteen of us on the Council remained capable of supervising the execution of the rules, strategizing on the behalf of our kind, and negotiating with humans. I have managed to keep most of my memories as well. However, the fresh, creative thinking that requires significantly deviating from the rules and creating anything entirely new is still hard to attain for unmated Incubi. Only now, watching how quickly Andras comes up with new ideas, have I become aware of my own limitations."

"Why didn't people think about a better way then, instead of you? I would think humans, first and foremost, should have the women's interests at heart"

"I don't know. Incubi are excluded from the inner dealings at the Priory, or from anything at all that doesn't concern us directly. We stopped all kidnappings on our own, finding alternative ways to feed, without any further input from the Priory. They did, however, take it upon themselves to help integrate the released women back into society."

"How can a relatively small group of people represent all humanity in their talks with Incubi?" I wondered out loud. "Don't you think the Priory has lost its usefulness? Wouldn't it be more prudent at this point for you to come out to governments and deal with them on a global scale?"

He shook his head slowly.

"Earth's governments are varied, their interests are largely limited to their own countries, and the speed with which they change is impossible for us to keep up with. The Priory has been the one stable partner for us. Their last Elder was in his position for fifty years. The current one is going into his third decade now."

The wine must have begun its work, filling my veins with warmth and making me reckless.

"You know what, who cares about the Elders and their stupid Priory? Why don't you just do what you know is right?"

"I am very tempted to do just that." I heard a smile in his voice.

"What's stopping you?" I got off the bed.

"Caution. I wonder what is there that allowed them to hold power over us all this time."

"Well, since they're not fighting what you have been proposing, their attitude and mentality must be changing, too."

"Must be. The lack of proper communication still bothers me, though. They have called face-to-face meetings for far less significant reasons in the past, but have been avoiding it lately."

"Just keep doing what you're doing, I'd say. And if it bothers them, I'm sure they'll let you know." I stepped around him, crossing the threshold of the bedroom.

The barrier must have vanished as soon as I was in the hallway with him. Vadim lost its support at his back and would have fallen backwards if he hadn't quickly propped himself with his hands on the floor.

"So, what now?" I asked, sitting down next to him.

"That was what I was going to ask *you*." He glanced at me.

The way he lifted his eyebrow gave him an almost playful expression, despite the serious tone of his voice, and I smiled.

Our honest conversation—no doubt, combined with the wine I'd had—eased my concerns and melted away any lingering fears about him. I felt comfortable sitting next to him, as if we'd known each other for years. The same sense of connection I'd had at the restaurant during our dinner together took over me . . . then sadness filtered in.

"Vadim, I'm moving early next year."

"Where?" His brows furrowed, forming that crease again.

"To Moscow, it looks like. My company is closing their office here, for good."

"Really?"

"I'm afraid so. You know I do like you, very much," I confessed to him and, finally, to myself.

"I can see it." He nodded, confidently.

"You can, huh?" My smile grew wider as I thought about Andras describing human emotions to me. "What colour is it? Pink?"

"Coral, with a hint of orange and sunshine."

"Is it?" At that moment, I believed I could really feel the warmth of sunshine inside me while gazing into his jade-coloured eyes.

"But that bright red streak in it is what I find particularly intriguing." Something very much like hope tinted his voice.

Hope for what? Lust? Or love—like the other Incubi had managed to evoke in their women? Did Vadim hope I would fall in love with him?

'When an Incubus loves, he gives you his heart and his soul. You have to be careful not to damage that gift.' Natasha's words came to mind once again.

"I tend to outgrow all my relationships, Vadim," I warned, deciding to be brutally honest and possibly save him from a huge disappointment in the future. "It applies to everything—things and people. What seems new and exciting at first loses its appeal as soon as it becomes old and familiar. I've never been able to change this for anyone. If I try forcing myself into a routine—a stable life with someone—it only gets worse, inevitably ending in a nightmare for both of us."

"How long until you have to leave, Jade?" he asked, his expression pensive, but not devastated, I noted with relief.

"Um, about three and a half months."

"Will you give this time to me?"

"What do you mean by that, exactly?" I shifted on the floor, hands clasped in my lap.

"Be with me." He shifted to face me. "Let me see you whenever I want."

"Just for three months?" Surprisingly, I found myself disappointed that he seemed to accept my impending departure that easily. Still, three months of having Vadim all to myself was too tempting not to accept. "But you refuse to touch me."

"Not because I don't want to." He heaved a sigh.

"Do you think you could learn?" I tilted my head, taking in his face—the absolute perfection of his features that seemed to be permanently moulded into a stern expression with an ever-present hint of grief. "With time and patience, could you learn to control your appetite like the others have?"

"I don't know."

"Would you like to try?" I offered, catching a flash of something bright and beautiful light up his face at my words.

"Only if there was a way to keep you safe," he said resolutely, the thoughtful frown back almost immediately.

I considered that for a moment then lifted my leg over both of his on the floor, straddling his thighs to get closer.

"Well, you have your gloves on. Would that be enough?" Slowly, I slid my hands under his jacket and hoodie, feeling his muscles flex under his shirt. "I'll touch you through your clothes only. Would that be okay?"

His gaze slid from my eyes to my lips.

Quickly, I shrugged out of my jacket then pushed his off his shoulders too.

"We'll keep your shirt on," I murmured, getting him out of his hoodie. "Just like this." I lifted the collar of his shirt up, the way I saw him do. "See? To avoid any accidental touches."

Carefully, he circled my waist with his arms, and I leaned in closer, drawn in by his scent and warmth.

The desire to feel his bare skin under my palms grew stronger the closer I got, but I focused on what I *could* have instead of what I could *not*, welcoming the opportunity to explore his body thoroughly and unhurriedly, even if through the material of his shirt.

He slid his hands up my back, prompting me to arch closer to him. The heat of his breath fanned across the sensitive skin of my neck then spread lower through my body in a wave of hot ripples.

Suddenly my blouse was in the way.

"Since you're wearing the gloves," I whispered, "I don't think I need this." I tugged at the blouse, sliding it over my head, not even bothering to open the tiny pearl buttons in the front.

His breath hitched, but he didn't waste any time, sliding his hands along my torso, up my back, down my sides, then up again to cup my breasts through my bra.

The feeling of his leather gloves was eerily familiar, bringing to mind the hands of the two men at the Base. The way he moved his hands, however, with a frantic, hungry urgency, as if I were about to disappear from his grasp, was all his own. No one had ever touched me with this much hunger and passion before.

Spreading my legs wider, my skirt hiked all the way to my waist, I slid along his thighs. Closer.

My hands on his shoulders, his face was right in front of mine, his parted lips just a breath away. Closing my eyes, I savoured him with all my other senses. The growing bulge in his pants, pressing between my thighs, the hardness of his muscles under his shirt, his fresh scent wrapped all around me, luring me in.

Forgetting all about caution for a moment, I leaned in for a kiss . . .

My lips pressed into the leather of his glove instead, as he quickly placed two fingers between his mouth and mine to prevent me from kissing him.

"Vadim . . ." I leaned back, accidentally brushing the side of his nose with mine.

A surge of electricity seemed to pass between us when our skin touched. A freezing sensation spread from the tip of my nose through my face.

My lust instantly evaporating with a jolt of fear, I jerked back, sitting upright.

"Jade!" His voice sounded strangled, he grabbed me by my upper arms. "Are you okay?"

"I'm fine." I brought my hand up to my nose and rubbed some feeling back into it. The crestfallen expression on his face prompted me to add with a smile, "All good, see?" I wrinkled my nose, moving my mouth side to side. "Everything is working."

"I'm so sorry," he said somewhat mechanically, as if still frozen in horror.

"Don't, please." I patted his chest soothingly. "It's all my fault anyway. You're just so, um . . ." I wrapped my arms around his neck, making sure not to stray past the edge of his collar.

So irresistible, I wanted to say, but that would be putting the blame on him for my indiscretion.

"You're too tense," I said instead, rubbing his shoulders. "Tell me what do you normally do to relax?"

"I'm afraid I wouldn't know." His brows were still knitted together, but the rest of his features had eased a bit. "I don't recall being this on edge before."

"So, is it because of me? Do I make you anxious?"

"It seems that way. Although, it doesn't mean I don't want your company." He tightened his arms around my waist.

"What do you do when you're alone then? Do you get to be alone?"

"Often. Most of the time between the Feedings and the occasional Council sessions I am on my own."

"Right. You don't even have to sleep." I remembered from my conversation with Andras. "So, how do you spend all your time?"

My hands linked behind his neck again, I remained sitting in his lap. With my arousal gone, however, it felt simply nice and comfortable to be close to him. The fact that we were still on the floor hardly even registered with me at all.

"I read. A lot."

"Do you have a library at that place? What do you call it, *the base*?

"Yes, something like a library. Archives. They hold records of our history, but also a large number of books written by humans."

"Which ones are your favourite?"

"I would read anything, to be honest." The smile with which he said this seemed almost shy, as if he was a bit self-conscious talking about his personal tastes. "But I think I like to read novels the most. Historical fiction—what you would call 'classics' now. I'm still catching up." His smile grew a little wider, sweeping me in with its out-of-this-world gorgeousness.

"Like Alexandre Dumas?"

"Him, yes. Victor Hugo, too. And Leo Tolstoy, Stendhal, Thomas Hardy. Emile Zola, as well . . . Well, everything and anything, really."

"You've lived through the times they wrote about."

"That's what I find the most fascinating about their work—the human account of what I've watched happening from a distance. I didn't get to leave the Base often, but when I did, I paid attention to the things around me. Then when I read their books, I compared the ways in which humans and I saw the world."

"What are the differences?"

"That's the thing, Jade. There aren't that many. At the end of the day, we seem to like the same things and often find the same things appalling. I have no trouble following the human emotions in books or movies. I understand the heroes' pain, their happiness, too."

"You watch movies?"

"Yes. For the past few decades." With his thumbs, Vadim was drawing slow circles on the bare skin of my back, his arms still around my waist.

"What would you like to do now?" I asked. "Andras said some of you eat or drink occasionally. I can make us some tea if you want. It's a bit too early for dinner, but if you're hungry, for food I mean—"

"I am hungry," he said, his gaze firmly on me. Something in his eyes and his voice made me squirm in his lap. "But not for human food."

His hands under my backside, he rose to his feet smoothly, holding me to him.

"Well, that's all I have to offer," I teased. "Since you gobbled up my arousal way too fast, I'm not that horny anymore."

"I can change that." He carried me to the bedroom. "Just give me a minute."

Carefully, he laid me down on the mattress then climbed on top of me. One knee on each side of my thighs, he straightened, unbuckling his belt.

"No more touching, my precious Jade." His voice low, he looped the belt around both of my wrists, then stretched over me to tie the other end to the metal bar of my bed frame, bringing my arms over my head. "Much better. Now, stay still," he commanded and pulled his gloves off, tucking them in the back pocket of his jeans.

"This needs to come off," he murmured, unzipping my skirt then sliding it down over my legs. "This too." Carefully avoiding any contact of his bare fingers with my skin, he pinched the waistband of my pantyhose and dragged them down, tossing them aside. My underwear followed.

His movements were unhurried, he obviously delayed the process, dragging it on to savour each part.

Despite the lack of the skin-to-skin contact, the slide of each garment as he slowly peeled it off me made my whole body tingle with awareness once again.

"This too," he said softly, sliding his hands over the satin of my bra. His thumbs stroked my nipples through the thin material, making the tips harden with a sweet prickling sensation that spread through to my stomach.

"Yes. Please." My breath rushed out of me.

I arched my back for his hands to slide under me, his fingers traced the back strap of my bra, without straying onto my skin. Vadim deftly unhooked the closure then pushed the cups up, setting my breasts free.

I watched his expression change as he hungrily caressed my chest with his gaze, pleasure rippling along my skin in its wake.

"Beautiful," he whispered, his eyes lighting up deep magenta as he yanked the gloves from his pocket, putting them on again. "And all mine."

'Yours,' echoed in my mind. '*I'm all yours, Vadim. For three months.*'

The titillating sensation of his hot breath against one of my erect nipples chased away the sadness that threatened to overwhelm me at the thought of my inevitable moving away.

Vadim slid his hand up the inside of my thigh, and I gasped at the contact of his gloved fingers when they reached the most sensitive part of my body.

The sensation was new. The demons at the Base never went this far, bringing me to climax with different toys only, their hands never actually touching me there.

Heat rushed me at the dexterous slide of his fingers, and I thrust my hips up, searching for more.

With another flash of light in his eyes—this one bright red—he squeezed my breast with his other hand as his fingers continued to slide back and forth through my folds, the slick heat slipping out of me, soaking his glove.

He lightly pinched the hard bud of my nipple between his fingers. My eyelids fluttered closed under the onslaught of pleasure rolling through me in hot, blinding waves.

"So incredibly wonderful." I heard his whisper next to my ear then felt him nuzzle my hair. Carefully, ever so slightly, he glided his face over my temple, breathing me in deeply.

A soft moan caught in my throat as the movement of his fingers intensified, the pressure grew tighter inside me before finally exploding, released by him.

Straining against the belt that tied my wrists to the headboard, I pressed my thighs together, trapping his hand while I rode the pulsing ripples of my orgasm.

Finally, I dropped my knees apart—my leg muscles still trembling from the strain and pleasure he'd just put me through—and slumped back on the mattress, struggling to catch my breath.

Vadim stretched on his side along my body, a faint, satisfied smile on his face. Propped on his elbow, he left his other hand where it was —between my legs—still cupping me lightly. The intimacy of this gesture, protective and possessive at the same time, felt more intense than anything he had done to me. And I had no idea how to deal with the strong wave of feelings that rose in me in response.

My first instinct was to shift away from him, to break this lingering contact between us, so I could go back to being me again, with familiar thoughts and emotions.

This new sensation, however, caught me as if in a trap. Combined with the warmth of his gaze on me and content expression on his face, the effect of his heat seeping through the thin leather of his glove to the most intimate place on my body felt simply too enjoyable to give up so soon, and I let it be.

"You seem very relaxed now," I teased, keeping my voice light. "Being with me must beat reading after all."

"It beats everything," he easily agreed, and my face flushed warm with pleasure at his words. Even the tips of my ears felt hot.

"For someone who doesn't get out much, you are a smooth talker, Vadim. Is it a part of natural Incubus charm?"

"Natural?" He slid his hand up my stomach then to the belt restraining my hands. "If you're asking whether I was created the way I am now, and you find me charming, then yes, it is natural. None of us have changed much physically from the day we first came to earth."

He untied my hands, rubbing my wrists gently.

"Naturally charming." I sighed. "Breathtakingly handsome. Andras mentioned you speak any known language on earth, too. I know you were sent here for punishment for a crime none of you remember committing. Do you think, though, that whatever power sent you here, equipped with all these tools of seduction, meant to sentence you to centuries of fighting your own nature?"

"What are you saying, Jade?"

"I'm saying that maybe your punishment wasn't meant to be the pain you all have been going through all this time. Maybe the idea wasn't to punish but to teach you a lesson. What if your task was to learn to co-exist with humans by realising the value of life and love? I mean, since you view the Forgiveness as the ultimate prize that you get by making a woman fall in love with you, then maybe this was the point of it from the beginning? What do you think?"

"If it was that simple, why did we find ourselves in centuries of violence with humans, during those first few hundreds of years on Earth?"

"I'm not sure." The soothing, massaging movements of his hands along my arms and shoulders had relaxed my body, wrapping my mind into a sleepy haze. "Maybe all of you needed to grow to this level of understanding and acceptance first? Perhaps humans needed to grow, too."

"Maybe," he said in a half-whisper, sliding the straps of my open bra off my shoulders to take it off completely.

"Maybe now is finally the time in history when both Incubi and humans can accept each other without judgment, making relationships possible?"

"I would love for that to be true." He took a blanket from the foot of the bed and covered me with it.

"It's barely dinner time." I stifled a yawn. "Why do I feel this tired?"

"It is often physically taxing for a human to feed an Incubus." His even voice reached me, as my eyelids drooped. "And emotionally intense."

"Why, though?" I protested, half-slurring the words already, as sleep began to drag me under. "Without the skin-to-skin contact, you were just skimming. Andras explained—"

"There has been skin-to-skin contact. Did you forget?" He flicked my nose lightly, any numbing sensation in it long gone. "Sleep now, you'll feel much better in the morning."

"Will you be here when I wake up?" I rolled his way, snuggling against his shirt-covered chest, my hands tucked between us.

"If that's what you want."

"I do."

He draped his arm over my shoulders, keeping me close. "Then I will."

Chapter 20

DARK, AND WARM, AND . . . cozy. Something, no, *someone* big and solid at my back.

Vadim.

I recognized his scent in the darkness of my bedroom—I would recognize it anywhere by now.

My arms over my head, I stretched and rolled over to face him. "What time is it?"

"Still early," came the immediate reply, his voice clear and alert, in contrast to mine—rough from sleep.

He caught my wrists in his gloved hands before I had a chance to bring my arms down. "How are you feeling?" His eyes, like green jewels, shone mere inches away from mine.

"Good," I whispered, subdued by the awareness of him being this close to me. "Very good, actually."

God, I wanted to kiss him, now more than ever. Face to face with Vadim, my naked body separated only by a blanket from him, I couldn't think of a more perfect moment for a kiss.

"Would you let go of my arms?" I asked. "It's my turn to touch you."

"Jade—"

"I know the rules." I twisted my wrists from his fingers as he loosened his grip. "I'll stay away from your bare skin."

I eagerly slid my hands over his shirt, down his shoulders then to his chest and belly. Without taking the blanket off, I bent my knee, bringing my leg between his.

"What is it about you that makes me lose my head when you're near?" I murmured, without expecting him to answer.

"I believe that was in our design—you're supposed to find me attractive."

"Attractive, maybe, but not this fucking irresistible." I leaned into him to make him roll on his back. "I find Andras incredibly attractive, too. But even if he didn't have Natasha, I still don't think I'd want to do all these things to him as much as I want to do them to you." Holding the blanket to my chest, I threw my leg over his middle, settling on his thighs. "This . . . hold you have over me. I've never felt anything like it for anyone. Not even close."

"Good," he growled, grasping my hips through the blanket and yanking me closer to his crotch.

With a soft cry of surprise, I propped my hands on his abs to keep my balance. The cover fell off my chest, exposing my breasts, and I sensed the unmistakable hardness under my thigh.

Slowly, I slid my hand down his torso, my fingers skimming the waistband of his pants.

"Boxers or briefs?" I asked, a little breathless from anticipation, then added, prompted by his questioning stare. "Or do demons prefer to go commando?"

"Commando?"

"Are you wearing any underwear, Vadim?" I flicked the button of his pants open and took hold of the zipper. "I need to know to make sure I stay safe, remember? So, what will I find in here?"

"Boxers." He cleared his throat as I slid my hand inside his pants.

"Holy mother of . . ." I gasped, my fingers closing over something hard and so massive I had no idea how it fit inside his pants. Through the fabric of his underwear I could feel the throbbing heat of his straining hard-on. "I'm so sorry, baby." I slid my hand up and down his length. "This must be painful."

"Trust me . . ." he gritted through his teeth. "What you're doing right now is only making it worse."

"But I can also make it better," I cooed soothingly, gently massaging his erection through his underwear. The way he filled my hand felt amazing, and I tried not to think about how wonderfully he could fill me from the inside, too.

With a pained groan, he arched his back.

"Hold on," I ordered, letting go of him, then grabbed the waistband of his pants and yanked them down.

"What are you doing?" Despite a clear note of alarm in his voice, he lifted his hips to help me ease his pants down.

"No worries. No touching, I know." Carefully pinching the sides of his underwear, mindful not to brush by his naked skin, I tugged them down, too. "Here we go." I sat back admiring the majestic sight of his erection bobbing in the air, freed from the constraints of his pants. "Just . . . um, give me a second." I swallowed hard and jumped off the bed, leaving the blanket behind.

In the hallway, I quickly rummaged through the basket on top of my shoe rack, fishing out a pair of leather gloves.

"All set!" I waved the gloves in the air triumphantly as I returned. Crawling on top of Vadim again, I threw the blanket over his lap, lest his hard-on poke my naked stomach.

Watching me don the gloves must have put Vadim's mind at ease a little. He stretched under me, folding his arms on the pillow, his hands under his head.

"Have you ever had anyone touch you like this?" I asked, splaying my hands on his stomach.

"You mean wearing gloves?"

I nodded.

"No."

"I have." I winked. "It can be rather enjoyable. If the person knows what they're doing. It helps if you're into that person, too," I added, remembering how the excitement of the strangers' hands on me had worn off.

Taking the ends of his shirt, I tried to yank it open, but the buttons held.

"I'll need your help with these, babe."

He tossed his gloves aside then unbuttoned his shirt, unhurriedly, as if he wasn't in danger of literally exploding with lust at any minute, which was exactly where he was if the condition of his hard-on was any indication.

"Much better," I groaned with approval, leaning forward and sliding my gloved hands up the front of his naked torso then to the side to shove his shirt off.

"I need these . . ." He reached for his gloves, but I shook my head, slowly massaging his wide chest.

"Just keep your hands to yourself, mister. This is all about you."

"You're sitting naked on top of me," he protested. "I want to touch you, too."

"You can watch." I slid down his legs, my hands tracing the hard 'V' of his lower stomach. "But I'm the one doing the touching this time."

Tossing the blanket aside, I caught his thick shaft between my palms. Gliding my hands up and down his impressive length, I imagined what it would feel like if I didn't have the gloves on. Hot. The delicate skin would be tight and silky in my bare hands. The thick, protruding veins would be right under my fingers.

With the gloves on, I couldn't feel any of these. Shoving aside the disappointment that threatened to sink my mood, I focused on things I *could* feel, instead. The sizable weight of him in my hands, thick and solid, so hard there was barely any give when I squeezed, firmly but gently. It felt as if I literally had the power of a demon at my fingertips.

Vadim's breathing had rapidly accelerated, signalling to me he was close. With a strained groan, he threw his arms to the side, fisting the bedding.

Through the leather of my gloves, I sensed him pulse in my hands. Head back, his whole body shook with strain as he shot his release in long, erratic spurts.

As if all the tension drained from him with each pulsating shot, his body finally relaxed in a last wave of shudders.

"Jade," he moaned, throwing his arm across his face.

"I won't even ask if it was good for you." I giggled and leaned in to kiss his hard abs only to halt myself an inch or so away from his skin, startled by the realisation I'd come this close. The thought that I may forget to stop next time was sobering.

Was it even possible to maintain any level of intimacy with someone I couldn't touch?

"I'll need to clean this," I mumbled, climbing off him. "Be right back."

Vadim was still lying on his back, his forearm over his face, when I returned with the cleaned gloves and a washcloth soaked in warm water.

"Are you okay?" I asked when he jerked at the touch of the cloth against his lower stomach.

"Okay?" He peeked at me from under his arm. "I . . . This . . ." He rose on his elbows, regarding me as if I were some museum rarity. "It wasn't even about feeding, Jade. I didn't skim anything," he said, an expression of utter shock on his face.

"Well, it can't always be about food, can it?" I smiled.

There was something odd but rather endearing about seeing the big and mighty Vadim losing his cool composure because of one hand job.

But then again, who knew how I would feel getting an orgasm after centuries of celibacy.

"Are you hungry?" He sat up in bed. "Sleepy?" He grabbed his gloves, putting them on quickly then yanked his pants up, moving closer to me.

"Horny?" I mimicked his concerned tone and expression, before breaking into a smile again.

"Are you?" His voice deepened.

Truthfully, a small tendril of arousal still tickled somewhere deep inside me.

"I can make sure you are." The self-assurance in his voice flowed over my skin with the promise of more.

Except that I knew there couldn't be much more. A touch by a gloved hand, even if that hand belonged to Vadim, didn't feel like it would be enough at the moment.

"I, I don't want the gloves right now," I confessed.

He stared at his hands for a few seconds as if seeing the gloves for the first time.

"Without them . . ." he said. "I can't."

"What makes others able to touch their women without hurting them?" Andras and Natasha's kiss came back to mind again.

"Better control." The way his expression fell showed me he viewed his own lack of control as a weakness, a failure.

"They weren't created with any better control than you, though, right? Yours could be improved too. With practice, I mean."

"No."

"No, they weren't? Or no, it couldn't?"

"No, I won't practice," he said stubbornly, his mouth set into a firm line.

"You wouldn't even try?"

"I have tried—"

"It was long ago," I interrupted. "You weren't prepared. One can't expect much control over anything the first time—"

"Not long ago." He shook his head slowly. "Just yesterday, Jade. I was preparing myself in my head, hoping I could touch you. I longed to believe that as someone who cares about you, I would be able to stop in time. And I couldn't last night."

"You *care* about me?" It wasn't the only thing he said, but it seemed to be the only one stuck in my brain, ringing through it like a church bell.

"I do." He moved closer, placing his hands on my shoulders. "More with every minute of every day. I want to feel it all." He skimmed my neck with his thumbs. "To kiss you, to taste you. Everywhere. And I don't know how to go on without being able to do any of it. But there is no way I'd put you in harm's way."

"Vadim. Baby . . ." I shuffled on my knees towards him, and his hold on my shoulders tightened. He halted me from getting any closer, lest my naked breasts brush the skin of his exposed chest. "Last night, I caught you off guard. It was an accident for me, too."

"It doesn't matter."

"And I'm alive. See?" I lightly punched my chest with a fist in demonstration of my vitality then took his face between my gloved hands. "What if I did it one more time." I rushed to explain, cutting off his protests, "You will have due warning. If you know what is about to happen, you will make a conscious effort to stop yourself, right?"

"No." He shook his head resolutely.

"Listen." I dropped my hands to his shoulders. "Just one tiny touch. Like a feather. I promise to pull away if you don't. Faster than yesterday."

I realised I was actually begging him now. Since when had being touched by him become this important to me? I had no idea. I just knew that I wanted to be able to kiss him more than anything else in the world at that moment.

"At the very worst, I'd just fall asleep for another couple of hours, right? It's still too early for me to get up anyway," I added in a lighter tone, willing for him to relax a little, as tension seemed to be coming back into his every muscle.

He shook his head again, but the fact that he didn't voice his protest this time, gave me the courage to push for more.

"Put your hands behind your back," I instructed. "Sit on them if you must, so you don't grab me impulsively or something. Would it make you feel better?"

He was still gripping my shoulders, and I slid my hands down his arms.

"Please, Vadim. Just one tiny kiss." I circled his wrists with my fingers, prying his hands off me. "I've never begged a man before I met you."

"I'm not a man, Jade."

"For me, you are." That was true. It was the reason I wanted to go through with this—for him to be able to have me as a man in every single way.

Eyes on me, he appeared to study my expression carefully. No, not the expression, I realised. Vadim was searching much deeper than that—he was watching my emotions.

"Carefully," he conceded finally, dropping his hands at his sides.

"I will," I promised, leaning in.

Slowly, to give him enough time to get ready and react if needed, I brought my face closer to his. Gripping his biceps for balance, I kept some distance between our bodies, aiming for just one single point of contact—his lips.

"Now," I whispered, carefully angling my head to prevent our noses from touching. "Ready?"

My mouth hovered a hairbreadth away from his. I felt the warmth of his body against my naked breasts and strained to keep away when all I wanted was to press myself to him.

With another slight exhale, I leaned in just a fraction of a millimetre, brushing his lips with mine.

Light as a feather.

Just like I'd promised.

Freezing cold dusted my face, sweeping from my lips out in every direction, as if I stuck my head into a pile of fresh snow in the dead of winter.

Gasping, I leaned back, meeting Vadim's terrified stare.

"We're not doing this again," he said, his face white as the snow I imagined I felt on my skin.

"This is . . . unusual, though. Isn't it?" I mumbled, feeling confused. Why did it seem so easy for Andras and Natasha?

"Must be." He got off the bed and zipped up his pants—the cool, collected façade back in place.

"That one and only time you were with someone," I started and immediately regretted bringing it up as his expression tensed even more. "I mean, you *have* been able to touch, at least for some period of time, before . . . you know . . ."

"Before the murder?" he finished for me, buttoning up his shirt, his movements fast and determined. "My thirst for your energy is limitless. The more I take, the more I want. I don't see a way to decrease it."

I dropped my gaze to the quilt on my bed, going through what he said. The problem seemed to be closed into a circle. I believed if he took my energy on a regular basis, he might learn to regulate his hunger. Yet since there was a danger for me, he refused to take at all.

"Well, the good thing is, I'm still alive . . . So, when we try again—"

"It's not happening, Jade. I'm not playing some kind of demon version of Russian roulette with your life, just for a slight chance to gain control over this."

His reluctance was perfectly understandable.

What made no sense was my own willingness—even eagerness—to keep going, even despite the now familiar tiredness settling over me once again.

"I'm not giving up, Vadim," I promised stubbornly, climbing under the blanket again as sleep became harder and harder to fight. "Just so you know."

Chapter 21

A SMOOTHIE IN MY HAND, I was running from the Metro station to my office building.

Vadim had offered me a ride, but I only let him walk me to the Metro station this morning then took the train from there, as usual. That was my attempt at keeping things in my life normal, despite that there was nothing *normal* about the demon in my world.

He was the one who made the smoothie for me, with yogurt and frozen berries and whatever else he had found in my fridge. It was absolutely delicious, I had to admit, and probably significantly healthier than my usual breakfast of coffee and a protein bar.

I glanced at my phone and sped up on my run along the footpath. I was almost an hour late this morning. With my flexible hours, I often worked overtime. And with numerous social functions being a part of my job description, work often stretched into the night. Even with my leaving early the day prior, no one would mind my being late today, except me. I had planned to be in the office on time, the reason I was late was the man in my bed last night.

His touch had proved to be the ultimate sleeping pill. Even that one light kiss that felt hardly more than the brush of a butterfly wing, made me sleep in.

Instead of waking me up, Vadim had turned my alarm clock off and got busy making the smoothie.

I took another swig of it. Damn, it was good.

Something about the way he had said goodbye to me that morning didn't sit well with me. I could tell his failure at self-control had affected him more than it should have in my opinion, and I was worried he might decide not to see me anymore in some misguided attempt to protect me.

The thing was, I didn't feel like I needed protection from him. My thoughts kept flying to him ceaselessly, like a moth to the light, at any given moment of every day. And I didn't have it in me to fight it anymore.

What would be the point of fighting it?

In a few months I'd be out of the country, and Vadim would carry on with his immortal existence.

The fact that there was a firm time limit on our relationship made me feel protected. How much harm could be done in a few short months? None of my previous relationships lasted that long, anyway. With firm determination, I shoved away the sad feeling that tended to move in on me every time I thought about inevitably leaving Vadim.

The best I could hope for was to help him deal with his ravenous hunger before I had to move to Moscow. At the end of it all, maybe he would be able to touch a woman without the fear of hurting her.

The thought of some long-term good for him as a result of our brief relationship made me feel better. At the same time, the idea of him touching another woman after me scratched unpleasantly somewhere inside my chest.

The recurring thought of eventually having to say goodbye to Vadim pierced something inside me, and again I shoved it deep.

These months were all we had. And I was determined to make the most of our short time together.

"I THOUGHT YOU WANTED to keep things normal in your life and continue travelling by Metro." Vadim's voice sounded confused through my phone—rightly so, considering that my request he pick me up by car contradicted my morning statement.

The thing was, after thinking about him all day long in the office, I managed to convince myself that he had decided to stay away from me altogether. It seemed to be the only sure way he had to keep me safe from him.

By the end of my workday, the possibility of never seeing Vadim again had brought me to a near state of panic. I called him, needing to hear his voice, and ended up asking for the pickup, desperate to see his face, too.

"I've changed my mind. I'm giving up on *normal* for as long as I'm with you. Wear your gloves if it makes you feel better," I added hurriedly.

Wear a full-body armour or a hazmat suit if you wish, just please come to me.

The feverish need to have him near was quickly becoming un-bearable.

"HI." I JUMPED INTO the car, determined to keep my cool, yet feeling my insides melt at the sight of his smile.

"Did you have a good day, Jade?" Vadim enquired, impeccably polite.

"It was okay, but it's just got much better." I winked at him, making myself comfortable on the seat next to him. "Thank you for pick-ing me up. So, where are we going?"

"I thought you'd like me to take you home."

"I've never said that was what I would like." I gave him a playful smile.

His features strained into an expression of intense focus, as he obviously was trying to catch up with me. It probably wasn't fair for me to tease him, since he was definitely behind in social interactions with women, or with any humans for that matter.

"Would you consider it terribly rude on my part if I invited myself to your place tonight?" I asked tentatively.

"Rude? No." He lifted a dark eyebrow. "Careless? Absolutely."

"Good. 'Careless' I can handle. It's not the first time I've been called that." I shifted my backside closer to him and took his gloved hand in mine. "Can we stop at my place then, to pick up my overnight bag? It's my day off at work tomorrow." I threw a glance his way. "And knowing your touch, I may need to sleep in tomorrow morning."

"Jade, this shouldn't be taken lightly."

"On the contrary, Vadim. It should, and it will be. Many dark situations have been made easier through humour." I squeezed his hand. "I told you, I'm not giving up."

THE CAR DOOR OPENED, and I exited not wearing a blindfold this time.

The white, one-story building was plain and boxy, without any architectural adornments whatsoever. Behind the trees, in the distance, I caught a glimpse of a fence with coiled barbed wire on top. The term *fortified facility* came to mind.

To someone who didn't know what this place was, it might look like a military base, some secret research lab or even an insane asylum.

I shook the uncomfortable feeling off as Vadim walked around the car and stood by my side.

"Ready to go in?"

"Yes." I took his hand in mine for reassurance.

I distinctly remembered going down the stairs on my previous visits to this place. And true enough, I caught a glimpse of concrete stairs straight ahead upon entering the front door. However, Vadim led me to the left and along a main floor corridor instead.

Grey concrete walls and floor.

Bare light bulbs under the ceiling.

Plain, white doors. All closed.

This did not appear cozy or welcoming in any way. Although, I never got to *see* the lower level, I had a feeling it wouldn't be any more inviting, either. Could that have been one of the reasons for the blindfold in the first place?

"Are you hungry?" Vadim asked casually. "I can order dinner served immediately."

"No. Not right now, thank you," I replied, still too subdued by the atmosphere of this place to feel hungry. "Maybe later. Where do all these doors lead?"

"Rooms." He stopped in front of one, at the end of the hallway. "This one is mine."

Turning the handle, he shoved the door open with a visible effort. The hinges screeched with an ear-splitting sound, and I threw both hands up to cover my ears.

"Sorry, it hasn't been opened for um . . . a very long time." He gestured me in. "We don't use the doors much on this floor."

I remembered him walking through my closed apartment door again.

"Why have them at all?"

"Privacy. We all have our inner *demons* to deal with at times and prefer to do it on our own."

Vadim's room seemed especially large after the narrow corridors. The wide barred window opposite the door would have let in plenty of light through the day, I imagined, making it bright, too. Right now, though, the glow of the dying sunset painted the inside of the room in a red-orange haze.

"I'll have to get a bed in here," Vadim said, flicking the light switch.

I swept the room with my gaze, taking it in. Scarcely furnished, it appeared even more spacious. A wide armchair and an antique looking writing desk by the window were the largest pieces of furniture.

"I know you don't sleep." I took another step in, my feet sinking into the thick fur of an animal hide on the floor. "But do you never feel like lying down, either?"

"Not really." He shrugged. "I can relax in the chair just as well as in a bed."

He had lain in my bed most of last night, though. Now it appeared he did it purely for my benefit.

"How much time do you spend in this room?" I asked over my shoulder.

"Most of it."

"Right here? In this chair?" I traced the intricate gilded carvings on the frame of the armchair.

"Yes. Reading, working, thinking."

Centuries.

Just thinking about him sitting here all alone—years trickling by like hours for mortals—made my heart swell with compassion. I moved my gaze to the wall on the right, which was lined with bookshelves, floor to ceiling.

"Have you read all of these?" I pointed at the spines of the books, some of them more worn than others. And I would bet anything that some were made of real leather and embossed with actual gold.

"Much more than just these." He nodded. "Here I keep only my most favourite books." He came to stand by my side. Reaching out, he slid a finger along one of the spines carefully, like a caress. "Until recently, reading was pretty much the only way for us to learn human culture in detail and examine the events taking place in your world. These here are my personal collection. The library and the archives are in the north wing. A few decades ago, we also had a television installed there. It helps us to stay current with your news, even though world events don't affect us much."

Now, his complete and utter isolation became even more apparent to me. Vadim's life in here could very well be compared to that of a creature living deep under the sea, watching the world go by with the detached curiosity of a spectator.

"Going to the city must feel odd to you." I thought about making him walk me to the Metro station on the crowded street this morning, and guilt twisted inside me.

"It's . . . different," he replied. "Not unpleasant, though. And definitely exciting. Especially, if the reason for my going to the city is you."

He turned to face me.

"Valefor!" a male voice suddenly yelled from the corridor. "Purson and Agares are cooking chicken in the kitchen." A man barged into the room through the closed door, filling the space with his presence like an ocean wave crashing into a cave on the shore—all at once.

Still unused to the Incubi way of ignoring doors when entering, I shrank back and into Vadim's arms.

"They said you told them to—" The man cut himself short, his gaze stopped on me. "Are we keeping Sources at the Base again?"

"So much for privacy." I glanced up at Vadim with a short laugh.

His chest heaved with a deep inhale at my back.

"Zagan . . . I mean, what human name do you go by again? I don't remember."

The newcomer rubbed the back of his neck, his eyes—the colour of dark chocolate—darting from me to Vadim and back.

"Well, the last one I used was *Zayne*. And that was shortly before we moved here, a few centuries back."

"Right. Jade, this is Zayne, the other half of my team. When we were a team, that was."

"Hello, Jade." He seemed to have fully recovered from his initial surprise of finding me in Vadim's room and even bowed politely in greeting. "Nice to see you again."

Again.

The word shot through me like an eclectic charge. Zayne must have been one of those present in the room with the blindfolded me during my previous visits to the Base. He'd seen me on the cross. Naked.

"Um. Nice to meet you," I croaked, as my cheeks flushed with heat despite my best efforts to control my unease.

Thankfully, Zayne didn't seem to notice my flustered state, or if he did he hid it well.

"I have to apologize." He brushed his hand over his close-cropped dark hair. "I didn't know Vadim had a visitor."

"Very understandable," I replied, keeping my tone light. "It doesn't seem to happen often."

"No, not often!" Zayne huffed a laugh, humour bouncing with the golden flecks inside his eyes. "More like never."

"Jade is staying for dinner, Zayne. *Her* dinner," Vadim specified. "Do you like chicken Kiev?" He turned to me.

"Yes. Sure."

Would you join us? The invitation to Zayne almost left my lips, but I stopped it in time, remembering the difference between my own and their definition of *dinner* and afraid that coming from me it might sound more like a proposition.

"I have the dining table set in the meeting room, unless you prefer to eat here," Vadim said to me.

"No. Meeting room is fine. Whatever is easier." The atmosphere around us had thickened somehow.

"Jade." Zayne made a formal bow. "Once again, I beg your pardon for interrupting." He tilted his head Vadim's way, too. "Grand Master."

"Have a bed for Jade made in my room," Vadim tossed his way. "She is staying the night."

With another brief bow, Zayne exited the room, this time opening the door first.

"Is he your friend, part of *your team* or an underling?" I had some difficulties understanding the dynamics between them.

"All three," Vadim replied simply. "Come. We may as well go to the meeting room. Your appetizer should be ready by now. I'll show you the bathroom, too, on the way."

Chapter 22

"HOW DO YOU FIND THE chicken?" Vadim inquired, holding a knife and a fork over his plate.

"Thank you. It's excellent." I mimicked his formal tone.

During the appetizers, I'd figured out the behaviour of the demons around me. They simply weren't accustomed to entertaining anyone on their turf. If falling back into formality made them more comfortable with my presence in their space, I decided to play along for a while until they got used to the idea of having me around.

"You have some amazing cooks here. Especially, considering that none of you eat much."

According to Andras, Incubi didn't need to eat food at all, which was easy to believe, watching Vadim listlessly shove the food across his plate. The only reason he had anything in front of him, I suspected, was so I didn't have to eat alone.

"We've all learned to cook at some point." He took a drink from his glass of sparkling water, and I mirrored his gesture, taking a sip of my wine.

We sat at the opposite ends of a large table covered in red velvet. Vadim wore his usual army-green shirt, and I still had my work clothes on. Despite the size of the table, it still seemed too small for the spacious room. With the only light coming from the two large candelabras on the table, with twelve candles each, the walls and the ceiling of the meeting room sank into deep shadows.

An Incubus walked in to pick up my empty plate. Silent and stealthy as a shadow too, he set a bowl with dessert in front of me.

Unlike the armoured 'robots' I recalled from my last visit, he wore a pair of black dress pants and a white tunic.

"Did you cook the dinner?" I stopped him before he had a chance to leave.

"Yes," he replied, with a quick glance at Vadim first.

"So, are you Purson or Agares?"

"Um . . ." He blinked, seemingly lost for a moment. "Andrei. My human name is Andrei."

"Right. Of course. Well, thank you Andrei. The chicken was delicious."

"I'm glad you enjoyed it." With a deep bow and another quick look Vadim's way, he left the room.

"What is it with *human names*?" I asked Vadim when we were left alone again. "And what kind of a name is Valefor? That's what Zayne called you, didn't he?"

"Valefor is my demon name, the one I came here with, to this world."

"How did you get to be Vadim then?"

"I simply picked the first local name I liked when I became the Grand Master. In this position, I get addressed in places where humans may overhear, like the meetings with the Priory representatives, for example."

"So these names are solely for the benefit of humans then?"

"They are to protect us from them." He placed his hands on the table in front of him. "It's not as important nowadays. The proper rituals have been long forgotten. But the tradition to take human names goes way back to the times when demon summons was a real threat to us."

"How?" I had a hard time imagining Vadim considering anything or anyone a threat. The confidence and authority exuding from his tall frame made me believe that being near him was the safest place on earth. "How could anyone harm *you*?"

"We have no choice but to appear if ritually summoned by our demon name. Once there, we are at the mercy of the one who summoned us, the conjurer. And once we are under his will, we can be commanded to do whatever they please."

"Like their own supernatural servant?" I took a moment to consider this. "What if you don't agree with what is asked of you? What happens if you refuse to do their bidding?"

"You can fight the summoner's will for a period of time, how long depends on their strength, but it is nearly impossible to refuse it if the ritual is performed flawlessly."

I shuddered at the thought of being reduced to no more than someone's mindless soldier.

"Have you ever been summoned?"

"No. But Zayne has."

"Really?" I nearly dropped my spoon, staring at him in shock. "How did he get away?"

"He fought. Until the monk made a mistake. Then Zayne was able to kill him and escape."

"Kill?" I gasped.

"It was the only way to break the bond created by the conjurer to bind Zayne to him."

Gripping the silver dessertspoon in my hand, I shook my head. "It's hard to believe things like that are real."

Yet, this was now my reality.

"I should not have called him by his demon name in front of you," Vadim said with regret. "Not because he wouldn't trust you, but because ever since that time, he has been painstaking in avoiding mentioning it anywhere near a human ear. It was very inconsiderate of me to forget it. It's just that we have been on our own here for so long, I simply was not used to calling him by any other name."

"I understand. And I promise never to reveal his or yours or any other demon's name to anyone."

Lost in thoughts about what I'd learned, I mechanically cracked the sugar crust on my crème brûlée with the spoon. "How many of you are here?"

The place seemed rather quiet. We never ran into anyone in the long hallways on the way to his room or to dinner.

"Very few now. Less than two dozen. The building used to house several hundred Incubi before."

"What happened? Where did they all go?"

"West. Andras has been implementing the idea of a dance show there. If it works, more of us will be able to stay awake, experiencing less pain."

"By doing a dance show?" I lifted an eyebrow at him in question.

"All-male dance show." He nodded. "To entice the imagination of humans in the audience, so the Incubi on the stage can feed off their emotions."

"You mean like stripping?"

"Does dancing always equate to stripping?" He tented his fingers, gazing at me with some challenge.

"No. Of course not." I faltered. "Sorry for the assumption. I guess it's the *all-male show* and *to entice the imagination* that led my mind to wander that way."

"One doesn't need to strip naked to *entice*. Isn't there a human expression 'to leave something for the imagination' that implies some clothes on the body may actually be more seductive than full nudity?"

"There sure is." I took another sip of my wine, my mind going straight to *his* body, with all its seductive parts, and the way the layers of clothing he insisted on keeping between us enticed me into desperately wishing to get naked with him, despite the danger that would bring.

The thought brought back images of his bare skin under my gloved hands, and I swallowed another gulp of wine in an attempt to calm the glowing embers of desire before they fanned into a flame.

"We have been searching for other ways to keep ourselves fed," Vadim continued calmly, as if he couldn't see what his words had stirred inside me. "Although sexual energy in any form is our preferred source of nourishment, there are plenty of other positive emotions in humans capable of sustaining us."

"Like what?"

"Any of them, as long as they're positive. Natasha had the idea of a charity project at the hospital. She's organized a few public events, which gave us the chance to deliver treats, medicine, and hospital supplies as well as monetary donations. During the first visit, the delegation of seven Incubi spent a few hours, socializing with staff and patients."

"Were they feeding all this time?"

"Skimming. Gratitude, appreciation, good humour are all potent emotions, especially if felt by a group of people at close proximity."

"Interesting." My mind latched on to the idea, moving away from lustful thoughts about him for a moment. "I'll try to think of more places like that where there are an abundance of positive human emotions."

"Thank you. That will be helpful."

I considered all the things that normally brought good feelings in me, personally.

"You know, besides doing the shows yourselves, how about going to see one? Maybe a comedy show or a funny movie? Although, you'd have to be careful with your eyes sparkling in a dark theatre, like that." I pointed at the bright, blue-white lights flashing through Vadim's gaze on me and took a spoonful of my dessert. "Mmmm," I couldn't hold back a small moan of pleasure, closing my eyes. "I didn't compliment Andrei's cooking enough when he was here. This is fantastic!"

"I'm glad you like it." The deep, velvet note in his voice prompted me to open my eyes to catch his still twinkling blue in the candlelight. His gaze on me, however, grew heavy, his eyes hooded, unblinking.

"This wasn't sexual," I pointed out, squirming in my chair.

"It didn't taste like a sexual emotion," he agreed. "But it looked and sounded very much like it."

"It did?" I swallowed hard, a tendril of heat licked through my chest and slipped down to my stomach, making my inner muscles clench.

The next series of sparkles in Vadim's stare on me had an unmistakable pink hue.

"Here is another idea." I cleared my throat, crossing my legs under the table. "How about going to a restaurant that serves good food? You could order your glass of sparkling water and feast on people's enjoyment of their meal."

"I prefer to feast on you." His head low, he stared at me from under his thick eyebrows, his hands fisted into the scarlet velvet of the tablecloth. "On your enjoyment of . . . anything, really."

Emptying my wine glass, I got up from the table.

"Is that what you have been doing? Feeding on my emotions?"

"Yes."

I walked around the table and headed to him.

"Exclusively?"

"Yes."

"How about the prostitutes? Do they still come here?"

I hadn't talked to Tanya for the past couple of days, but I was fairly certain she would have called me had she been *fired* from the job she treasured.

"A few. As well as a couple of women who come whenever they please. The way you used to—"

"But *you* don't feed off them?"

"No."

"Why?"

"I don't want anyone else's emotions to mix with yours inside me."

A sense of deep satisfaction stroked my soul at his confession.

"You like the way I 'taste' then?" I was standing right over him now, and he lifted his head to meet my eyes, turning with his chair to face me.

"I wish I knew how you taste," he rasped, his gaze sliding down my body. "Everywhere."

The last word came out with a deep pained groan. Wrapping his arms around my hips, he drew me in, burying his face in my stomach.

"Vadim." I swayed off balance in his sudden powerful embrace, my heart bursting with compassion and desire for him. "We can try again." I hovered my hands over his head, wishing I could sink my fingers into his hair, then smoothed my palms over his shoulders instead. "We can just keep trying."

Silent, he shook his head, his forehead pressed into the fabric of my blouse.

"No more trying. I'm not risking it again."

"Baby." I sank to my knees in front of him, fitting myself between his legs to get closer. "What happened *then*, in the seventeenth century, I can't even begin to imagine how it must have felt . . ."

Chilling horror crept up my spine at the image of Vadim holding the lifeless body of the woman in his arms, realising what he had done the moment the passion was gone.

I closed my eyes for a second, willing that picture out of my head and the fear away from my heart because he didn't need that from me at the moment.

"You can't hide from your past forever, though. An eternity is too long to spend it here, all alone. What will happen to you when all the others leave? Because that's what they are doing right now, aren't they? Leaving, in throngs, to find love and new life out there, in the real world."

"It's safer for everyone if I stay here," he replied, sternly.

"How many people have died in this building?"

"Many. Hundreds."

I inhaled a shuddering breath, refusing to let the dark history of this place affect me.

"How many of them did *you* kill?"

"None."

"Do you realise what you ended up doing?" I gripped his forearms, willing him to understand what I was saying. "You stopped it all. Why? Because what happened back then made you see the change was needed. After all the abductions and murders, you were the first Grand Master who let women walk free."

I swept the shadows of the room with my gaze. This place didn't scare me. The horrors hidden in these walls hadn't touched me. My own memories tied to this building were pleasant. Could I help Vadim build some new connections with this place, too? Some that would move the grim past into the background where it belonged and finally set him free?

"Andras said you all have to wear gloves in public, to avoid taking from strangers during accidental touching."

"True." He nodded. "The self-control varies from Incubus to Incubus. Being in public, surrounded by humans, any situation can quickly turn unpredictable. It's best to be safe than sorry."

"Yet those Incubi who have girlfriends are able to touch them skin-to-skin without concern."

"Yes, they have learned to do that."

"How?"

He shrugged his shoulder, shaking his head. "They have practiced. Especially, we noticed that if a demon cares about the woman, he is able to stop himself from harming her. Once it happens, he can eventually learn to gain more control over his hunger."

"You said you cared about me."

"I do," he said softly. His arms around me, he caressed between my shoulder blades with his thumbs. "Still, I can't stop from harming you."

"It's been awhile since you fully touched someone. And the first and last time you did ended in tragedy, which was obviously traumatizing." I slid my hands up his biceps then along his shoulders. "Let me help you build new memories filled with light and pleasure. Yours and mine." Carefully avoiding touching his skin, I tugged at the buttons of his shirt, opening them one by one. "We'll go slow." I lowered my voice, trying to soothe him and keep him calm.

Leaning closer, I savoured his scent, fresh and warm, with a hint of the ocean. I kissed the hard muscles of his chest through the thin fabric of his shirt, feeling his heart beat frantically under my lips.

"You are a very stubborn woman," he gritted through his teeth.

"So I've been told." I smiled, diligently working on the rest of his buttons. "Many times."

"Stubborn. And tantalizingly enticing."

"*That* I have not been called." I laughed, leaning back to open his shirt wide.

His hands flexed on my shoulders, keeping me at a distance.

There was no question, I could not overpower him physically and he seemed dead set on keeping me at bay.

"Stand up," I ordered, rising to my feet.

"What are you doing?" he asked, but followed me, standing up, too.

"Come here." I took his gloved hand in mine and tugged him to follow me to the centre of the room. "Do you know how things work around here? I want those chains down." I pointed at the coils of chains gleaming in the shadows high under the ceiling.

"I've never operated them myself." He headed to the far wall. "But I've watched it done many times. Let's see."

He picked up a flat metal box from a rolling cart and pushed a few buttons. With a low humming noise, the coils turned, and two chains slowly descended from the ceiling.

"If you want handcuffs, I can look on the shelves under that balcony—"

"No." I stopped him on his way to one of the wooden balconies constructed along two opposite walls, with seating for spectators, I imagined. "The handcuffs will be too small for your wrists. Are there any padlocks, though?" I asked innocently.

"*My* wrists?" He stopped in his tracks and turned around to stare at me.

Without replying, I sauntered past him to the shelves under the balcony and rummaged through the various sex toys and equipment laid out there.

"What are you planning to do?" Vadim's deep voice sounded uncharacteristically uncertain.

Finding a couple of padlocks in a crate under the shelf, I walked back to him, stopping a breath away from his bare chest.

"This time, I will have *you* in chains, Grand Master."

Chapter 23

HE LET ME LOCK HIM in, watching my every move, as I wound a chain around each of his muscular arms then brought his hands up and attached the makeshift restraints to the ends of two chains hanging from the ceiling.

From what I knew about Incubi strength, the chains wouldn't hold him against his will, but I hoped they would add one more step, just a moment before he freed himself, which might be enough for him to stop.

"I don't want you to break the chains, Vadim. No matter what I do, keep still." My hands on the belt of his pants, I spoke calmly even as my heart raced, my emotions in turmoil.

So many things rushed through me.

Appreciation at the sight of this strong, powerful man, bound and at my mercy.

Trepidation of the danger always lurking under the surface when one was about to play with a demon.

Excited anticipation of things I knew he was capable of making me feel.

Worry. For him. Despite the strength and confidence he exuded, he was fractured inside, and I dreaded inadvertently breaking him. My aim was to help, not to harm.

I slid my hand over his shirt and up his sides.

He tensed under my palms. "Say *stop* and I will," I promised softly. "But don't stop me for as long as you can stand this. I need to feel you."

Everywhere. I had to feel him everywhere.

I needed his hands on me. I wanted to taste his lips . . .

Patience.

I drew in a long breath and took a step back.

"It would only be fair if I had my shirt open, too." I tugged my blouse out of my skirt and opened the small buttons. Taking it off, I unhooked my bra, too. "Even better—I'll go completely topless." I shrugged out of my bra, tossing it to the floor.

His eyes bright, Vadim devoured me with his gaze. My breasts tingled as my nipples hardened under his hungry stare.

"I promised this wouldn't happen again," he rasped, as I stepped back to him. "Don't come any closer."

"Is that what you really want? For me to stay away?" I splayed my hands on his shoulders again. He jerked back, yanking at the chains, which rattled and squeaked in protest. "Tell me to stop," I challenged, but he kept quiet. "You know I want this, very much. And I know you long to give me what I want." The truth of this statement became perfectly clear the moment the words left my mouth.

I wanted him more than anything in the world right now. And he wouldn't stop me even though he was infinitely stronger than me, because he *needed* this.

"For the love of all that's holy," he growled. "Put some gloves on at least."

"Gloves would protect my hands, but how about the rest?" I leaned in slowly, the tips of my breasts coming less than an inch from his bare chest.

He breathed heavily, watching the shrinking distance between us.

"Careful," he begged, his voice pained. "If something happens to you, it'll wreck me."

"I want you whole, Vadim. Healed, not wrecked," I whispered, my breasts swaying at his chest with every breath I took.

The heat from his body broke against the biting needles of frost that plucked at my nipples as I leaned in too close.

"Jade." Terror strangled Vadim's voice, making my name catch in his throat.

"I'm good," I reassured him, shrinking back a little, breathless. "Really good, actually . . ."

The stings of cold turned into warm tingles, rapidly spreading from my breasts to between my legs.

Kicking my red pumps off, I lifted my leg and hooked it around his hips.

"I want to make you feel good too." I circled his waist with one arm for balance, clicking his belt buckle open with the other hand. "Just hold still, baby. And breathe," I murmured, leaning into his side, his open shirt between us.

Sliding my hand between his pants and his underwear to keep from touching his skin, I found his pulsing hardness. "How can you be this hot and feel so freezing cold to touch?" I squeezed him gently, enjoying the tight resistance in my fingers.

"I take . . ." he panted, "through skin-to-skin contact. It causes the chilling sensation in you."

"Right." I moved my hand a little faster.

I wanted to keep his mind on what I was doing rather than on his fear or worry about self-control. My aim was to make him focus on what was physically happening between us and to distract him from everything else, including the visual of my emotions. As hard as he was, I knew he wouldn't last long.

"But how would you explain these flushes of heat in my body whenever you're close to me?" I rocked my hips into him, shamelessly riding his leg now in sync with my hand gliding up and down his length. "Tell me, why I all but lose my mind with you around? My whole body aches for you, constantly. And no matter how much you let me have, it's never enough."

With a loud growl, he yanked at the chain that held his right arm, swinging it back and away from me, as it fell from the ceiling. Hiking my skirt to my waist, he tore at my panties before sliding his gloved fingers between my thighs.

"How do you expect me to hold still? When all this crimson lust is practically dripping off you?" he gritted in my hair, rubbing between my legs faster and faster. I moaned, feeling his finger slide inside me, the leather of his glove slick and cool. "You're all hot and wet. For me."

Closing my eyes under the onslaught of pleasure spreading through me from his fingers, I pressed myself to him, trying to match the speed of my hand on his erection to that of his between my thighs.

I was no longer fully aware which parts of our bodies touched, and which ones of them were covered or not. Violent waves of heat and biting frost rolled through my skin at will, and I clung to him, striving to stay upright as the surge of pure ecstasy rocked through my body, threatening to crush me.

"Vadim . . ." I moaned, flexing my leg hooked around his hips to bring him closer and to keep my balance through the tremors of my orgasm.

His heavy breathing turned erratic then halted, as he pumped his own release into my hand, soaking the fabric of his boxers.

"Baby . . ." Lost in the moment, drunk on him to the point of being nearly delusional, I craned my neck and caught his mouth with mine in the kiss I'd wanted for so long.

Cold slipped between my lips along with his tongue a moment before he jerked back, and I slacked against his body, my muscles disobeying me and my bones as if dissolving at once.

"Jade!" The second chain came crashing down as my eyes closed and I slid to the floor. "My treasure." Strong arms caught me just before I hit the ground.

Then the world went dark.

Chapter 24

A LOUD SCREECHING NOISE woke me up, as if someone had shoved a heavy piece of furniture across the floor.

Squinting in the bright light filtering through my eyelids, I made an attempt to open my eyes and only partially succeeded. Peeking with one eye half-open, I spotted the familiar large figure of my demon by the window. He seemed to have shoved the armchair back on his way up from behind the desk.

"Morning," I muttered, rubbing my face.

"Jade." Spinning on his heel, he rushed to me.

"How long has it been this time?" I asked, as he crouched by the bed I was on. "What time is it?"

"Three in the afternoon." His voice came out hollow.

"So, just like . . . less than twenty hours then?" Exact math was not going to happen for me right then. There was no point in trying.

"How are you?"

"Not bad." I rose on my elbows. The embroidered bedspread in luscious violet dropped away from my chest, exposing my breasts. "I'm naked," I stated the fact, feeling no clothes on me at all. "Completely."

"I undressed you for the night," he dismissed and repeated, "How are you? Any pain? Hungry? Still tired?"

"Calm down, Mister Nanny." Holding the bedding to my chest, I sat up. My head swam a little then settled as I got my sense of balance back. "Nothing hurts. A bit lightheaded—"

"You need some food." In two long strides Vadim reached the door then shoved his head and torso through, without opening it.

"Zayne!" His voice boomed through the concrete corridors outside the room. "Lunch for Jade. Now!"

No *please* or *thank you*. Vadim seemed to reserve all his pleasantries exclusively for me, with none left for his fellow Incubi.

"Here." He picked up a mug from the desk. "Herbal tea with honey for you." He sat on the bed next to me. "Well, it's more like ice tea by now. I had it made much earlier."

"Thank you." I took the mug from him. Even lukewarm, the tea was pleasant and sweet. "It's good." I inhaled after taking a few sips then leaned back against the headboard of the carved wood bedframe. "This is gorgeous." I slid my gaze along the poster bed, taking in the intricate carvings on the dark wood and the rich fabrics of the bedding. "I've never seen anything like this. Where did you get it?"

"What? The bed? We had it in one of the storage rooms downstairs." He glanced at the piece of furniture, critically. "Not sure how it got there, must have been left from a visit by someone from the Priory." The focus in his eyes sharpened. "We must have got it sometime around the eighteenth century, by the look of it. Seventeenth, maybe. The mattress is newer, of course," he added quickly. "And the bedding was washed yesterday."

"Cool." I stroked the silk embroidery, noticing that the threads had faded in places, betraying the age of the piece. "What else do you have in this treasure room of yours?"

"Um, lots of things," he replied distractedly, his focus fully on me. "Do you feel tired at all?"

I rolled my shoulders back, taking another drink from my mug.

"Not really. I had an almost twenty-hour nap, remember? A little hungry, maybe."

"Jade." He sat next to me. "I—"

His expression fell, and my heart squeezed painfully.

"Don't. Please stop blaming yourself."

"I promised you I wouldn't let it happen again."

"And I promised I wouldn't give up trying," I echoed. "This is definitely not on you. At all. Last night, I tied you up and took advantage of you. Did you forget?"

A flush of dark heat in his stare made my breath hitch.

"I'll never forget last night." His voice, deep and sombre, stroked something inside me. "You are the only one—demon or human, dead or alive—who has ever made me break my promise. I have no strength or willpower to deny you. And you keep putting yourself in danger. Carelessly."

"Well, it was a very bad promise to begin with. You shouldn't have made it in the first place," I retorted. "Look. The way I see it, I keep getting mind-blowing orgasms from you—"

"At what price?"

"At the price of a long and restful nap." I took another drink from my mug. "Seriously, Vadim. Try to look at it objectively, not through the gloomy prism of all the perceived dangers out there. Please. Last night . . ." I dropped my gaze to my lap, my face and my insides heating again at the memories of us together. "It was beautiful. Our skin touched, pretty sure more than once. And that kiss . . ." I sighed, bringing my hand to my lips where the sensation of him still lingered.

He followed my gesture with his eyes, an expression of intense concentration on his handsome face.

"Don't tell me it can't happen again," I warned. "Because I want more of this. Don't you feel how great we are together?"

"Amazing," he agreed. "Being with you, Jade, could never compare to anything I've ever experienced. But—"

"Listen." I lifted a finger between us, prompting him to stop. "Just think about how it all happened last night. Do you remember fighting it? Because I swear the cold wasn't there all the time. It came and went, in waves. Not scary enough for me to stop. You held it back, until I kissed you. Which I admit might have happened a little too soon."

Not that I'm sorry.

That kiss alone was worth it all.

"Maybe, I shouldn't have let it go that far yet," I conceded. "But the truth is, Vadim, I simply want you so damn much . . ."

"Jade." He hovered over me, prompting me to press my back into the headboard behind me. The storm in his eyes both frightened and drew me in, all at once. "I love how unapologetic you are in your desires. The way you go after what you want . . . You have no idea how much—"

"Lunch!" The announcement came with a loud knock on the door. Then the now familiar shape of Zayne emerged into the room.

Dressed in a long white tunic, black pants and a pair of embroidered slippers, Zayne carried in a tray with some dishes.

"Chicken broth, veal meatballs with potatoes and gravy, and fruit compote," he announced proudly, approaching the bed. "Compliments of Andrei and Ilya, with best wishes for your speedy recovery."

"This is a lot of food," I gasped as he set the tray in my lap.

Midday meal was the largest one, according to local custom. Still, I didn't think I could eat all of this even if I ate all day.

"You need food to get well." Vadim stepped in, handing me the spoon.

My fingers brushed by his gloved hand as I took it from him.

"Can you sit with me?" I patted the cover at my side. "Please?"

Zayne cleared his throat. "I'll be back for the dishes when you're done." He left, with a short bow.

Vadim sat next to me.

"I'm not feeling anything overly sexual for you right now," I said.

That was true. The pleasure of having him near, the enjoyment of his company was warming my heart, but the usual burning desire for him simmered on low at the moment.

"I've taken most of it," he gravely reminded me.

"That may be a good thing." I put the spoon on the tray. "You see, I believe we might have started too strongly. Let's try this from the beginning."

"What do you mean?"

"Instead of rushing into sex, when both you and I lose our minds to lust, how about we start with casual touches first? Whatever emotions I have in me right now must be easier for an Incubus to resist than the raging sexual energy burning hot and wild."

"You may have a point." His smile at me was warm, if a little sad. "Except that my own *raging lust* for you hasn't faded. To be honest, I don't think it ever will."

The intensity in his eyes, combined with the quiet resignation in his voice, coiled around my heart with wistfulness and longing. Both were new emotions for me, and I had no idea what to make of them at the moment.

"Well, only one of us is raging with lust right now, then." I decided to stick with the topic at hand. "If I remain focused, it may be easier for you. Right?"

His chest rose with a heavy sigh as he seemed to consider my words.

"You won't quit trying?"

"I said I won't. The thought of you being left here, all alone when everyone leaves and I move away . . . I can't stand it. It would make me feel so much better knowing you could . . ."

'Touch any woman without the fear of hurting her,' was what I was going to say. However, the unwelcome image of Vadim with someone else rose in my mind. My throat tightened painfully, and I just couldn't squeeze these words out.

". . . knowing you could live in this world freely," I said instead. "Without the fear of hurting anyone."

His hands clasped in his lap, he stared at me—through me—searching somewhere deep inside, then stretched his hand. "Try again then."

His glove was on, and I didn't pry it off. Instead, I took his hand in mine then traced with my finger the edge of the glove around his wrist.

"Are you ready, darling?" My voice came out softer than I intended. I wanted this for him, so much.

He nodded, his focus firmly on my finger inching towards his bare skin.

"Light like a feather . . ." I whispered, skimming atop the fine dark hairs on his forearm, all the way to the rolled up sleeve of his shirt then back, the pad of my finger barely touching his skin here and there.

A fine dusting of frost prickled under my finger whenever I came too close. I glanced up at Vadim, finding his gaze on me, no longer on his arm. His eyes seemed unfocused, but I recognized that look by now—he watched the emotions he took, keeping an eye on my life force, too.

"More," he whispered, his breathing stilted, a hard expression etched on his face.

I stopped my hand over his arm and gingerly pressed my finger to his skin. The frost still skirted around the tip, but then the whole area of our contact warmed up slowly, as if melting from our touch.

"Don't move it away," he requested as the tiny blue lights flashed through his eyes. "I'm skimming only, Jade. Not taking."

"Yes, you are, baby." I smiled, my chest feeling suddenly much lighter. "And I'm touching you. Skin to skin."

Chapter 25

OVER THE NEXT FEW WEEKS, we developed a pattern. Vadim would visit me after work through the week. He had my permission to enter my apartment to wait for me there if I was late.

I found myself looking forward to coming home, knowing he might already be there, getting dinner started. My enjoyment of the domestic aspect of our relationship thrilled me, but I knew it would pass. Sooner or later, unfortunately, I would get bored with the routine. The fact that it was inevitable filled me with deep sadness, and I made sure to fully enjoy every day we still had together.

December came and went. With my office closing, I didn't get enough time off to make it back home for Christmas to see my family this year. Instead, I connected with them through the Internet and watched my nieces and nephews open the presents I'd sent for them.

The Incubi invited me to the Base for Christmas dinner. Sitting at the large table in the dining room with Vadim, Zayne, and the twelve demons who still remained there, I felt not a trace of awkwardness whatsoever. By then I'd gotten to know all of them well enough to feel absolutely myself in their presence.

Zayne told me it was the first Christmas dinner that had ever taken place at the Base. The fact that Incubi made it for me—complete with roast chicken and plum pudding, like my mum would make, and even a small decorated Christmas tree as a centrepiece—filled me with gratitude the moment I entered the room.

For New Year's celebration, the biggest night of the holiday season in Belarus, I went to Tanya's apartment. I told her I was seeing someone but didn't explain who he was, afraid of the questions I wouldn't be able to answer without revealing the Incubi's secrets.

Every weekend in January, Vadim sent a car to take me to the Base. There we would spend the two days together every week.

I made it to the basement one day, to the wing opposite from the meeting room where we normally had dinner.

It was a sombre visit.

My mood subdued, I walked along concrete corridors similar to the ones upstairs except for slightly lower ceilings. All doors were open here, room after empty room. Only the grey walls remained, and the lingering sense of isolation, despair, and death.

"Why?" I whispered, reaching to touch the doorframe of one of the rooms, then yanked my hand away, afraid that the morbid essence of this dungeon would seep into me with the contact. "I am more than happy to feed you." I turned to face Vadim, who was accompanying me. "Natasha and the others are doing it for their demons, too. Why did *this* have to happen at all?"

He splayed his hand on the wall.

"For someone who has lived for a mere thirty years, it may be impossible to understand."

"Try me," I challenged, not at all offended by him basically calling me too young to get it.

"The world has changed drastically in the past couple of centuries—the past one hundred years, really. When the treaty was signed, back in the fifteenth century, it was actually viewed as a salvation for some. Not just to ensure our isolation from human populations, but also a way to take care of women whom society might not have been able, or didn't want, to look after."

"What are you saying?" I narrowed my eyes at him.

"Incubi never took random people off the street. You know that all our acquisitions were sanctioned by humans."

"The Priory." I nodded.

"Right. Centuries ago, the prospects of a widowed or unmarried woman, who was not allowed to hold property and often couldn't provide for herself without a man, were grim."

"Huh!" I scoffed, pointing at the cells. "Don't make it sound like you were providing some kind of a sanctuary for them in here."

"But for a while, I believe we were, Jade. You have to understand, we did not kidnap nobility from castles. The women who got approved to be taken often came from the very fringes of the society, someone no one would miss when they were gone. The Priory monks turned many of those who showed up at their church begging for charity to us. Those women often were at the end of their rope, with no means to survive—the most likely future for them being an untimely death from violence, disease or hunger.

"For someone like you, who learned about this part of history from a book, it might be difficult to grasp this. Because the women we took have never been mentioned in any history books. They came and left, their lives but a tiny blink on the timeline of the world, with society paying as much attention to them as to a speck of sand in the desert. We skimmed their emotions, held them in isolation, but we gave them food and shelter, the safety from all the things that plagued their existence on the outside. In some cases, I truly believe, we extended their lives. They were safe here, physically sheltered from harm."

"Until they weren't," I pointed out.

"Human life has always been painfully short, but the Sources rarely had to be drained back then. They died from other causes. Before modern medicines, disease and infections still found their way in here, wiping out all our Sources a few times. Still, generally, their time with us here used to be longer in those earlier centuries."

Hands on the doorframe above his head, Vadim stared inside the cell, recalling the life that took place here for so long.

"As society developed, life outside became better for everyone, including women, single and otherwise. The survival time of our Sources actually shrunk. They died or had to be drained sooner. It was the isolation that would kill them eventually. Humans need interaction to thrive, we know it now. Also, women had much more to miss from the outside world. It's no longer the men who provide and care. Widowed and unmarried women are full members of modern society, with all the rights that go with that."

It was bizarre to hear him talk of fundamental rights like some new, modern concept, as if they had just happened now. Trying to see it from his perspective, though, I imagined it would seem pretty recent. On the timeline of his ten-century existence, the decades of women's rights movements would be like the blink of an eye.

"At the end of the day, though, it never mattered what we believed and how we felt about the way we were forced to feed. The treaty came from the Priory. And they have been unwilling to revisit it until now."

"How could they not search for better ways to solve this?"

"We have been trusting the Priory to look after the best interests of humanity. However, I now suspect there has been more than simply keeping humans safe in their motivations and in their ways to make us stick to the rules."

"What do you mean?"

"I've met with Raim, the Grand Master of the Western Council, on several occasions since becoming a Grand Master myself. He is the most zealous follower of the rules of the treaty. Raim has been in his position since before the treaty, and he's been essentially governing the actions of both our Councils all this time.

"Andras and I have been going through the archives, piecing together from the records of our Council meetings as well as the meetings with the Priory, what exactly has been happening between us and them. Raim has always been arrogant, ambitious and hungry for power. However, since the treaty was signed, he appeared to follow the ruling of the Priory flawlessly."

A thought flashed in my head.

"Maybe they have something on Raim. Some way of controlling him?"

"You think so?" He didn't seem overly surprised by my suggestion.

"They must have." I gripped his forearm. "I mean I've never met the guy, but you described him as powerful and arrogant, and definitely not someone who'd submit that easily to any decree made by humans much younger and weaker than himself. Look, even you talk to me sometimes like I'm some clueless *thirty-year-old* babe in the woods—"

"Sorry, I never meant to offend you." The mortified expression on his face gave even more sincerity to his apology.

"I know, I know." I patted his arm, pacifyingly. "And I'm not offended. Not really. My point is there must be something that gives the Priory its power over Raim. Has he ever been summoned, do you know? Maybe they have made him do their bidding, and he's been serving them ever since?"

"I don't think so," Vadim dismissed my idea. "Raim is too strong for any conjurer to force him into submission. That's the main reason he is the only one who never bothered with a human name in the first place."

"Raim is his demon name then?"

Vadim nodded. "The only name he's ever used."

"Hm." I frowned in concentration, trying to think harder. "There is something fishy going on with him, I'm sure of it."

"I'm beginning to think there is, too. He seemed to be absolutely against allowing relationships between Incubi and humans. He only relented when the Priory approved Andras's proposal."

"See? That doesn't make sense for someone like Raim. What do you think they could be using against him?"

"No idea. As far I know, Raim has nothing he treasures enough to submit to anyone over it."

"Could it be blackmail then?"

"What could the Priory blackmail him with? What secret would Raim have that he'd want to keep away from us?" Vadim moved closer, wrapping his arm around me. "Whatever it is, Jade, as long as he doesn't get in the way of these changes, Raim is nothing for us to worry about."

"ANDRAS CALLED FROM America," Zayne rushed to us as soon as we got upstairs. "Raim quit."

"Quit what?" I asked.

"When?" Vadim's expression darkened.

"Just now, pretty much. Andras has been elected to lead the West instead of him."

"Andras? Good. Why did Raim quit, though?" Vadim rubbed his forehead. "Actually, let me call Raim right away." He made a move to his room, but Zayne stopped him.

"He left."

"Raim left? Where?"

"No one knows. He didn't say. His phone is dead, too."

"Just like that?" Vadim stood, his arms crossed over his chest. "He quit and took off, vanishing without a trace?"

"According to Andras, he gave a warning before leaving. Something about the Priory not being what they seem and that no one with Incubi blood in them is safe. Andras believes that includes the offspring of the Forgiven."

To my knowledge, there were no known offspring of Incubi yet. Alyssa was in her last weeks of pregnancy, and there were now several more couples who were expecting.

How low would someone go, to threaten babies?

"Our children . . ." Vadim stared at me, his expression stern.

"I'm on the pill," I blurted out, immediately regretting what I said.

It was stupid. He obviously was considering the situation in general and how it would affect the children of all established human-Incubi unions. Besides, technically, Vadim and I had not come to that point in our physical relationship yet where babies could be made.

"Never mind." I waved my hand, wishing I could just sink through the floor from embarrassment.

"I need to call Andras. To get the details." Vadim seemed to shake off whatever heavy thoughts had furrowed his features into a deep frown, his body and expression filling with energy as he took off along the corridor.

"Andras has been moving all the Incubi currently in the Western hemisphere to Vegas, in case anything happens," Zayne was filling Vadim in on the way to the room. "He mentioned something about bringing both Councils together for the time being, too."

"It may be a wise idea to stay close." Vadim sounded as if he was thinking out loud.

"Should I start preparations for our move, too?"

Vadim paused with his hand on the door then glanced my way quickly.

"Those who want to move now are free to go," he stated. "I'll remain here until the end of March."

THE NEWS OF THE BIRTH of the first human-Incubi baby came just a few weeks later.

"Healthy baby boy," Vadim announced when I got home from work one night, late in February.

"Really?" I followed him to the kitchen, lured by the mouth-watering smell of the dinner he had been preparing.

"Both the mother and child are well."

"How is the father?"

His calm expression melted with a huge smile.

"Wrecked!" He huffed a laugh. "Sytrius is a complete mess according to Andras."

"Aw, poor guy," I cooed, taking my seat at the table as Vadim placed a bowl of fragrant stew in front of me. "One of my brothers spent the whole night in a bar drinking after his first baby was born. Needless to say, his wife is still pissed at him for that! Oh, and my other brother passed out at the first sight of the baby's head crowning . . . Childbirth is so hard on men!" I chuckled.

"Watching the woman you love go through pain would be the hardest part, I imagine." Vadim's smile faded.

I rested my gaze on his handsome face for a moment. Suddenly, there were so many things I wanted to know. Had Vadim ever thought about being a father one day? Would he want to have a family of his own?

I deliberately avoided any talks about the future with him, because I knew it wouldn't be *our* future, so there was no point in discussing it.

He didn't bring it up either, never questioning my own or his impending relocation, leading me to believe that he didn't mind us parting soon.

Less than a month now.

Way too soon.

I cleared my throat, lifting the spoon he'd given me.

"What is the baby's name?"

"Phoenix. Alyssa chose it, as the symbol of the re-birth of our future from the ashes of our past."

Chapter 26

"NOT TOO TIGHT?" I TUGGED at the chain that held Vadim's wrist at the corner of the padded table where he was lying. "We don't want to obstruct your blood flow," I muttered to myself, inspecting the other wrist and then the chain that secured his torso to the table. "If I do it right, you'll need your blood flowing elsewhere."

My demon was naked, sprawled on his back, hands and feet chained to the corners of the table in the middle of the meeting room at the Base.

The fingers of my bare hands brushed by his skin, without so much as the cold of one single snowflake to be felt, making me proud of our progress. It had taken us weeks—many trials, requiring endless patience from me and lots of determination from him—and here we were now, able to be completely naked together without worrying about me passing out any minute.

Vadim grew more and more confident about touching. And lately, we had been working on other forms of contact, too.

He seemed to worry less when he gave control to me. I suspected that lying on the table, tied hand-and-foot, he believed I'd have a chance to get away from him if things got too cold for comfort.

As for me, I was happy to do whatever would help him to relax.

"Alright, baby." I hopped on the table, too, crawling on my hands and knees over him. "All your chains are fastened. Hold on while I take you on a ride."

Carefully, I brushed my lips across his, once then twice, giving him a chance to adjust, but he lifted his head to meet my mouth, forcing me to deepen the kiss.

I smiled inside at his eagerness—despite his best intentions, my Grand Master had a hard time truly relinquishing all control.

"Ready for more?" I rocked back on my knees, his hard-on slapped against my butt cheek.

"Always am," Vadim replied, his voice husky.

Crawling backwards, I settled between his spread legs and took in the view for a moment.

Spread-eagled, all muscles tight in anticipation, his magnificent erection straining up in the air, Vadim was a sight to behold.

"Come here." I slid my palms up the thick muscles of his thighs, closing in on his shaft standing upright.

"Careful," he gave me the usual warning.

"Don't worry. I'll make sure to stop before your dick freezes my mouth."

"Jade." He shook his head with a chuckle. "The way you speak sometimes—"

I didn't let him finish. Sticking my tongue out, I gave his tip a long lick, and the air left his lungs with a loud hiss instead.

We had done this before, on two occasions. Both ended with me passing out on the floor and Vadim fussing over me for days afterwards.

I was more optimistic this time. He'd been doing so much better generally lately. The fear and horrible memories that terrorized his mind, paralysing his ability to control his hunger, must be receding as he wrestled free from their power over him.

Thoroughly enjoying the feel of his skin under my palms and his taste on my tongue, I moved my hands up the hard ridges of his abdomen and wrapped my mouth around his hard length, taking in as much as I could. Just the fact that I could do this filled me with pride at our accomplishment.

Vadim's abs tensed under my hands as I moved my head faster, sliding up and down over the thick veins on the surface of his glorious dick.

God, I loved the way he filled my mouth, but I had agreed to be patient about having him inside me. Vadim still seemed terrified by the idea of inadvertently pinning me under him in a moment of passion and draining me from the inside.

I flicked my tongue along his length, twirling it around his tip, and his hips bucked. His hard breathing halted for a moment, before erupting in a series of rugged grunts as he climaxed in powerful spurts. He jerked his legs, bending them at the knees, and the chains snapped to pieces around his ankles.

The chilly sensation ghosted my lips, numbing them for a moment.

Before the last tremor of orgasm fully rolled off him, I heard the rest of the chains crash to the floor.

"Jade?" He sat up, lifting me by my arms to him. "Are you okay?"

"I'm fine." I smiled, rubbing my mouth and cheeks with both hands to chase away the chilly numbness. "Just a bit frosty around here. Very little this time, though. You did good, baby."

"Are you sure you're okay?" He rubbed my arms then squeezed my sides, hips, thighs, as if checking for any broken bones. "Not sleepy? Dizzy? Hungry?"

"Honestly, I'm fine." I laughed. "Not horny anymore, though. But I know you can fix that."

"I'd be delighted to." The frantic movement of his hands along my body slowed down. Instead of squeezing, he was massaging now.

My thighs. My hips.

Then he slipped his hands up to my breasts, cupping them and kneading gently.

I wrapped my legs around his waist, and he rose to his knees on the table then lowered me down on my back.

"Kiss me," I whispered, reaching for him. All sounds above a whisper seemed too loud right now.

"Always." He took my mouth the way I imagined he would take me one day, with a greedy hunger and delightful care.

I spread my legs wider, cradling him. The hardening ridge of his renewed erection rubbed between my thighs, brushing against my core and making a sweet jolt of pleasure ripple through me.

I lifted my hips, pressing myself to him, and he rocked against me, sending another charge of liquid heat through my veins.

Breaking the kiss, Vadim slid down my body, leaving a trail of small, hot kisses on the way—along my neck then down to my left breast. He sucked the tip in, twirling his tongue around my nipple, then moved along my belly, past my navel, and lower, between my thighs.

My heart skipped when he dipped his tongue inside me. I arched my back with a moan as the heat began to pulsate wherever his tongue touched me.

"Payback time." His voice was thick with satisfaction as he glanced up at me, his chin pressed against my most sensitive spot.

Through the warm haze of lust enveloping me whole, I saw his glowing red eyes. The sight of them only spurred my arousal. Then he dove back down again, licking, nibbling, and sucking, until I could no longer take it.

"Please, please, please . . ." I chanted, rocking my hips against his tongue as he kept filling me with sweet torture.

He slid a finger in me, rubbing from the inside as the pressure of his mouth on me intensified.

The heat coiling low in my belly exploded, rocking my whole body with pleasure, and he grabbed my hips to stop me from falling off the table as he squeezed every last tremor and shudder of my climax from me.

"Vadim . . ." I panted. "Baby . . ."

He pulled himself up my body, gathering me, happy and absolutely boneless, into his arms.

Everything about being with Vadim was amazing, but this right now was one of my favourite parts. Him being able to hold me—my naked body pressed to his, skin to skin—was something I could never take for granted.

Being here, wrapped into him like this—safe and warm, my body flushed with the mind-blowing orgasm he'd just given me—was the only place I wanted to be at that moment.

"Dinner now and into bed." Vadim got off the table, with me in his arms.

"We already had dinner, remember?" My arms over his shoulders, I settled against his chest. "I had salad and cabbage rolls, and you had a whole bottle of sparkling water."

"You'll need a snack after what we just did."

The tone of his voice didn't allow for arguing, but I still did. "I'm not hungry yet."

He yanked the silk sheet off the table, tucking it around me on his way to the exit from the meeting room.

"A cup of tea with honey then?" His tone softened. "You need some calories to help you recover."

"Fine, *daddy*." I actually pouted, fighting a giggle.

"Daddy?"

"Well, taking your age into account, you'd be more like a many-times great grandpa . . . Oh, no," I groaned, rolling my head on his shoulder. "I can't think about you that way, but it's true! You are hundreds of years older than me. It's insane."

His chest vibrated with a chuckle. "It's a little too late to worry about that now. Don't you think?"

"Right." I leaned against his shoulder, savouring his familiar scent, the warmth of his body, the strength of his arms holding me.

The ever-present sting in my chest had been growing sharper with every day that brought me closer to my moving day.

I'd never felt the need for a man to complete me. In fact, I always thought my destiny was to have fun and end up alone. These prospects for the future never used to make me feel sad. I imagined myself as a cool, forever-young aunt to my nieces and nephews—someone who wouldn't be stopped by wrinkles from wearing a bikini to her dying day and would surf the ocean until she needed a walker to get around.

I knew that a relationship with a demon extended a person's life by centuries. Impossible to fathom for someone like me, whose relationships never lasted long enough to even speak of them in years. Spending an eternity with one person—be he a man or a demon—was just not realistic for me, I knew myself far too well to have any delusions about this. I liked and respected Vadim way too much to pretend otherwise.

Surely, he took my initial warning to heart, because he never brought up the possibility of my quitting my job and coming with him. He hadn't offered to come to Moscow with me, either.

I felt his affection and his growing attachment to me every day. But I was the first woman he had been able to touch and enjoy without fear. It was to be expected he would develop some special feelings for me. Wasn't it?

As to my feelings for him . . .

At the very least, I could be happy for him when we parted. With more freedom for Incubi than they'd ever had, Vadim would be able to skim the emotions off anyone he wanted when he moved to the States. And I could rest assured it wouldn't take long before some lucky girl in Vegas claimed him for her own.

Something twisted painfully in my chest at the thought, and I gripped his shoulders tighter as he carried me up the stairs and into his room.

"A cup of tea would be great, baby." I pressed my nose into the side of his neck. "Thank you."

Chapter 27

STARTLED AWAKE I SAT up in bed, trying to figure out what woke me.

The greying sky behind the large barred window indicated early morning—way too early for me to be up.

"Vadim?" I called softly, realising that he hadn't reacted to my jumping up in bed.

He never slept and seemed to be fully alert whenever I opened my eyes in the morning.

"Are you here?" I patted the bed next to me, finding his arm.

The extreme stiffness of his bicep sent a shot of alarm through my chest. It didn't feel natural.

"Baby?" I called softly, roaming my hands over his chest and shoulders, his whole body seemed to be tensed. "Are you okay?"

Not getting an answer from him, I jumped off the bed and flicked the lights on.

"What's happening?" I climbed back in bed and crawled to him.

A rumbling noise, similar to the one that must have woken me up, rocked through his chest and made it through his clenched teeth with a hiss.

"Vadim?" I shook him by the shoulders as horror seized my heart. "Wake up!"

Demons don't sleep.

Unless it was the static state they called Deep Sleep, but I'd heard it took days if not weeks of complete starvation for an Incubus to fall into Deep Sleep. Not like this, literally overnight.

"Baby, baby, baby . . ." I patted his arms and shoulders, cupped his face. Everything I touched was hard as rock. His features sharp, jaw clenched, eyes shut so tight, I could barely see the tips of his long, thick eyelashes.

A violent shudder ran through him, rocking his body, head to toe. Another groan ripped from his chest, strained and tortured.

This was like nothing I'd seen or heard of before. Vadim was clearly suffering, and I had no idea what to do to help him.

Afraid to let go of him or to leave him alone even for a moment, I yelled over my shoulder, "Zayne!"

Demons didn't die. But what if whatever brought him to this world was taking him away from me now, back to where he came from?

My concern shot into panic, crushing my heart.

"Vadim, baby, please wake up." I shook him harder. "Zayne! I need help!"

Where was everyone?

Had the same thing happened to all of them?

"Anyone! Please!"

Finally, the sound of heavy footsteps booming through the hallways reached me. I exhaled with relief—I was not alone.

"Jade?" Zayne emerged through the door. "Are you okay?"

"It's Vadim," I sobbed, pressing my demon's head to my chest. "Look at him."

Zayne rushed to the bed as another wave of shudders rolled through Vadim's body. As violent as a seizure, the convulsions were not sporadic—the rhythmic swells rolled through the whole length of his body, one after another.

"What's happening?" I whispered, as my voice broke, my face wet from tears I hadn't even noticed overflowing from my eyes.

Zayne splayed his large hand on Vadim's convulsing chest. The expression on his face turned grave, knowing.

"He is being summoned."

His words plummeted my insides into an icy void.

"Where? Why? By whom?"

"There is no way to tell." He shook his head.

"Is there a way to get him out of this?"

"He is fighting it." Zayne removed his hand, and I cradled Vadim in my arms, pressing him to me as hard as I could, despite the shockwaves of convulsions that violently rocked as both.

"What can we do, Zayne?" I begged.

"Nothing." He shook his head, my heart sunk with a heavy feeling of dread and helplessness. "We just have to wait for him to find a way through."

"Through what?"

"His demonic essence is being restrained by the spells of the ritual. If performed properly, there is no escape. However, the summoner is always just a human, and humans often make mistakes. If Vadim can fight long enough until an error is made, he can break the circle and escape."

"Break the circle?" I repeated mechanically, my mind buried under a thick haze of despair.

"It means he'll have to kill one of those who hold him captive."

Kill.

I remembered Vadim telling me about Zayne being summoned once, too. "That's what you did when it happened to you. You killed the one who summoned you."

"Yes." He heaved a sigh, his voice sounded leaden.

"There is no other way?" Vadim had been striving to move away from a violent past. I was afraid about the damage a murder, even one of an enemy, would do to him now.

"Unless the conjurer lets him go. But that's not why he called a demon in the first place."

"Why would anyone do this?" I slid my hand up and down Vadim's trembling arm.

"To gain access to the power of the demon unleashed from his physical form," Zayne explained, sombrely. "Once the conjurer gets the demon under his control, he can make him do anything he wants."

"Like a genie released from a lamp?" I whispered, frozen in fear.

"Except that it's not limited to only three wishes. The summoner can ask the demon as much as he wants, as long as he can hold him. A demon can never deny his master."

"What would someone want from Vadim?"

"Knowing humans, their wishes tend to revolve around money and control of others. Hopefully that's all it is this time, too."

"Hopefully?" I stared at him.

"If all the conjurer wants is a fat bank account, it'd be easy enough to accomplish. Then we can hope Vadim would be released after he has complied."

I realised Zayne made it sound simple for my benefit. Still, the hope of having Vadim back soon calmed me somewhat.

"I thought there wasn't anyone left who'd know how to perform the ritual."

"People die, but their knowledge is preserved in books. Someone must have gotten a hold of one and figured out how to use that knowledge." He glanced at Vadim's struggling body. "Someone who seems to know what he is doing, too. How long has it been?"

"Just a few minutes. At least that's when I woke up from his groan."

"All we can do is wait now."

"How long?" I asked, although I knew that Zayne had no answer to this question. No one did.

I rocked in bed, holding Vadim to me.

"He is a powerful demon," Zayne said, his voice turning soft and comforting. "Strong and smart. He'll fight for as long as it takes for the summoner to make a mistake, and I have no doubt he'll use the chance once the error is made."

"What can I do to help him?"

"Nothing. Just be here when he returns."

VALEFOR

Pain burned, slashed, and twisted his essence. Though he had no physical body to feel it, the agony seared through his soul, and there was no escape from it.

"*Deditionem . . .*" chanted the conjuror, every word of the litany a slash of a fiery dagger that felt like it would cut him to pieces. "*Vestre dominum . . .*"

His physical body never tired. The ethereal spirit was all he had control of at that moment, though, and it was worn out after hours and hours of resisting the spells that held him captive.

Desperate to escape the lashes of pain, he lurched up, only to be slashed by more chants, every word a razor-sharp arrow cutting through him, forcing him to stay put.

"*Daemonium . . .*" Demon.

But that wasn't all he was. Somewhere, he remembered, in another world, he was a man. *She* saw him as a man.

The distant memory of that place, near her, was what gave him the strength to keep fighting.

His place was *not* here.

With everything he had left, he forced himself to strike against the power holding him. Ignoring the pain, he launched towards freedom.

"Hold him." A firm command came from somewhere outside the circle he was confined to.

"Deditionem..." Sounded louder, with more force.

Surrender...

The impact of the words crushed him, depriving him of the strength to fight.

Beaten, weakened, and torn. Tossed around inside the prison of the circle and the pentagram.

Held in place by the chants the conjurer kept throwing at him in Latin.

All he had left was his will to go on, the burning desire for freedom, to be with her. And he clung to that desire like to a lifeline.

Chapter 28

IT WAS THE EARLY MORNING of day three of Vadim being essentially gone. His body was here—tense and obviously in pain, but visibly intact.

His spirit, or *demonic essence*, as Zayne had called it, was elsewhere. And without it, my man could never be whole. Split apart, frozen in time, and suspended in his existence, it must have been worse than being dead.

After hours of holding him to me, rocking in bed, begging any higher power that might be out there to release him from this torment, I finally gave in to Zayne's pleas to get up, get changed, and have some of the food they had made for me.

There was no way I would go far from Vadim, though. I left a message for Harry, letting him know I was not going to work that day, possibly not that week either. With less than two weeks before our office closed for good, the last days were supposed to be spent on closing any legal contracts still outstanding and liquidating whatever assets we had.

Despite having his assistants, I knew Harry could always use my help, but I couldn't bring myself to leave Vadim, even for a moment.

Sitting on the bed next to him, I held his hand. Watching his beautiful face contort with agony and his strong, powerful body bend and twist under the will of a stranger killed me. The helplessness I felt was crushing.

"Talk to him," Zayne had said earlier.

"Why? You told me he can't hear me. He is not here."

"Not for him, for you. Talk to him to distract from the thought of what he is going through. You're driving yourself insane."

I had scoffed at Zayne then. Who cared about my thoughts and what they did to me if Vadim was the one who was really suffering?

Now, I could no longer stand to sit idly by him, doing nothing.

The pain of him being this close yet worlds apart was unbearable. Suddenly, words seemed like the only connection I could build between us.

"Vadim." I lay in bed next to him, ignoring the waves of disturbing convulsions raging through his body, and focused on the familiar things instead—the warmth of his skin under my hands, the scent of him all around me, the feeling of comfort and safety I always had when being close to him. "I miss you, baby," I whispered, my throat all but closing with pain. "You see, the thing is, I need you with me. I no longer know how to be happy without you."

The full meaning of that rushed me. It was the truth.

Being forced to part with him for almost three days now showed me how miserable I'd be without him when I moved to another country.

I had thought I'd be ready to leave him in just under two weeks time, never to see him again. I had made myself believe it was for our mutual benefit to part.

My heart, however, refused to be without him.

Even if I tore myself away from him, moved a thousand kilometres, and forced my life to go on, without him, I knew I would never be truly happy again.

"I need you, baby. Right here, with me. Always."

Holding his face between my hands, I kissed his pale, firm lips, putting the full power of the longing I felt into this kiss and in my words.

"Come back to me, Vadim."

VALEFOR

Chant after chant, the words brought him lower to his knees. His power shrivelled under the pain, his spirit had shrunk. Any light inside him had been reduced to nothing.

"Vestre dominum . . ." Surrender to your master. Came the order, impossible to disobey, for he had nothing left to fight it with.

"Tell him who his master is. Now." Came the imperious voice from outside of the circle.

Through the immobilizing web of chants, he strained his awareness to focus on his surroundings. The reality outside of his prison seemed more like a dream compared to the sharp pain inside, still he tried to absorb the images that flashed through the red fog of his vision.

The pentagram drawn in blood on the stone floor—fresh human blood glowing red and drawing him in like a magnet with no means to escape.

A high dome above, with ceiling caved in in the middle. The sky outside mocking him with the promise of freedom.

The circle of robe-clad monks, all holding hands to keep him inside.

The conjurer, his new master, standing just outside the circle, wrapping long chants around him, chaining the demon to himself.

And one other, by the wall, giving the orders. The true master here. His voice and face so familiar.

He'd seen this man many times before, talked to him, shook hands with him. The man never used to wear the robe he was wearing now, only a suit, still Valefor recognized him.

This was his master. The one to dictate all his actions from now on, because he was his demon now.

'Come back to me, Vadim . . .' The feminine voice, filled with longing, flew in with the breeze through the gaping ceiling and reached

for him. Soft and delicate, it carried the power stronger than the conjurer could ever muster.

The pull of the call was unstoppable, drawing him in, up to the light, fresh air, and freedom.

Her claim carried the only order he could obey from now on. And he willingly surrendered to it, without a fight.

He could never be anyone's demon—he already belonged to her, his body *and* his spirit.

"You are no master to me!" The words shot through him and out into the room, reverberating against the worn, stone walls under the dome.

The chants lost their power, the fiery words scattered off him like embers, setting him free.

The ring of monks wavered, as he lunged at them again. This time he easily incinerated one of them, breaking the circle.

"I already have a Mistress!"

Chapter 29

VADIM'S BODY STIFFENED in my arms with another wave of ominous shudders then unexpectedly slumped to the mattress, as if life had left him all at once.

"Vadim!" I grabbed his shoulders, afraid to think what this sudden change could mean.

Did he lose?

Was he gone?

"Zayne!" I called again, forcing the panic down.

"What? Zayne?" Vadim's voice was harsh and rough—words slurred, as if he were talking with a mouth full of sand—still, it was *his* voice.

"Baby? Can you hear me?"

"Why Zayne?" He lifted his arms and rubbed his eyes with the heels of his hands. His movements jerky, still he was obviously in control of his body once again.

"Oh my God!" I climbed to my knees at his side. "Vadim?"

With a groan, he opened his eyes, and I recoiled in terror. The brilliant jade colour was gone. Black and grey swirled and churned through his irises, flooding the whites of his eyes, too.

"What's wrong with you?" I asked tentatively, unsure whether I had to stay away or throw myself at him and never let go.

He blinked, the horrifying swirls melting away, dissolving into the usual warm green.

"Are you really back?" I whispered carefully.

"I had no choice." He met my gaze. "You called me to you."

I had no idea what that really meant and, at that moment, I didn't really care. All that mattered was that the expression on his face was true and familiar, the blood returned to his cheeks, and there was awareness in his eyes, their colour a dazzling jade again making me choke up with relief.

He was here, and he was whole again.

"Oh, thank God!" I exhaled, lunging into his arms. "You really *are* back."

VADIM

Her body relaxed in his arms, and the turmoil of her inner emotions began to settle, the colours turning lighter and brighter. The familiar red glow flickered deep under the dark shards of worry and pain, as he glided his hands up her back.

The silk of her camisole slid smoothly under his palms, but it couldn't compare to the wonderful sensation of her skin. Eagerly, he slipped the thin straps off her shoulders, touching the expanse of her neck, back, chest.

The sound of hurried footsteps in the hallway brought Zayne through the door of the room. "Is he back?"

"Leave!" Vadim barked the order, sending Zayne back where he came from. The demon could wait.

The whole world could wait. Right now, all he needed was *her*.

"Vadim?" Jade asked softly, arms wrapped around him, her fingers in his hair as he buried his face in her neck. "How are you feeling, baby? Should you rest?"

This voice. Sweet, kind, calming. This was what saved him from the hell on Earth he had endured for days that felt like centuries.

She saved him.

"No rest," he rasped. "Just you."

He kissed her neck, with increasing urgency, as his hunger for her grew.

The phantom stabbing pain of chants still burned through him, and he needed her sweet essence to cleanse it from him.

He rose to his knees in bed, lifting her in his arms, as he claimed her lips with his mouth, hungry to feel her and taste her at once.

She gasped softly when he tossed her to the mattress, the red flared up inside her, teasing him, luring him in.

"Are you sure that's what you want?" her voice came out a little breathy this time. She rose on her elbows, her gaze sliding down his naked torso. He could almost feel it like a caress against his skin.

"Not just *want*." He tore at the ties of his linen drawers. "*Need*, Jade. I have to have you." He shoved the pants down his hips, freeing his painfully throbbing erection. "Please, let me take you. Now."

His voice sounded rough and low, foreign even to his own ear. His eyes must have been glowing the unsettling red, as he was skimming every single tendril of her emotions.

Relief, affection, budding lust, and the most wonderful of them all—love. The newest emotion in her, the one that he was fairly sure she hadn't acknowledged to herself yet.

He wanted it all.

"Now?" She sat up, letting the straps of the camisole slide further down. The edge of the neckline caught on her full breasts, and she tugged at the fabric, freeing her arms and exposing her chest to him. "Take me then." She smiled. "I'm all yours."

She was his. All of her. Even if she didn't fully realise it herself yet.

The all-consuming hunger for her churned inside him. His control slipped, and he lunged.

Instead of shrinking away from his attack, she leaned in, welcoming his hands and his mouth.

"I missed you," she moaned into his kisses, her hands roaming over his naked body. "You can't leave me again. No one can take you from me . . ."

Sucking on her breast, he yanked the hem of her camisole up, finding his way between her legs with his hand.

"No one can," he echoed, sliding a finger in her slick warmth.

With a sharp exhale, she lifted her hips up to meet his touch.

"I won't let them. You hear me?" The fierce determination in her voice wouldn't allow for any doubts even if he didn't see it already in her emotions. "I don't know who took you or how they did it, but I'll do anything to stop them from ever doing it again . . ." she panted as he pumped his finger in and out of her—hot, wet, *his*.

"I know you will." He rolled them over, just to feel the weight of her body on top of him. He needed that reminder of her physical presence here with him.

She had stopped the summons, broken the ritual, got him back. The power she had over him was all hers.

And this power he had no intention of fighting.

Her hips trembling, she pressed her legs tighter around his middle as he rose to catch the other swaying breast in his mouth.

The crimson light of desire swelled through her, flooding him. Hungrily, he lapped at it, like a starving dog, needing more the more he took.

She was his. All of her. And he wanted it all. Craved it. Starved for it.

The madness of this all-consuming need blinded any caution in him. Tightening his arms around her, he flipped her on her back again. Her legs spread wider, cradling his hips in invitation.

Willing, eager. And so trusting.

His head swam with the unrelenting need to take. It warred a merciless battle with his fear of hurting Jade, his most precious treasure, the only one he ever cared about more than himself, his hunger or anything else in this world and the next.

Stilling over her, he forced his eyes closed, shutting down the delicious picture of naked Jade under him. As long as he touched her, he could still 'see' her emotions, though. There was no way of escaping that.

In the maddening avalanche of feelings that crashed over him, he chose lust and diverted all his focus to it in a desperate attempt at controlling his insatiable appetite.

Shoving aside the visual of her tempting arousal, he took none. Ignoring his hunger, he tuned in all his other senses on her.

He *listened* to the sound of her accelerated breathing as she panted under him. Her frantic heartbeat racing under his hand when he cupped her breast.

He *felt* the slick, silky warmth inside her, as he entered her, slowly, savouring every inch.

He let the sounds and sensations of their bodies fused together guide him, making love to his woman like a mortal man would, using nothing but his human senses.

When her moans grew louder, he sped up.

When her body rose to meet his, he thrust harder.

And when she shifted her hips, he angled his until he hit the spot that turned her moans into screams of wild passion and she exploded into the shudders of orgasm.

"No one . . . will take you . . . away from me." She breathed heavily, drawing him to her as he let it all go, surrendering to his own climax.

"Never."

"Because I love you, Vadim."

Something hot shot through his system at her words, melting into achy warmth that spread through his veins like hot butter.

"I know." He kissed her hair, marvelling at the renewed flare of that wonderful feeling he'd first glimpsed in the eyes of Alyssa for Sytrius months ago.

This time it was all his, and his alone.

"I've been learning to love you, too, my treasure. Every minute of every day."

Chapter 30

SITTING IN THE MEETING room, Vadim leaned back in his chair—ankle crossed over knee, elbow on the armrest, hand under his chin. "Speak," he ordered Zayne.

"Andras has requested a meeting with the Priory, but was granted a phone conference instead." Zayne filled him in on everything that had happened during his three-day absence.

During the Incubi Council Meetings, I would normally be reading in the library or searching in the storage room for some old, pretty things to decorate Vadim's room. Today, however, Vadim insisted on my presence here.

"They are hiding something." He released a frustrated huff. "Hence the refusal to meet face-to-face—they don't want us to read their emotions."

"The Elder assured Andras that the Priory has severed all ties with Steffen Keller from the moment they learned from the Western Council about his kidnapping that Source in September."

"What happened?" I asked.

"Keller, a monk from the Priory of Grimien, attempted to kidnap a Source from the Western Base in September."

"Attempted?"

"They took her, but she ran away while they transported her along a road in northern Alberta."

"Smart." Vadim nodded approvingly.

"Or lucky, but probably both. She is fine now, paired up with . . ." Zayne shot a cautious glance my way before continuing, obviously deciding me worthy of his trust, "Eligor, an Incubus from the Western Base, I don't know the human name he goes by. Are you saying Keller was the one who summoned you?"

"No, I've never seen this conjurer before," Vadim replied. "Keller was the one giving him orders, however."

"Are you certain?" Zayne narrowed his eyes, leaning in. "Your vision and your awareness wouldn't be the best in that state."

"He was there, Zayne," Vadim insisted. "I recognized his voice and his face."

"If The Elder is lying and Keller organized the summons under their orders . . ."

"I have no idea why they would do this. They have been supporting us. If they weren't happy with something about the new agreement, the first step would be to approach me directly, through the usual channels." He shrugged his broad shoulders as if shaking off the lingering pain of the ritual. "There was no need to resort to that."

"A most brutal way of *negotiation*, I'd say," Zayne agreed. "I'm just glad you managed to get away."

"Did you have to murder?" I asked Vadim quietly. "To get free?"

He stared at me for a moment, an intense focus in his eyes. I wasn't worried about what he'd see inside me—I had no fear, no judgment left. If he had to kill to get away, it was on those who took him in the first place, not on him.

"Yes," he replied simply. "I killed a man to break the circle."

"Good." I took his hand in mine, and he squeezed it as if in gratitude for my acceptance.

"But it was you who set me free."

"Me?" I gazed at him in confusion.

"I chose you, and you claimed me." The intensity of his stare on me conveyed the gravity of the moment. Still I didn't quite understand.

Vadim turned to Zayne. "I believe we have a way to be absolutely free now. The woman a demon chooses for his Mistress apparently can take the power away from the summoning ritual."

"The conjurer didn't make a mistake?" Zayne asked with a confused frown, too.

Vadim shook his head. "The ritual was performed flawlessly. I searched for a breach, but there was no way out. Until Jade called me to her—her call deprived the chants of their power."

"Is that what happened?" I gaped at him in shock. Was that all it took? "Oh God! I should have done it sooner."

"It couldn't be rushed." He stroked my hand soothingly. "You did it when you felt it. Thank you for freeing me."

"The power of a demon's Mistress supersedes that of the conjurer's?" Zayne said slowly, as if testing the new concept in his mind.

"More than that. It completely deprives another human of having any power over the Incubus who has a Mistress. She is his one true master, no one else."

"This is . . ." Zayne rubbed the short, dark stubble on his chin. "This is huge, Vadim. Enormous!" His gaze shot to his Grand Master again. "You have to let the others know right away."

"I will."

"Do you realise what that means?" Zayne focused on me for a moment. "If the woman we choose can stop anyone from summoning us, we no longer have to live under the threat of it happening. As slim as the possibility of anyone figuring out how to conduct the ritual properly is, it has always been there." The grave note in his voice when he mentioned the ritual reminded me that Zayne experienced first-hand the pain of the summoning chants.

His relief at discovering a way the ritual could be stopped was almost palpable, the gratitude on his face when he stared at me unmistakable.

"Thank you for discovering this, Jade."

"Um . . . you're welcome." I blinked, thinking he was somewhat overdoing it with the gratitude. Although I felt like I would physically fight for Vadim's life and freedom, all I did was call him to me.

"Raim's parting statement worries me, though." Vadim rubbed his face.

"Andras is concerned, too," Zayne agreed. "He has assembled all Incubi in Vegas and cancelled Demon Army's European tour until we have figured out exactly what the threat is. He feels that when we're all together, we'd be easier to organize and could act quickly if required."

"He may be right," Vadim replied slowly, as if lost in thought.

"Do you think Raim may be in the conspiracy with the Priory against his own kind?" I asked softly, wondering where exactly his concerns lay.

Zayne glanced my way, then turned to face Vadim again.

"You've been in the meetings with both Raim and The Elder of the Priory," he said. "You know them both better than any one of us here. What do you think?"

Vadim took a moment to respond, pressing his mouth into a firm line before saying, "I wouldn't put it past Raim to have private meetings with the Priory through the years. He was the one who ended up signing the treaty and has been enforcing it ever since. Every Elder seemed to know him well, although that could be explained with Raim being a Grand Master for so long. Still, I don't see what he could be gaining from it. What would be the purpose of the conspiracy for him?"

"Getting everyone back where you all used to be, back to the Bases, with himself in charge again?" I ventured a guess.

"He *was* in charge." Zayne rubbed his forehead. "No one forced him to resign. Also, why would he bother with the warning at all if he was planning something against us?"

"Out of spite? Being the big meany that he is." I shrugged.

"I recall Raim having an early preference for aggressive human emotions when feeding," Vadim replied, thoughtfully. "I've seen him in battles. He's always been ruthless to the enemy. However, I haven't witnessed any deliberate cruelty or deceit on his part. He'd kill in cold blood if necessary, but not for the *sake* of killing. Raim is not completely without compassion, either. I saw him drain a Source once. He took the pain that drove her to madness and let her die in peace—bliss even."

Personally, I wasn't sure if I would classify that as *compassion*. Ultimately, Raim still ended up killing the poor woman.

"In any case, I'll have to speak with everyone who is still left here at the Base." Vadim's gaze stopped on me. "I want you near me, at all times." Despite his usual commanding tone, I could sense the hidden plea for me to work with him in his voice.

"I'm not sure . . ." I started.

"Zayne," Vadim ordered, without taking his eyes off me. "Get in touch with everyone who is off Base, tell them to come back here ASAP. I'm with Andras on this one—if anything happens to any Incubus, I want the rest of us to know immediately."

"Yes, Grand Master." With a brief incline of his head, Zayne got out of his chair and left the room.

"SPEAK," VADIM ORDERED to me this time, as soon as Zayne was gone. His voice remained firm, but the anxious flickering of his eyes between mine betrayed him.

My Grand Master was obviously nervous and hiding it behind the true, tried, and familiar—command.

I drew in a lungful of air, bracing myself. "I need to show my face at work, have a proper conversation with Harry, my boss. Tanya was supposed to come by my apartment this afternoon. Sure I can call her and ask her not to come . . ." I lifted my hand between us to stop his obvious attempt to interrupt me, "but that's not the point, Vadim. I have a life outside of the Base, and it's not that easy to drop every-thing." I patted his hand on the chair's armrest. "Not even for you."

"That's not the real problem, though," he dismissed, staring at me expectantly, as if awaiting the *real* explanation. "It's not just about to-day. Your worry is bigger than that. What is it?"

"Fine." I exhaled sharply. "I'm scared. The events of the past three days aside, I'm still worried for you. For us. I know myself too well. The feelings I have for you are new and wonderful. No one has ever made me feel this way, not even close. Ever. But nothing lasts with me." I'd never hidden the truth from him, but maybe he needed a reminder. "All my relationships have failed. Some never even lasted long enough to be called a relationship, to be honest . . ." I sighed heavily, hating every word coming out of my mouth, hating myself as well. "It seems to be in my nature, Vadim. Sooner or later, I know that even this wonderful feeling would fade, leaving nothing but dis-appointment behind. Gone. Just like all the other short thrills in my life."

"Except for surfing," he stated evenly.

"What?" I blinked, trying to figure out what that had to do with anything.

"You said you love surfing and never get tired of it. Why?"

"I—I don't know." Confused, I gave him a smile. "I just do. It's different."

"You said what we have is different, too. The love you have for me is unique—you've never felt that for anyone else. How can you be so sure it will be gone then?"

"I don't want it gone." I shook my head, tears prickling behind my eyelids. "But I'm afraid it will . . . And I don't want to hurt you."

"Don't let the fear kill what hasn't had a chance to flourish yet, Jade. Let it take root."

"If I let it, it will take over my entire being," I replied with conviction. "Then when it's gone, the emptiness will destroy me."

"What if it doesn't go anywhere? Have you ever thought about such a possibility? Because I truly believe in that."

His mouth curved in a light smile, and warm sparkles played in the green of his eyes. He didn't seem to be nearly as concerned as I was, and I wished I could lean on his trust in us.

"Was that why you never asked me to stay?"

"I never asked because you're not the type of woman who could be forced to do anything against her will. Instead, I've waited until you realised you wanted to be with me."

"What if I didn't? Would you have really let me leave for Moscow?"

"If that was what you wanted to do." He nodded. "I hoped you wouldn't go, but if you left, I knew it couldn't be the end for us. Sooner or later, I knew I'd be with you."

"How? Would you have gone to Moscow with me?"

"To Moscow, to the end of this world, and to any other one beyond this one."

Something had been lightening inside me at his words, despite the tears swelling in my eyes.

"Look, Jade." He took my hand in his. "If ever I have to be away from you, it would always be only temporary. I knew it from that night in your apartment when I told you the darkest moments of my past and you accepted me despite it all. You simply needed some time to realise that, and I gave it to you."

I inhaled a shuddering breath, squeezing his hand tight, as hope curled warm around my heart. "Do you really think this could last?" I didn't believe I could ever survive the disappointment of losing him now.

He got up from his chair, tugging at my hand for me to follow.

"I have full intentions of making it last, for as long as we both shall live." He placed his hands on my shoulders. "Do you?"

"Well, I can see myself surfing until the day I die." I smiled through the shimmering haze of my tears. "So I think I could definitely envision loving you for as long as we both shall live."

He drew me in for a kiss.

Slow, deep, and tender, it made my head spin. With every glide of his lips and with every brush of his tongue against mine, I sensed the tension between us dissipate and drain from his body and mine.

"Always," he whispered his vow against my mouth, and I swallowed it with a kiss of my own.

Chapter 31

WE RAN INTO ZAYNE IN the hallway, just outside of the meeting room. Andrei followed close behind him. Ilya and the few others still left at the Base were approaching, too.

"These are all the Incubi we have here," Zayne reported to Vadim. "I've sent the summons to the few who went to the city, most should be here within the next hour or less."

"I'll call Andras right now and put him on speaker." Vadim turned to go back in the meeting room. "I want everyone to hear about Keller and the ritual. About what Jade did, too."

"Um . . ." I lingered in the hallway, not following him in.

Knowing that I could call him back anytime someone tried to take him away again, brought a definite relief, like being in possession of a strong antidote to a poison. Yet I still worried about leaving him, even for a short period of time.

"What are the chances of you being summoned again?" I asked quietly.

"Well, they know they won't get anything from me now. I don't think they'll bother again. But I'm worried about the other Incubi. If summoned while outside, they would drop down on the street in convulsions. I want them all here, where they are safe."

"Good. Could I borrow a car for a few hours then? I need to get some things done in the city."

"Today?" Vadim stared at me as if I had just told him I was an alien from another planet.

The past three days had passed in a blur of fear and worry. I had a number of missed calls and texts from work. Tanya was supposed to be at my place soon to help me pack. The lease on my apartment had expired, too. I'd let everyone know I was alive to make sure no one would file a missing person's report or do something else just as drastic, but things had been piling up, requiring my attention.

"You're not going anywhere." Vadim used his most authoritative tone of voice, and I dug in my heels.

"Listen, I was still supposed to be at work this week, helping Harry close up the office. Instead, he's been doing all of it on his own, most of the staff have already been let go . . ."

"I don't care," he replied, unyielding. "Call him."

Bossy *and* stubborn.

"Well, I do care. Harry has been a great boss. At the very least he deserves a personal goodbye from me."

The stern expression on his face didn't ease.

"I'll also need to pick up my things from the apartment," I continued, "and hand in the key to the landlord, and generally, you know, show my face to everyone, to prove I'm alive and to give some kind of an explanation for my sudden change of plans. As far as my work goes, everyone still thinks I'm leaving for Moscow within weeks. I'll need to sign some paperwork, cancel the transfer request." Which would also mean quitting my job.

I didn't say the last part out loud. We hadn't discussed this in detail yet. I understood that in order to stay with Vadim I would have to quit working, at least for now. I'd been ready to leave the country and part with my co-workers, but there was no time to prepare myself for saying goodbye to the job I actually liked.

"Does this have to be done today?" His mouth set in a firm line, Vadim definitely looked displeased, and I knew he was worried. Something in the curve of his bottom lip, though, brought to mind a petulant child.

I sighed, calling on my patience.

"Would you let me go tomorrow?"

His jaw flexed, and he kept silent for a moment, betraying something I already knew. It wasn't the timing for him. Vadim simply didn't want to part with me. Ever. Part of me liked that, way too much, despite the frustration at his resistance.

"Vadim, I am going to be with you, but I had a life before I met you, and I can't drop everything just like that."

"The sooner you go, the sooner you'd come back," he spoke as if talking to himself.

"Can I have the car then?"

"No." He turned to Zayne, who lingered in the background, letting us sort things out. "Take Jade to the city."

"Me?" The Incubus raised his eyebrows in surprise.

"I trust you the most," Vadim replied, still with a displeased frown on his face.

Zayne inclined his head. "I'm flattered."

"Don't take your eyes off her. If so much as a hair falls off her head, I'll kill you then wait until you come back to and kill you again. Do you understand?"

"Yes, Grand Master."

"WELL, TAKE CARE OF yourself, Jade." Harry shook my hand then pulled me into a bear hug. "Keep in touch, will you?"

He leaned back, his eyes flicked to Zayne standing silently by the office door with his arms crossed over his chest.

"I will," I promised, taking the folder with my paperwork off the desk.

Following Harry's advice, instead of quitting completely, I had applied for a leave of absence for six months.

Many things still needed to be sorted out in the Incubi world as well as in my new life, with some possibly taking longer than others. I knew I would choose Vadim over anyone or anything. Still, not burning all my bridges right now felt comforting.

As Zayne and I left Harry's office and took the lift down to the lobby, I hoped there would still be a chance for me to come back to the job I liked and was sure I'd miss.

Not finding any free parking around my building, we ended up leaving the car at the next apartment complex then walked back to mine.

"There you are!" Tanya's thin, wiry figure jumped from the steps to my entrance to greet us.

"Sorry, are we late?" I patted my jacket pocket for my phone to check the time.

"Nope, I'm early." Her voice remained cheerful, even as she glanced Zayne's way suspiciously.

"Tanya, this is Zayne, he . . . um, he'll help us pack."

"Is he your boyfriend?" She lowered her voice, avoiding another look at him. "The one you've been seeing on the weekends?"

"No. It's his friend. Zayne, this is Tanya—" I stopped, faced with Zayne's intense stare fixed on Tanya. "Have you two met?"

He just blinked and swallowed hard, without replying.

"No, we haven't," Tanya answered, instead, then added under her breath, "I would've remembered meeting someone like him. That's for sure."

It hit me that being a Council Member, Zayne must have seen Tanya in the meeting room during her weekly visits. Something about that must have impressed him enough to render him practically speechless when meeting her face to face now.

"Well." I cleared my throat. "Shall we go in then? It's rather cold and windy out here."

IT DIDN'T TAKE US LONG to pack. All my belongings fitted into a couple of suitcases and a few boxes. I was used to traveling light and always made sure that all my earthly possessions fitted in one car at all times because, sooner or later, I knew I would have to move again.

"There are just my mugs left," I said, rearranging some of the folded clothes inside one of the suitcases, in order to zip it up.

"I'll get those," volunteered Tanya. "There is still some space left in this box." She made a move to lift the box, but Zayne beat her to it.

"I've got it," he mumbled, heading for the kitchen with it.

This was the first thing he'd said during the whole time we had spent in my apartment. He also proved to be rather useless in packing, mostly getting in my way.

"What do you know, he *can* talk." Tanya's voice was quiet but filled with sarcasm.

"Could you help him, please?" I asked, shoving my knee onto the lid of the suitcase to force it to close. "It's my collection of souvenir mugs on the shelf over the sink."

"He didn't ask for my help." Tanya sulked. "I don't think he needs it."

Something was definitely going on between these two, but I had no time for sorting out their differences at the moment.

"Sure he does." I waved her to follow Zayne. "It's definitely a two-person job."

Mumbling something about stuck-up, snobby men, Tanya shuffled into the kitchen.

"I'M ALL DONE," I CALLED to Zayne and Tanya about twenty minutes later. "Just need to take the garbage out and we can go."

"I'll come with you." Zayne emerged from the kitchen, with Tanya on his heels. He heaved two packed boxes from the floor, one under each arm. "I may as well take these to the car, too."

"Okay." I gestured him to follow me out of the apartment.

"Vadim texted me, he is on his way to pick you up," Zayne casually informed me in the lift.

"What? Why? We have the car right here."

"I don't know." He shrugged, seemingly unconcerned. "He said the meeting was over, so he decided to come here to fetch you himself."

"*Fetch me.*" I couldn't hold back an eye roll. "We'd be back in an hour."

"Well, this way he'll get to see you in fifteen minutes instead." Zayne grinned, obviously teasing me. "He must be missing you."

"Right. A serious case of separation anxiety. That's what it looks like."

Instead of going to the car right away, Zayne insisted on following me all the way to the garbage bins first. Remembering the orders he received from Vadim, I didn't argue, although it felt weird having Zayne shadow me like a bodyguard.

The sun was setting, streetlights flickered to life, illuminating the courtyard surrounded by the five apartment buildings of my complex.

It definitely took Vadim less than fifteen minutes, since on our way back from the garbage bins, I spotted the black car pulling over at the entrance to my stairwell.

"I bet he was speeding to get here this fast." Zayne shook his head as we approached the vehicle. "I'll put these in his car instead of walking all the way to ours." Shifting the boxes in his arms, he headed for the trunk.

The back door opened and I leaned in, expecting to be greeted by the familiar outline of Vadim in the dark interior. My heart sped up with the anticipation of seeing him again.

Obviously, whatever case of separation anxiety he might be suffering from was severely contagious—I already missed him, too.

"Get in!" The order came in Russian as someone grabbed me roughly and yanked me in before I managed to exhale a sound.

With a loud screech of spinning tires, the car took off, the door slamming closed on the way.

Kicking everywhere, I struggled against the hands holding me down.

"Let me go!" I yelled, as rising panic jumpstarted my ability to speak.

"*Blya!*" Someone cursed in a strangled voice. "The bitch just kicked me in the nuts."

This was followed by a sharp punch in my ribs that knocked the air out of my lungs for a few seconds, forcing me curl in on myself.

"Here," came from the front seat. "Give her the shot."

A hand roughly shoved my head down and a sting of a needle burned the side of my neck.

"What do you want with me?" The end of my question came out muffled to my own ears. The twilight thickened around me.

Then the night came.

Chapter 32

I WAS LYING ON A HARD surface, which was moving. My head hurt, my wrists did, too. And my shoulders felt like the joints had been wrenched out of their sockets.

The floor under me lurched again, jolting my body with a renewed wave of pain everywhere.

A loud moan reached me, then the realisation that it was *me* moaning filtered through to my brain—like thunder following the lightning.

"She's awake," a male voice announced too loudly for my aching head, making me wince. "Should we put her under again?"

"No." This was another one. "We didn't get that much of this stuff from the German guy."

"German? I thought he was from Switzerland—"

"Whatever. Same shit. Don't waste it on her. I'll find a better use for it. This is some good stuff, man." The voice filled with appreciation. "The Germans really know how to do things, I tell ya. One shot knocked her right out for hours."

I understood the meaning of their conversation. However, it took me a few moments of painful concentration to determine they spoke Russian.

The awareness of my surroundings slowly trickled in. We were no longer in the car. The plush seats had gone. I lay on a cold metal floor of what must be another moving vehicle, as the shaking and lurching of it hadn't stopped, making my insides churn.

With a groan, I made an attempt to rise, afraid I'd throw up.

"She's gonna barf," someone stated calmly.

"Hey, give her the bucket, Shorty!" This one came from the driver's seat and sounded much more panicky. "I'm not driving for a whole hour with her fucking stench in the van."

I opened my eyes just in time to see the one who must have been referred to as Shorty scurry with the bucket to me.

He grabbed my hair, yanking my head up, and I scrambled to get my knees under me to heave myself off the floor.

My stomach emptied itself into the white plastic bucket that he'd shoved under my face.

"Fucking gross," he squeezed through his teeth in disgust. "What do I do with this shit, boss?"

"Toss it, you idiot. Do I have to spell everything out for you?"

Shorty kicked the back door open and hurled the bucket full of vomit onto the dirt road outside.

It was dark out there. Since they talked about hours, not days, I figured it must still be the same night. I spotted no headlights on the road behind us. If Zayne or Vadim had followed us, my kidnappers must have managed to evade them.

I was on my own.

The van shook on the uneven ground. Fear tightened my stomach. I had no clue where they could be taking me and opened my mouth to ask, but the words refused to form into sentences yet.

"Water," I croaked instead. The inside of my mouth felt dry and disgusting after vomiting.

"Boss, she's asking for water," Shorty forwarded my request, taking his seat on the bench along the wall opposite from me.

Left a few feet away from him, by the back door of the van, I briefly considered shoving it open and jumping out. We couldn't have been moving that fast, considering the condition of the road.

Shorty had locked the doors, though, after tossing the bucket out. With my hands tied behind my back, I wouldn't be able to unlock them.

As my head cleared a little, jumping out of a moving vehicle on a deserted road in the middle of nowhere no longer seemed like a good idea after all. Even if I managed not to break any bones in the process, the fact that the goons would simply stop the van to pick me up again made me abandon this plan for now.

"Thirsty, is she?" the Boss asked mockingly, tossing a plastic bottle of water my way. "Here you go."

The bottle hit my shoulder and rolled under the bench. With my hands tied behind my back, I was unable to catch it, not to mention open the lid.

The two of them found it hilarious, guffawing loudly at my helplessness. Shorty bent over, laughing so hard, he nearly fell off the bench.

I caught the eye of the Boss. Glaring at him, I gathered whatever saliva I could and spat his way, getting rid of at least some of the foulness in my mouth.

The gesture, combined with the resentment I was sure was imprinted on my face, infuriated him.

"*Suka!—You bitch*," he hissed, launching himself from his seat towards me.

A hand in my hair, he yanked my face to his.

"I may *have to* deliver you alive," he gritted through his teeth, assaulting my senses with the stench of stale tobacco. "But no one said you have to be well and sound on arrival."

His eyes shone wild and unhinged as he squeezed my throat with his other hand— hard—his whole body shaking with strain.

Choking and struggling for oxygen, I realised he was lying.

It took him visible effort to contain the obvious rage coursing through him right now. His own willpower would hardly be strong enough to hold him back, I suspected. The type of person that he'd been proving himself to be wouldn't hesitate to beat the living hell out of me were it not for the orders of someone with more power forbidding him from harming me.

"No one can stop me from fucking your ass right now, so you better behave." Every word dripped with irrational hatred.

Defiance burned through me, urging me to do something stupid, like spitting straight into his rage-distorted face. I forced my gaze away from his, lest he spot the hatred I felt for him, too.

Unstable as he was, I had no desire to test how well he'd follow orders. If they indeed had been to deliver me in one piece, I preferred he stuck with that.

Probably taking my avoiding eye contact with him as submission, he gave me another shake and jeered with satisfaction, "There you go, *suka*, know who is the boss here."

He tossed me to the wall of the van and returned to his seat in the front.

For a while I kept quiet. When I could trust my tongue to obey my brain in forming the words, however, I turned to Shorty, who was sneering at me all this time from his seat on the bench.

"Where are you taking me?" I asked quietly, not wanting to attract any more attention from the Boss.

"Fuck if I know," Shorty replied cheerfully, displaying chipped, yellowed teeth in a smirk. "I'm gonna get paid in an hour. After that, you can go to hell for all I care."

"Great."

Curling up in the back corner of the van, I huddled inside my coat from the cold and the fear and tried to ignore Shorty's mocking stare crawling all over me as we kept bouncing along the dirt road on the way to the unknown.

Chapter 33

DESPITE THE COLD, THE uncomfortable floor, and the stress of the situation, I must have actually dozed off for a little while. It might have been due to the residual drug in my system or the fact that it was deep into night already.

The sound of the front doors opening and closing jolted me awake. I opened my eyes, realising that the van had stopped.

In a moment, the back doors screeched open, too.

"Time to get you to your rightful owner, bitch." Boss held on to one of the doors.

Suddenly paralysed with fear, I pressed my back to the wall of the van. As much as I'd detested this vehicle and the men inside it, right now they seemed the lesser of two evils—with them at least I knew what I was up against.

"Come." Shorty gave me a kick in the ribs. "What? Do you need a special invitation?"

Boss took hold of my arm and unceremoniously dragged me out of the van.

I staggered unsteadily on the frozen ground, my feet immediately freezing cold in the tennis shoes I had on, making me wish I had put my boots on to take the garbage out with Zayne.

Zayne.

Where was he now? Had he and Vadim been looking for me? Would they be able to track me down?

A brutal yank on my arm nearly knocked me off my feet, cutting off my thoughts of the demons. Paying no attention to whether or not I was in any condition to keep up, Boss roughly dragged me around the van and towards a string of lights in the distance.

I saw, as we got closer, that the lights marked an airstrip with a private jet parked on it, its doors open, with the air stairs lowered to the ground.

A group of men approached through the dark. The one in the middle stepped forward, giving me an assessing once-over.

"What do you know," he said in a slightly accented English. "These thugs actually got the job done."

I took him in, trying to figure out if I'd ever met him before. Middle-aged. Well-groomed, with neatly styled receding blond hair. Dressed in a long wool coat, he seemed harmless in his middle-class appearance—if it weren't for the cynical, cold expression in his pale eyes.

"This is kidnapping," I attempted to talk some sense into him. "There will be consequences—"

"I hope there will be," he interrupted me, gesturing to one of the several men accompanying him, all dressed in identical long, brown robes.

One of them moved forward, grabbing me under my arm.

"I'm an Australian citizen." I made another attempt to resist.

"I know exactly who you are," the one in the wool coat replied calmly.

"Hey." Boss shifted from foot to foot nervously, not letting go of my other arm. "I need my money first," he said in Russian, and one of the brown-robed men translated his request to the man in the wool coat.

He nodded curtly, without sparing a glance for Boss, then headed back to the aeroplane.

One of the robed men shoved a duffel bag in Boss's hands before helping the other one wrench me away from him. The two then dragged me along, hurrying after the one in the wool coat, who must be their superior in some way.

"Well . . . um," the uncertain voice of Boss quickly faded in the background behind us. "It was nice doing business with you . . ."

The pair of monks—for that was what they all looked like to me, dressed in the robes tied with a piece of rope around their waists—basically carried me up the few stairs then dragged me inside the plane.

One of them then shoved me into a plush leather seat, with definitely more force than was necessary.

"Demon whore," I heard him hiss under his breath as he turned to leave.

"What did you just call me?" Shocked, I jerked my head to watch him stomp to the end of the cabin. The sound of his footsteps added to the noises of the aeroplane being prepared for departure.

"Delighted to have you here," a voice prompted me to spin around. The man in the wool coat took the seat across from me, a small table between us.

This time, I was able to place his accent as German, or maybe Swiss, if Shorty was right about him.

"Can't say the same," I snapped.

"That does not surprise me." He appeared unfazed by my anger, taking his coat off and making himself comfortable in the wide beige seat.

The engines came to life, shortly bringing the plane into motion. Thrown back against the seat, I winced at the pain from my bound hands digging into my spine from the acceleration at the take-off.

"Coffee or tea?" my companion asked as soon as the plane seemed to have levelled off.

"What?"

"You must be hungry. I'm inviting you to eat." It would have been polite had it not been said in a steely voice, the tone hostile.

Tempted to decline, I felt too thirsty to refuse a drink, any drink.

"Tea." I bit the word *please* back. "And some water."

He gestured to someone behind my shoulder.

"Where are you taking me?" I asked gruffly.

"*Where* is not the most important question here." He took a wet towel that one of his men had placed on the table between us. There was one for me, too, but with my hands still tied behind me, I couldn't use it.

My companion paused, as if only just noticing my predicament.

"Brother Lukian," he called to the back of the aeroplane.

A young man approached us, silently.

"Handcuffs." The man in front of me tipped his chin my way.

Brother Lukian produced a knife from the folds of his robe and cut the plastic ties off my wrists.

I exhaled with relief, and rubbed the soreness out of my arms. The freedom was short lived, though, as the monk took a pair of metal handcuffs next, and quickly locked my wrists in front of me.

"I believe you'll find them more familiar than the plastic ties," the man in the seat mocked me. "Although, I have to apologize, these might be rougher than what you're used to—they aren't padded with silk after all."

"And that makes all the difference." I couldn't hold back.

He levelled a heavy stare at me.

Glaring back at him, I took the towel and wiped the sweat and grime off my face and hands.

"Why am I here?"

"A much better question." He nodded, with approval.

"I really don't care for whatever game you're trying to play here," I snapped. "I want some answers. Who are you?"

He ignored my burgeoning rage, staring at me calmly.

Brother Lukian brought a tray with tea, a bottle of water and some finger food, setting it on the table, then picked up the used towels and left again.

Immediately, I grabbed the bottle, twisted the cap off and half-emptied it in a few thirsty gulps.

"My name is Steffen Keller." The man lifted one of the teacups. "Have you heard of me?"

It took just a moment for me to remember where I knew this name from, and when I did, the shock was too great to hide—Keller's expression melted into contentment as he watched my face.

"I see you have."

"You were the one behind the summons of Vadim."

"*Valefor*," he corrected, annoyance clearly audible in his voice. "Don't kid yourself, using human names doesn't make them human. He's been hiding behind *Vadim* for just over a year, but he's been *Valefor* for close to a millennium."

"The name doesn't really matter—" *to me*, I meant to say, but he cut me off.

"Oh, but it does make all the difference. Especially, when you know how to use it."

"What do you want with him?"

Keller leaned back, the teacup in his hand.

"Your questions are getting better and better." He smiled, but it never reached his cold, pale eyes. "I simply want things to go back to the way they were. Everything has been out of control lately, as I'm sure you know, and I need the Incubi Grand Master to bring his *fucking* demons back to order." His head jerked compulsively, any shadow of a smile gone.

"Why would you want to go back?" I asked in disbelief. "The changes have only been for the better—"

"That's what you think." His mouth curved in disdain. "But your judgment has obviously been impacted by lust."

"What is that supposed to mean?" I set my cup on the table. The undisguised contempt in his voice, combined with the earlier insult by one of his men, only set me more on edge.

"No need to feign being offended here. You, as well as a handful of other women of questionable morals, have decided to play with the demons, to risk your lives by jumping into bed with them. Unfortunately, your behaviour has bigger consequences. And I'm not just talking about filthy half-breed offspring." His features creased into a grimace of utter disgust.

"I don't see how letting Incubi and their families live in peace could result in any harm to you or others," I challenged.

"Oh, you will see soon enough, I'm sure. There are plenty of historical accounts on Incubi behaviour among people from the times when they were allowed to roam free. Before the Priory found a way to contain them, the Incubi lurked around towns and villages and entered the homes of innocents to force them into having lewd dreams so they could prey on them. When attacked, the demons killed in cold blood. Murders were rampant. Is that what you want to return to? Because once they are allowed anywhere near people, they cannot be trusted to keep their hunger in check. And I'm sure you're aware of their strength. No man is a match for a demon in hand-to-hand combat."

"That's not how it is, though," I protested. "They *can* learn to control their hunger. And once they find a partner, they're loyal to them. A married Incubus is not a danger to society in any way whatsoever."

"How can you be so sure?" He set his teacup on the table with a little more force than was necessary. "There is no data that backs up your belief. Even as a Forgiven, an Incubus is expected to live for centuries. How can anyone guarantee that the relationship would last that long? Marriages fall apart. Couples grow tired of each other. People want more, no matter how much they are given. Who is to know what demons would want a hundred years from now, two hundred, three?"

"You can't keep punishing them out of fear of some *what-if*." My blood heated with anger that had even shoved the fear aside. "The old ways were no longer working—"

"They can work again!" Keller exclaimed with force. "All Incubi will return to the Bases. The old and tried rules of the treaty will be reinstated. And peace will reign over all of us once again." He spread his hands in an all-encompassing gesture, as if delivering a blessing to the world.

"Except for those select few who'd be fed to the Incubi annually," I pointed out, flabbergasted he really seemed to believe in benefits of the old order.

"Some new rules will be required this time," he conceded. "We'll need to ensure Handlers and Sources are kept separate from each other, to prevent this mess from ever happening again."

"The women will die in isolation."

"What are the lives of the few for the good of many?" He tilted his head to the side, a serene expression on his face as he mentally sacrificed lives of others in his plans for the future.

"What's in it for you?" I squinted my eyes at him, as if I could read his true motives if I looked closely. "What are you really hoping to gain?"

"Is there a better reward for someone who has dedicated his life to the servitude of others?"

His saintly expression didn't fool me. I shook my head, making no effort to hide the revulsion in my voice. "There must be more in it for you."

He shifted uneasily in his seat but didn't reply.

"Did the Incubi Councils pay for the Sources?" I noted his facial muscles twitch at my question.

"The scale of operations that the Priory has been running to ensure the smooth acquisition of the Sources is enormous. You can't fathom the amount of work and planning it involves, as well as the resources it requires."

"So, Incubi paid, but not anymore. Right? Now that no *acquisitions* are taking place, I bet the Priory's income is dwindling. How about your own personal finances?" I dug deeper. "Was the request for more money on your list of demands for Vadim?"

His mouth curved in a crooked smirk, Keller seemed to have abandoned any attempt to give his actions some moral ground. Elbows on the table, he steepled his fingers in front of him.

"I am accustomed to a certain lifestyle, missy. One I'm not willing to give up just because a bunch of whores chose to fornicate with demons." A flash of contempt distorted his features for a moment. "We needed that source of income. The Elder fails to see that without the Incubi and their money, the Priory will simply cease to exist."

"Is that why you kidnapped that woman in Canada, in September? To re-sell her back to the Council eventually?"

"Kitty Jones was sourced and cleared just over a month prior." He stabbed his finger through the air at me, as if to better drive his point in. "She was already dead to the world. You have no idea how much work it involves not only to declare a person legally dead, but to make everyone truly believe that, too. And all for what? To set her free just five weeks later?" He shook his head, his face flushed with anger. "Likely, she had formed no ties with any of the demons at the Base where she was held. I happened to get there conveniently early, before anyone else. Unfortunately, my work can only be as good as the people I hire. The idiots I had with me in Canada let her go."

I leaned against the back of my seat to distance myself from him as much as possible.

"So, you're ready to start with kidnappings and murders again. For a buck."

"Oh, I assure you, there is much more at stake than that. The wealth amassed by the Incubi is enormous. Most of them aren't even aware of the true value of their riches. All of which ultimately came from humans, anyway, in one way or another. And to humans it shall return."

By selling other humans.

Anger vibrated in me at the thought. However, I reined it in the best I could, realising there was no point in arguing with him on this. Keller was too deep into his way of thinking—his actions proved it.

"How do I fit into all of this?" I asked, instead.

"I need you to ensure Valefor's co-operation," he said slowly. "The demon apparently obeys only you. So now *you* will obey *my* every word."

I flexed my jaw, my resolve hardening. "No. I won't."

"But you will. I will *make* you." Keller's eyes narrowed into slits, cutting me from the inside with his piercing gaze. "I've had enough setbacks lately. In addition to that Kitty Jones fiasco, I've just lost a supplier in Toronto, Canada. His operation went up in flames, literally. There was nothing left to determine the cause of the fire. I cannot afford any more mistakes. You spoiled our attempts at getting Valefor to submit to me. You *will* make sure he does it this time."

"No." I shook my head vehemently. "I know that the Priory hasn't sanctioned this. You have absolutely no right—"

"The Priory is weak," he snapped. "The Elder's strategy is too slow, and he refuses to listen to me when I say that more drastic measures have to be taken. Believe it or not, my idea for the future is actually more *humane* than his."

"What are you talking about?" A tendril of suspicion licked my insides.

"The official plan of the Priory is to exterminate every single one of your precious Incubi as soon as the very last one of them becomes mortal."

"What?" The cup dropped from my weakened fingers, as terror rushed over me like an avalanche at his sudden revelation.

"Whores like yourself gave the Priory a way to finally kill the demons—something our members have been searching for, for centuries."

"Oh my God," I whispered, staring without seeing, shock choking me.

I remembered how eager the Incubi at the Base were to be Forgiven and how hopeful they were with the new agreement.

"You really hadn't considered the possibility of such an outcome?" Keller tilted his head, obviously enjoying my distress—feeding off it, as if he were some kind of energy vampire himself.

I desperately hoped he was just toying with me, but what he said made sense. If anyone out there wanted the demons dead, now they had a way to accomplish it.

"But the Priory has been helping Incubi, even when at the expense of the lives of human women."

"The Priory has been *containing* them, my dear, by any means necessary, for a lack of any more effective ways of dealing with them. Until now."

"It can't be," I mumbled, clasping my shaking hands in my lap, terror gripping my heart with icy fingers.

"Yet it is happening." He paused, probably to let the full horror of this sink in me. "But there is still a chance for you to save Valefor. As long as he has not been Forgiven, he will be impossible to exterminate."

"I won't help you enslave him," I said, my voice firm.

Keller leaned closer across the table, fixing me with his glare.

"Unlike his," he gritted through his teeth, "your own life is fragile. And who knows what might happen to an Incubus whose Mistress is dead." Without taking his unblinking stare off me, he took a deep breath and leaned back in his chair again, arms crossed over his chest. "It would be a shame if Valefor was to suffer such an unfortunate loss."

My chest seemed to be closing in on itself, and I forced some air into my lungs, determined not to make too obvious the devastation his words had created inside me.

"A moot point—my life is not on the negotiation table here. I know you have no plans of letting me out of this alive either way. Why else would you be telling me all the things you have? You're not intending for me to live long enough to tell the tale."

"Smart." Something like a flicker of genuine admiration crossed his features for a moment. "However, your life is in my hands, and I may consider gifting it back to you if you do exactly what you're told."

Chapter 34

UPON LANDING SEVERAL hours later, Keller's monks dragged me out of the aeroplane and into one of the several all-terrain vehicles parked near what looked like a small airstrip in the middle of nowhere.

Whatever hope I might have had of escaping evaporated when faced with the deserted landscape interspersed with patches of short, grey vegetation and melting snow.

"Where are we?" I asked the monk sitting next to me on the bench inside the tarp covered back of the vehicle they'd shoved me into.

"Brother Valeriy has vowed an oath of silence," the one across from me spoke instead. "Not that we should be talking to you anyway."

The monk appeared very young, no more than twenty. However, the disdain on his face was way beyond his years.

"Well, since *you* are talking, where are we?" I asked in Russian, the language he spoke.

"Doesn't matter to you." He smirked, without looking at me, as though to do so was offensive. "It's a long way to your embassy from here—you'd have a better chance blasting into space than getting back to where you came from."

One of the other monks nudged him, and he went silent.

"How long is the drive going to be?" I asked anyway, but none of them replied this time—all avoided eye contact, too.

Unable to see anything through the few narrow gaps in the tarp, I did some quick calculations in my head.

I had nothing to accurately track the time, but by my estimation, the flight must have taken us about five to six hours. Except that I had no idea in what direction we had flown.

Since I was abducted in the late afternoon, taking the ride in the van and the flight into account, it should be early morning right now. However, I noted on the way from the aeroplane to the vehicle, that the sun was already a considerable distance above the horizon, which meant we flew against the sun . . .

East.

The chill that sneaked inside my coat seeped deeper into my bones. Keller had taken me East, not West. The desert I glimpsed outside could have been anywhere in the southern parts of the former Soviet Union. Some of which were scarcely populated states run by corrupt governments. That snappy monk was right, my embassy—any western country embassy—would be a long way away.

'You have a better chance blasting into space . . .'

I strained my memory. Baikonur, the Russian Star City where the spacecraft launch facility was located, was in southern Kazakhstan. Was this where Keller had taken me?

THE DRIVE FROM THE landing strip took us another couple of hours. The sun was considerably higher over the horizon when the caravan of vehicles stopped and I was allowed outside again.

The sun blinded me, as cool wind bit at my face and snuck under my coat.

"Get her ready," Keller ordered to the monks when the two of them brought me to him. "Keep her away from the others. We'll start as soon as everything is set up."

"This way." The same huffy monk who spoke to me during the drive yanked at my arm, dragging me away with the help of another one.

Blinking in the sunlight and huddling from the wind, I tried to get a better idea of where I actually was by examining the landscape.

At some distance, I spotted a large object of uneven shape that seemed to be half buried by dirt and sparse vegetation. Closer to us, there were several rows of dilapidated huts, where the monks seemed to be taking me. And to the side, there was a cluster of much more modern looking tents, where Keller headed with a few other monks accompanying him.

"Brother Grigoriy!" someone yelled behind us, prompting my escort to slow down.

Another monk caught up with us, a bundle of brown material in his hands.

"Here, ceremonial clothing for the witch." He handed the bundle to the monk at my side. "Per Father's orders." He bowed quickly and took off in the direction of the tents.

"Father?" I asked. "Is that what you call Keller?"

"We are all the children of men," Brother Grigoriy replied, his expression easing into calm serenity. "As demons are children of the Devil."

"Aren't we all children of God?" I said, in an attempt to provoke him into continuing to talk, in hopes he'd say something useful.

"God is weak."

"What?" I blinked, genuinely puzzled by his words. Whatever this little operation of Keller's was, he seemed to have given it the distinct characteristics of some religious cult.

"God has had his time. And his love for humankind only bred weakness and decay. It's the Devil's time now."

"Holy crap," I gasped. "Are you all Satanists?"

"Not exactly." He shoved me into a hut, farthest from the rest, then followed me in. "We are the chosen ones who know the truth."

"Sure you are."

I swept the inside of the hut with my gaze. It appeared to have served as a shed or a small cabin some time ago. Now, the floor was covered by a layer of dirt and debris blown in by the wind through gaps in the walls, and the whole structure seemed to be falling apart.

"The Devil's reign is approaching." Brother Grigoriy shook out the bundle in his hands, unfurling a long, brown robe similar to the ones they wore. "He has sent the demons—his children and his soldiers—to cleanse the Earth of the weak and feeble before his coming."

I had expected some brainwashing on Keller's part to keep the army of monks at his disposal. This, however, had exceeded anything I could've come up with.

"So this *cleansing* is what you expect the demons to do?"

"Yes. All the rot will be wiped off the face of the world, so the strong and the chosen ones can flourish. Get ready . . ." He thrust the robe my way. "For the meeting with the messenger of Hell—Valefor, the Devil's Soldier."

Chapter 35

SHIELDING MY FACE FROM the wind, I hurried behind the two monks tugging me through the desert towards a large domed shape in the distance. Struggling to keep up with the punishing pace the two had set, I could barely breathe, the cold air piercing my lungs.

"Worthless," Brother Grigoriy threw my way.

Barefoot, dressed only in the coarse brown robe they had forced on me, I couldn't keep my teeth from chattering and tried to ignore him.

Worry about Vadim fuelled me with anxiety, numbing me against the monk's insults. One didn't have to be a genius to figure out that Keller had planned another summoning ritual for Vadim, which I knew would hurt him.

"Your only purpose is to satisfy the desires of the flesh for men, nothing more." Brother Grigoriy wouldn't quit. "Even conversing with females rots one's mind."

I wished he would *stop* conversing. In fact, I would have preferred he'd taken the same vow of silence as Brother Valeriy. At this point, I was convinced the only purpose of the yappy monk chatting with me was to torture and demoralize me.

"Masculine strength is the true manifestation of power," he went on. "Weakness always comes from females."

A brand new religion they had here, however, the concept seemed age-old and painfully familiar—women were evil.

231

Tripping on the hard soil, I considered refusing to walk, making them have to carry me instead. Only, the thought of their hands on me filled me with repulsion.

"Sooner or later, the Father will let us share your flesh," he announced suddenly.

"Fuck you," I spat his way. His words finally riled me enough to abandon my resolution to ignore him.

"You are a demon's whore," he explained evenly. "You have lain with him. Through your flesh we will all get closer to one of the Devil's Soldiers."

"If you come anywhere near *my flesh*, you little prick," I squeezed through my chattering teeth, anger boiling hot inside me. "My demon will rip all of your tiny dicks off."

The flash of shock—no matter how brief—on his face brought me a strong feeling of satisfaction. My reply had finally shut Brother Grigoriy up, and the rest of the way was made in relative silence, save for him mumbling something about 'rotting of the mind' under his breath.

The structure we approached turned out to be the ruins of an old stone building, buried to the roof in the desert floor. Only the domed top and part of a wall, with an entrance carved into it, remained aboveground.

As if subdued by the anticipation of what was to come, both monks were completely silent as we took a long, curved stairwell down into a large round room lit by a number of torches on the wall.

The smoke from the torches made the air hazy, throwing an orange glow on a group of monks standing in a circle. Someone in the shadows beyond the circle recited something in a language I'd never heard before.

The monks shifted, letting us into the circle where Keller stood, dressed in the same long brown robe as the rest of us.

I tripped again on the slippery ground, my gaze fixed on a motionless, naked woman spread on the floor at his feet.

Without saying a word, Keller gestured and two minions lifted the woman off the floor, taking her out of the circle. The way her limbs flopped, like those of a rag doll, meant she was either unconscious or dead.

"Is she alive?" I gasped.

"No, she is not," Keller replied calmly. "And neither will be you if you don't keep your mouth shut."

His threat vibrated through the chilly air. The sinister atmosphere surrounding me rendered me speechless.

The sudden rush of cold against my exposed skin as they ripped my robe off brought me back to my senses, and I fought their hands as they dragged me to the place where the dead woman had just lain.

"Let go off me, you sick bastards!" I thrashed in their grip.

"Silence." The order came from Keller. Then one of those who held me kicked the back of my knees, knocking me to the ground.

Bent over on the floor, I realised I was kneeling in the middle of a pentagram painted on the stones. Short metal chains with rusted cuffs were mounted at the ends of four out of five rays of the star.

A shot of panic spurred me into action. I scrambled to get up, but my hands and feet slipped, unable to find purchase on something warm and sticky that coated the floor. I caught a whiff of copper in the air.

Blood.

With a grunt, one of the monks wrestled me to the ground, flipping me to my back, while the other quickly locked my wrists and ankles into the cuffs.

Fully restrained, spread on the floor with my arms and legs wide open, the helplessness of my position threw my panic into top gear.

"No! Let me out of here!" Blinded by fear, I thrashed on top of the pentagram.

"Quiet!" Keller landed a heavy kick to my ribs.

Gasping for air, I tried to curl into myself, but the restraints prevented me from that, keeping me open for more abuse.

The chants increased in volume, and the torchlight seemed to blur as the orange haze turned to red around me.

The centre of the dome above us had caved in at some point in time, leaving a gaping hole in the middle, with the bright sunlight shining through high above me. The light never reached me, though, overpowered by the hazy darkness below.

Mixed with the stench of blood, the air turned nauseatingly suffocating. Panting, I struggled to get any oxygen to my lungs, as my chest seemed to be compressed by some invisible weight.

"I can't do this," I squeezed the plea through my sore throat.

"Yes, you can." Keller knelt at my site. "And you will. Name me his master, and I'll set you free."

I knew I couldn't trust him, still the mention of freedom sparked a glimmer of hope and longing somewhere deep inside me.

Keller began to chant, too, his voice joining the one outside the circle. Then, with a flash of reflected light, he raised a long, narrow dagger over my chest.

My heart felt like it skittered in my chest and my breath stuck in my throat with a renewed wave of terror.

Unable to tear my stare from the glistening blade, I watched in horror as it descended lower with each foreign word coming from Keller's mouth.

"No!" I pressed my back into the stone floor when the cold tip of the blade touched the skin between my breasts, as if I could escape it by disappearing into the ground beneath me.

The circle of men around us tightened. Some energy seemed to be charging them and filling the room.

The thick, crimson fog churned and shifted over me, coagulating into a cloud. It appeared to be heating up from the inside, as the red had brightened to orange, then to fierce yellow and finally to a blinding white.

Keller kept his voice low. However, the conjurer's chants increased in volume once again, his tone firm and commanding.

Raising my head slightly, I caught sight of an elderly man just behind the monks' circle. Kazahk or Mongolian in appearance, his long, thin beard almost reaching his waist, he lifted a string of beads in his hands with a large pendant shaped like a half-moon.

The beads and the crescent began to glow as bright light silently exploded from the radiant mist above me. Blinded for a moment, I closed my eyes.

The dagger in Keller's hand jerked, scratching my skin, and a thundering roar shook the dilapidated building to its foundation.

The conjurer's incessant chants broke into short commands—forceful and loud.

A wave of warmth descended upon me from above, and I slowly opened my eyes.

The cloud above me had expanded. Its edges, however, seemed to be stopped at an invisible line in the air, the same size and shape as the circle formed by the monks around me. As if unable to penetrate the space outside, the glowing cloud shifted and churned with a rumbling sound somewhere deep inside it.

As I stared at it, the bright tendrils curled and squirmed, forming fiery images. At first, they seemed abstract and blurry, then the face of a roaring lion emerged clearly.

No feature of the face stayed in place, every line moved continuously. Its mane was formed entirely of licks of fire that spread in every direction, as far as the invisible circle would allow.

The yellow eyes of the fiery apparition stopped on me, and pain distorted the features of the glowing face.

Suddenly, the groaning noise that had been thundering through the walls under the prolapsed dome formed into words, "Release her!"

Neither Keller nor the conjurer paid any attention to the demand, both continuing their litanies.

The lines of fire shifted once again, making me gasp in shock as I suddenly recognized the features above me. Despite the burning yellow eyes and the golden flame of mane, it was the face of the man I loved.

"Vadim," I whispered, tears escaping my eyes.

With a renewed burst of energy, the conjurer lashed out with another string of chants, and my man's face became a lion's once again as he roared in pain.

I recognized the convulsions that distorted the features of the animal. They were identical to the ones that tortured Vadim while I held him in my arms during the previous summons.

The tormented creature leaped down to me, but another barrier over the pentagram seemed to enclose Keller and me. The lion's tortured groans bounced off the walls as he crashed against it in vain.

"Oh, God, please stop this," I sobbed.

"God won't help him," Keller's coarse whisper reached me. "But you can." He nudged me with the blade pressed to my chest. "Tell him who his master is."

As if sensing the break in Keller's chants, the fiery lion lunged for me again the moment Keller renewed his string of foreign words, yanking the demon back up again. His roar was filled with agony and frustration when the barrier stopped him from reaching me once again.

"Now," Keller hissed, the fingers of his free hand digging into my shoulder.

Another tortured growl was wrenched from Vadim's chest.

"Mistress," he rumbled, his eyes on me full of sorrow.

The blinding cloud of fire shaped as a lion was the essence of the man I loved. I knew Vadim was the one enduring every painful lash of chants, his physical body twisted in agony out there somewhere. And I was not with him to help him this time.

"Go!" I ordered, desperate to release him from this torture. "Leave here."

Anguish distorted the flames of his features. "No."

Yet the circle that held him in place seemed to have disappeared, following my command.

Uncontained, the flames of his mane unfurled, spreading to the walls. One tendril speared through the chest of a monk, breaking the circle as his body fell to the ground.

Keller continued with his chants, though, maintaining the invisible barrier above the two of us and keeping Vadim away from me.

My demon couldn't save me, but I still had the power to set him free.

"Go," I whispered, watching Vadim's face rise and thin into the gloomy darkness of the dungeon, the relief for him spreading through my limbs.

"Stupid bitch!" The insult came with a sudden blow to the side of my face, filling my head with ringing pain. "That was a fucking stupid thing to do. Even for you."

Keller's face, red and distorted with rage, hovered over me. His chilly composure had deserted him completely.

"Do you think you're in any way safe?" Another blow knocked my head to the side, completely disorienting me for a moment.

"You think I *need* you, so I'll think twice before killing you?" He raged on. "Just because you've been fucked by a Grand Master doesn't make you indispensable. There are hundreds of fucking demons, growing complacent about keeping their names a secret. Sooner or later, I'll find someone else."

Lost in rage, he didn't seem to be that selective where he hit, his fists raining punches to my arms, chest, and ribs.

I twisted away as far as the restraints would allow, trying to hide my face behind my shoulder.

The monks had tightened their circle, gathering around us to watch in silence.

"I swear I'll kill you." Keller grabbed a handful of my hair, yanking my head up. "But you don't deserve a quick, clean death."

Panting, he rose to his feet. "Get her to the cabin. We'll do it one more time when *ata* recovers." He gestured at the elderly conjurer, who sat on the ground nearby. "No matter how it goes, she is all yours at the *Gathering* tomorrow night."

In an apparent attempt to collect himself, he smoothed his hair and straightened his robe.

"See how being fucked by a demon compares to being raped by two dozen demon worshippers." He shoved his boot in my ribs again, sharp pain shot through my side. "Who knows, you may like it. The whore that you are."

Chapter 36

LISTENING TO THE WIND whistling through the holes in the walls of the hut, I huddled under a bunch of old blankets on the cot. A heater, powered by a generator outside, hummed softly in the corner. With the temperatures dipping for the night, Keller obviously intended for me to survive until the morning.

Tomorrow was another story, though.

One more summoning ritual was all that stood between me and certain death now.

Worse than death.

I remembered Keller's threat about the *Gathering*. Despite the layers of clothing and blankets, I still felt the leering stares of the monks on my skin. Hugging my knees, I curled into a ball from cold and from the fear of what was to come.

I had the power to release Vadim from a summoning. The trouble was that Keller remained immune under the protection of his own chants. Even if I ordered Vadim to raze that place to the ground, I doubted Keller would lose his composure long enough to let the barrier lapse. With his knife at my chest, I'd be as good as dead then.

I shuddered under the heavy blankets, the meagre dinner of bread and water they'd given me roiled in my stomach.

Recalling Vadim's demonic essence, I thought about all that power rolling and churning under the dome, like a thunderstorm ready to erupt.

'God won't help him, but you can.'

The power of my demon was at my disposal.

I just had to find a way to use it against Keller somehow. And then maybe we both had a chance.

"ONE MORE TIME, DEMON whore," Brother Grigoriy hissed in my ear, dragging me down the stairs to the ceremony room late the next morning. "Father will not give you another chance."

"What's in it for you?" I had no idea how all this little clan of crazies fitted with Keller's plan of getting the Incubi back into submission.

"Valefor, The Devil's Soldier, will take us all into the Devil's Army," Brother Grigoriy haughtily explained. "We'll be the chosen ones, ruling the world with the Devil himself when he comes."

"Alrighty then."

Crazies, indeed.

A sharp female scream pierced the air, sending a shot of reactive panic through my chest.

"Wait!" I heard Keller's voice as we descended. "I want *her* to see this."

There were at least twice as many people here today—the monks stood by the walls, outside the circle formed by young women.

Unlike the men, the women were hunched and cowering, shaking in their robes. Some cried softly, others stared blankly, with muddy tear-tracks on their cheeks.

"What's going on?" I asked, confused and worried by the change, but no one answered me.

The conjurer started chanting as we entered.

Keller stood inside the circle, next to the pentagram. In front of him, two monks held a naked female under her arms.

Catching my eye, he raised his dagger over the naked girl.

She screamed again and jerked to the side in a desperate attempt to escape, but the monks held her steady. Her screams turned to whimpers.

"Stop this!" I lunged towards her, but the ones holding me tightened their grip, keeping me in place.

The girl prayed rapidly in Russian as Keller suddenly thrust his dagger into her throat, slicing it open. Blood sprayed in an arc. The prayer bubbled in crimson foam from her lips. The monks took their hands off her, letting her drop to the floor.

"No!" I screamed in horror. "You can't . . ."

"I can," Keller bit out sharply. "I did. And I'll do it again. As many times as necessary to get what I want. Think about this before you make another stupid decision. The price of your idiocy is human lives."

Unable to peel my gaze away from the girl's body, I slumped in the monks' hold, as if my own life was already seeping out of me, too.

One of Keller's minions moved hurriedly into the circle with a wide brush in his hand. Chanting something under his breath, he dipped the brush into the pooling blood under the poor woman's body then spread a fresh layer over the lines of the pentagram.

"Demons love human blood," Keller murmured with satisfaction, stepping aside as two monks carried away the dead body.

Demons want none of this,' rushed through my brain, my knees weak from the horror of it all.

"Get her over here," Keller commanded, and I was dragged to the centre of the pentagram, as my feet refused to move.

"We're all leaving here shortly. Changing locations," Keller said, ripping my robe open. "If you don't fulfil your purpose today, you won't be coming with us." The monks let go of my arms, and Keller shoved against my shoulders, pushing me to my knees. "If my men don't end you during the Gathering tonight, I will." He yanked the robe off me and tossed it aside. "Either way, you won't get to see the morning, unless you do what I brought you here to do." He kicked me in the side, knocking me to the ground, then stepped off the pentagram, folding his arms across his chest.

A group of monks quickly spread me on the floor again, in the cooling blood of the murdered woman, and locked me in chains.

My whole body shook, teeth chattering, from shock as much as from the cold.

Keller knelt at my side again, the dagger in his hand.

"Name me his master," he ordered, steel in his voice and in his eyes on me. Then I felt the chilly prick of the blade against my chest again.

The conjuror's chanting grew louder. The light from the torches blurred and thickened into a blood-coloured fog.

My head swam, my vision went fuzzy, and my heart raced, pounding as if it was about to jump out of my chest.

The thought of my passing out from stress ironically jolted me to my senses. I could not afford to lose consciousness right now.

Breathing in and out against the dagger pressing into my sternum, I forced myself to focus, shoving aside the stench of warm blood and the horrific images of the murder in my mind.

The circle was formed by women this time. Some were sobbing and whimpering, but all held hands firmly. Behind each female a monk stood, pressing a knife to her neck. After what we had all just witnessed, I was certain the girls were holding each other's hands tight, terrified of having their throats slit, too.

If I ordered Vadim to break the circle this time, he would have to kill a woman. My chest tightened in horror. For my demon to be free, an innocent would have to lose her life.

Starting his own string of chants, Keller's voice brought my attention to him.

I swallowed hard and cleared my throat, gathering whatever was left of my strength. "All this . . ." I said, adding a hefty dose of sarcasm to my words, "for some cushy lifestyle for you."

He glared my way, but kept his composure, the chants flowing smoothly.

The fiery entity already formed above us, roars crashing into the walls, as Vadim's essence lashed at the two barriers, one formed by the circle of whimpering, terrified women, the other conjured by the man with the dagger at my chest.

I remembered the way the lion creature lunged our way the moment Vadim sensed the break in the chants yesterday. Keller's muttering of Latin words was what maintained the shield over us, protecting him from Vadim's wrath. The care he took to keep the dagger in contact with my body at all times, hinted to me that this must be an essential part of the ritual, too.

From the corner of my eye, I noticed the lion's fiery eyes emerge from the blood-red cloud, flaming tendrils morphing into a face.

"Look at all the work you've done," I mocked my tormentor through my chattering teeth. "You have your own little cult going here and are about to get your very own demon, too. And all for what?"

"Silence," Keller bit out between the chants, digging the tip of the blade into my skin.

"You went not only against the Incubi," I continued, ignoring his order, "but against humanity as a whole, and you know it. You betrayed your own organization, and for what? For money. You have the morals of a common thief."

The demonic fire brightened from above, washing us with light and heat, but I was no longer watching the marvellous transformation.

My eyes on Keller, I continued to taunt him. "You're far from a spring chicken, you know. In a few years you'll die, alone and forgotten. Your money useless, just like you are."

His eyelid ticked, still he didn't break stride with the chants. However, I knew his composure was but a thin veneer. I learned the full extend of his volatile temper and lack of self-control yesterday when he beat me, as I lay there defenceless and unable to escape.

"You're worse than a parasite, deprived of morality and compassion." I called on all the anger I felt for him and turned it into words, as sharp as his dagger. "You're a coward, terrified of anyone stronger than you are. Sure it's easy to terrorize defenceless women, but would you take on a man? How about a demon? You'll never have the guts to kill me, because you're afraid of *him*. Scared shitless, you're a pathetic old man with a shrivelled dick and no heart."

I kept my gaze on Keller's face, watching every small twitch in his expression. At the same time I sensed Vadim thrashing inside the restraints of the chants, ready to be unleashed.

"Name me his master," Keller gritted through his teeth, his face turning an angry shade of red. "Or I swear . . ." The tip of the dagger pierced through my skin, scraping against the chest bone with an agonizing shot of pain that only fuelled my anger.

"I won't," I spat the words at him. "And you can't force me—I'm stronger than you."

At that moment, I fully believed in that. Power coursed through me, uniting me with Vadim, feeding me his strength.

"I am my demon's Mistress. He is mine." Holding Keller's gaze, I put the full force of my conviction into my every word. "You'll never have him. I won't let you."

The remnants of his composure blown away like a sandcastle in hurricane, Keller's whole body jerked, shaking with rage. The chants stopped abruptly.

"I'll end you, you bitch!" he yelled instead.

I didn't watch him raise the dagger, ready to stab me. As soon as I felt it lift off my chest, I slid my gaze above Keller's shoulder, finding the burning eyes of the lion in the clouds of flames.

"Kill him," I ordered.

An avalanche of fire and fury descended on Keller, the second the barrier over us must have collapsed.

I closed my eyes, turning my face away from the shower of hot ash that rained on my skin. But there was no escaping Keller's blood-curdling screams as my demon ripped him to shreds.

The conjurer's voice trembled with panic as he threw chants at the beast raging inside the circle. The walls shook from demonic roars.

I opened my eyes again.

The women screamed, shrinking away from the raging fire, breaking the ring of handholding in several places—the monks, too terrified themselves to do anything about the breach, retreated back, some started running for the stairs.

"Kill them all," I said to Vadim softly, all emotions drained from me. "Spare the women."

The lion leaped out of the rapidly deteriorating circle, attacking the men at the women's backs. With claws and teeth of fire, he ripped the monks to pieces of charred flesh.

In moments, the room filled with the stench of burned bodies and screams of utter terror from the crying women as they rushed the stairs to escape this nightmare.

His back plastered to the wall, the conjurer kept chanting mechanically, an expression of pure horror frozen on his face.

My glorious lion swept the room with his fiery gaze.

The floor was littered with the smouldering remnants of the monks. All the women had run up the stairs, leaving no one but me, him, and the conjurer in this underground hell.

Slowly, the lion approached the old man, and I realised why he had been spared until the end. The chants that he continued to spew in a desperate effort to protect himself were also what kept Vadim here, with me.

The lion turned to me over his shoulder, the fire in his eyes wavered with an expression of sorrow.

"Mistress . . ." the word formed in the rumbling noise vibrating through the room as he raised his paw to finish fulfilling my order. The long flames of his claws slashed clean through the bone and sinew of the human, severing the conjurer's head off his shoulders.

The chants stopped and the lion leaped through the air to me, but his shape dissolved, never reaching me on the floor. He was gone.

The silence that followed was deafening, as I realised I was completely alone, with only the charred, torn corpses.

I'd done this. Vadim might have been my weapon, but I was the one responsible for this massacre.

My whole body shook, even my brain seemed to be vibrating with shock and adrenaline. I yanked against the restraints, the full horror of my situation filtering through to me.

I was left naked and chained to the floor. "Hey!" I screamed at the top of my lungs, hoping to attract the attention of anyone who might be outside. "Is anyone out there?"

The dome teased me with the sight of the pale sky through the breach. But since it was way too high for the daylight to reach me down here, I doubted my voice would make it up that far either.

"Help me, please!" I yelled as loud as I could, the chilly numbness of fear seeping through to my bones.

The howl of the wind through the broken roof was my only answer.

Chapter 37

SPREAD ON THE FLOOR, in the puddle of drying blood that crusted under my back and in my hair, I watched the uneven patch of sky above me darken as the hours passed.

The heat from Vadim's fiery rampage had eventually cooled from the stone floor and walls of the room, letting the cold of the approaching night seep into my naked body.

With a hissing sound, the flames of the torches started going out one by one. And soon I was left surrounded by chilling darkness.

I'd screamed for help for hours, until my throat hurt and my voice left me.

Now the last vestiges of energy were leaving me, too. The cold around me had been stealing whatever body heat I still had, the stone of the floor aiding in this torture.

I shivered, clinking the rusty chains, as scary thoughts churned in my brain.

Immobilized by the restraints, I couldn't even curl into a ball. It would be just a matter of time until the night chill fully descended through the breach in the ceiling. With the cold stone floor under my back, it wouldn't take long for hypothermia to set in and eventually claim me.

Even with the heater in my hut last night, I could tell the temperatures in this area had dipped close to zero. It seemed that Keller might be right after all—no matter what, I wouldn't live long enough to see the next morning.

Spurred by incessant, panicky fear, I rotated my wrist in the handcuffs for the millionth time in the past few hours. The skin had been rubbed raw by now, with no effect on the cold metal whatsoever.

The women present at the ritual were the only ones who knew of my whereabouts. They appeared to be long gone, fleeing from this place as if the Devil himself had chased after them.

Deep inside I understood. I couldn't really blame them for running away, after whatever horrors they might have endured at the hands of Keller's perverted monks and after what they'd witnessed in this room. On the surface, though, I couldn't help feeling anger at them burn through me for leaving me here to die.

The sorrowful gaze of the fire lion rose in my mind once again. Was Vadim self-aware enough in this state to figure out how to find me?

He had been able to accurately identify Keller during the first summons. But would his mind be sharp enough and his memory clear to note and remember the exact geographical location of this place?

And if so, would the demons be fast enough to come to me in time?

DID I HEAR SOME DISTANT voices outside, or did my frozen mind play tricks on me?

Footsteps? My eyes closed, I jerked as the first drop of icy water hit my skin.

Not footsteps. Raindrops pounded the packed dirt on the top of the dome outside.

Lifting my eyelids, I felt big, fat drops of water hit my body in vaguely stinging shards that barely penetrated my awareness. Everything inside me was numb by now. My body seemed to have lost any feeling to cold or pain, too.

Mesmerized, I watched light sparkle on the raindrops that floated down through the air as if in slow motion to splash against my skin.

The thumping sound I'd heard grew louder, sounding like boots hitting stone. Had the rain gotten heavier?

It didn't seem to be the case . . . The sound got louder and closer.

Warm light moved from the stairwell and into the room, but I paid no attention to it, hypnotized by the flying raindrops.

"God Almighty! Jade!"

Someone ran to me, touched my face, cupped my neck.

"Say something, please."

Zayne, the name rose in my mind, connecting the voice to a face.

I tried to do what he told me, but I couldn't even open my mouth, let alone move my tongue. My body no longer felt like it belonged to me at all.

With a screeching sound, the cuffs were wrenched from my wrists and legs.

That's right, demons are strong. It's good to be strong, no one would ever keep you in cuffs against your will.

He lifted me carefully off the ground, and I jerked from the agony of it. A weak moan left my sore throat.

"Thank heaven, you're alive." Zayne lifted me in his arms, pressing me to the hard chest plates. He must be wearing Incubi armour, although I was positive he had no helmet on.

I groaned again.

"You'll be fine now. I promise." Holding the flashlight and me, he ran up the stairs, making an effort not to jolt my aching body too much. "If this is the last thing I'll do in this world, Jade, I'll make sure you're well and healthy again soon."

OUTSIDE, THE NOISE increased by a thousand, with red and yellow lights hovering above us. It took me a few seconds to realise it was a large, black helicopter descending from the dark night sky. Its blades hurled shrapnel pieces of sand against my naked body, the stings felt strong enough to pierce my skin.

Zayne turned his back to it, shielding me from the wind and rain, and I spotted several demons in their charcoal uniforms bring a group of women from the direction of the huts.

An Incubus rushed to us, armoured but also without a helmet. *Ilya.*

"Found her!" Zayne called to him over the noise of the helicopter.

"How is she?"

"Alive. I'm going to take her to the house now. Can you handle things here?"

With a nod and a wave, Ilya jogged back to the women as Zayne jumped into the helicopter with me.

"Get me some electrolytes and a blanket," he ordered to someone inside.

"Just a moment." Boris, another Incubus I recognised from the Base, crawled from the front to us with a bag in his hand as the helicopter took off with a sway through the air.

Settling on the floor, Zayne held me with one hand, taking his armour off with the other. He unzipped the grey jacket they all wore under the armour, and cradled me closer with only a thin t-shirt separating his skin from mine.

The warmth of his body heat prickled over me as sensation returned to my limbs, bringing a new wave of pain.

"How is she doing?" Boris asked, handing Zayne a bottle with pink liquid in it.

"Some degree of hypothermia, dehydration," Zayne reported before screwing off the lid of the bottle with his teeth. Boris inserted a drinking straw, and Zayne brought it to my lips. "Bruises . . ." He shifted my head to the cabin light. "She's been beaten." He heaved an inhale, the hardness of his chest pushing against my side. "I couldn't even spot the life force in her right away. Wasn't sure she was alive at all until she moaned."

I took a drink through the straw. The sweet-salty liquid washed the dryness from my mouth, my tongue felt like I could move it again.

"Vadim . . ." My throat burned with pain.

"He is with the search group up north." Zayne stretched his jacket over both of us, and Boris tucked a reflective blanket all around me.

"Dmitry and I," Boris pointed at the pilot in the front, "will go get him after we drop you off."

As if he could hear his name through the headphones he was wearing, Dmitry looked over his shoulder with a wide smile. The chipped tooth in his mouth, as well as the signs of aging on his face, betrayed him as human.

"Vadim has probably started hiking to the house already, the moment he got the message," Zayne muttered.

He shifted on the floor, settling both of us in a more comfortable position, then leaned back, his body relaxing. "He went berserk there for a while when he learned that you were gone. No, *taken*," he corrected himself, with a wince.

A flash of light from the front brushed across us, bringing out a huge, purple bruise on the side of his face.

"Are you okay?" I gasped, making an attempt to lift my hand. "Did . . . he do this?"

"I deserved it," Zayne replied gloomily. "For letting them take you."

"Oh no." I dropped my hand back into my lap, the effort proved too exhausting. "I'm so sorry."

"No. It's me who should be sorry, Jade. And I *am* so, so much . . . I don't know if you can ever forgive me, I'm sure I'll never forgive myself."

"You're not to blame," I said quietly. "There is nothing to forgive."

The last thing I wanted was for this terrible experience to drive us all apart in any way.

"I'm still sorry," Zayne whispered stubbornly, placing his chin on the top of my head.

Chapter 38

"WE RENTED THIS PLACE as soon as we got to Kazakhstan, to store equipment and re-group as needed," Zayne told me when the helicopter landed about an hour later. "Vadim made sure it was comfortable enough to bring you here when we found you."

When not *if.* They had kept hope.

Zayne gestured to the small cluster of lights far to the side as he walked from the helicopter, carrying me in his arms. "The village over there used to be a fishing town before the Aral Sea was drained in the last century. The water is coming back slowly now, but the life is slower to return here still."

The low, white structure, with small square windows, sat surrounded by sand dunes interspersed with short, sparse vegetation.

He carried me through a spacious main room. The floor and walls inside were covered with large, colourful rugs. The bedroom had a low, wide bed where Zayne placed me on top of the quilt.

"How are you feeling?" He brought more blankets over and wrapped me in them. While on the helicopter, I'd started to shiver violently, and the shakes wouldn't seem to ease. "Much better. Thank you," I managed, despite my chattering teeth.

"Well, 'better' doesn't say much, considering how I found you." His features settled into a deep frown. "I'll warm up some broth for you that Ilya left in the fridge."

"Is there a way to have a shower here?"

"Yes." He nodded. "But it may take a few minutes. The house has cold running water, I'll have to start the heater to warm it up."

Shaking uncontrollably, I wrapped my arms around my knees, drawing my legs in, and lay on my side as Zayne exited the room.

Boris had said it would take them about an hour to get Vadim. And right now it felt like an eternity. I desperately needed him with me. If I thought I could walk any distance, I'd start out hiking through the desert myself if it meant I could see him sooner.

I was glad it wasn't Vadim who found me, though. Knowing how strong his feelings for me could be, I was afraid that seeing me in the condition I'd been in would have crushed him.

"In this part of the world, they drink from bowls." Zayne walked in with a small clay bowl in his hands. "They don't use spoons for drinking broth, but I can bring one if you prefer."

"No, I'm good. Thank you." I smiled. "Chances are I'll spill more using the spoon."

He sat on the bed next to me, holding the bowl out. Only now did I spot the bandages on his hands. Each finger was wrapped individually, and some were shorter than they should have been.

"Zayne, what happened?" I leaned back, searching his eyes.

"It will all heal in time," he dismissed. "Drink."

The fragrant broth warmed me from the inside when I took a sip.

"How did you get hurt?" I insisted. "Was it Vadim, too?"

"No. It wasn't him." He stared at his hands for a few seconds, as if seeing the bandages for the first time. "I tried to stop the car."

"The night they took me?"

He nodded.

"I punched through the trunk with my fingers, but cut them when the car took off."

I stared at him in silence for a few moments, trying to imagine how it all happened.

"I'm so sorry, Zayne," I whispered. "It must have hurt so much."

"They'll grow back." He shrugged it off.

"You regenerate body parts?" I knew Incubi didn't heal quickly, and that they felt pain, just like humans did. This, however, was new.

"There'd be much less of me by now if we didn't." Zayne smiled. "I've lost each limb at least once through the centuries."

"It must be awful."

"The truly awful thing is that I failed to stop them from taking you." He got off the bed. "I'll check if the water is warm enough. You finish your broth."

ZAYNE PUT ME IN THE tub and used the hose with a shower-head on it to wet my hair. I shampooed it the best I could. Then he scrubbed my back while I quickly washed everything else.

At this point, I was way past feeling shy or self-conscious about being naked one on one with him. Well aware that Zayne had seen me writhing in the throes of passion on the table in the meeting room months ago, I hardly felt any trace of awkwardness being cared for by him now, just a sense of deep gratitude for helping me do what I couldn't do on my own yet.

The fact that he didn't seem to be bothered by any of it either put me even more at ease. His movements were quick and efficient. Gentle enough, the touch of his hands with surgical gloves over the bandages was similar to that of a medical practitioner—caring but far from sensual.

"What is going to happen to the women now?" I asked, as he rinsed the grime and dried blood off me, letting the dirty water drain. "I thought they all had run away."

"No, they hid in the huts." He plugged the drain and started fill-ing the tub with clean, warm water. "A few took off and hiked for hours to the nearest village. I heard about some women escaping a *demon cult* and managed to get someone from the village to show me the location the women talked about."

"So they still ended up helping me, even if unwittingly."

"It would have taken us much longer without them," he agreed.

The thought of the possibility of not being found at all came with an icy lick of fear.

"Vadim didn't know where the summons took place?"

"No. When you're summoned, you simply follow the call, without any clear sense of the geographical location or direction. Vadim made a conscious effort to memorize as much as he could see, though. So he was able to recognize the desert from the satellite shots, but we had a hard time narrowing it down. He kept talking about a building with a high dome ceiling, and that was what we searched for. That building, however, turned out to be mostly buried in the ground, with only the top of the roof partially visible from the air."

I hugged my knees tighter, watching the clean, warm water rise in the tub.

"Will the women be able to go home?"

"From my quick talk with some of them, most seem to be from the surrounding countries. Some are Russian, a few spoke English. Ilya and the others will question them all and see if they can be returned to their families."

"When can we go back to Minsk?"

"As soon as you're well enough to travel any sort of distance." Zayne brushed his hand over his short, dark hair. "I hope before Saturday."

"Why Saturday?"

He hesitated for a moment, then replied with a shy glance my way, "I have a date."

"You do? A date?" I stared at him in surprise. "Have you been seeing someone?"

"Well, technically, no. Not yet." He rolled his wide shoulders back and rubbed the back of his neck. "This would be our first date. Tanya is taking me to the movies."

"Tanya?" I'd thought they didn't like each other, but they had obviously worked things out. "Do you like going to the movies?"

"I've never been." Sitting on the edge of the tub, he leaned forward, his elbows on his knees. "I've watched a lot of television but haven't been to a movie theatre yet."

"I'm sure you'll enjoy it." The warm water almost reached my shoulders now. With most of me submerged, my shivering had slowly been subsiding. "Tanya is a good person, she's been a great friend. Do you like her?"

His chest rose with a deep inhale. "I do. But even though I can see her emotions, I'm still not sure what she thinks about me."

"Are you worried?"

"Yes. All the time she spoke to me, I haven't said much. It's so stupid, but I seem to forget all my words, in any language, when I'm one-on-one with her."

"Well. Going to the movies is a good choice for a date then." I smiled, wishing to cheer him up. Talking about something as mundane as going to the movies brought a sense of normalcy to my reality, calming me, too. "You won't be expected to talk much there—"

The sound of loud footsteps caused panic to spike through me. Zayne rose to his feet, his damaged hands fisted at his side.

"Jade!" Vadim burst through the closed door.

In full uniform, with his helmet under his arm, he wildly swept the small bathroom with his gaze, stopping it on me—his eyes a dark-green storm.

My heart thundered, and I gripped the edge of the tub with both hands, under the onslaught of emotions that filled me all at once at the sight of him—achy yearning, warm affection, blissful pleasure, and an overwhelming relief at seeing him, in flesh and blood, once again.

"Leave," he growled at Zayne, without taking his eyes off me. His chest heaved so hard he must have run to the house. I doubted he even waited for the helicopter to lower all the way to the ground before he leaped out of it.

"Well." Zayne calmly took the rubber gloves off, tossing them in the garbage. "If you need anything, Jade—"

"She won't." Vadim threw his helmet in the corner.

Zayne slapped his shoulder on the way to the door, and Vadim caught his hand, holding it in his for a second in a silent *thank you*, I realised.

It was by far the biggest display of emotion I'd seen between the two—after spending centuries, living side by side, they didn't appear to need words to communicate. I was glad to have the proof that there were no hard feelings between them after all. Zayne's bruised face had me worried.

As soon as Zayne left, Vadim moved my way, silently unclipping his armour. Chest and shoulder plates, bracers, the wide belt around his waist—with a loud clank each, he tossed them all into the corner with the helmet, one by one. He then ripped the rest of his clothes off.

"My treasure," he breathed out softly, getting in the tub with me and taking me into his arms.

And I finally lost it.

Wrapped in the warmth of his large body, safe and secure at once, I let all the fear, stress, and horror of the past two days drain from me in a torrent of tears.

"He killed people there, Vadim." I sobbed as he held me. "Slaughtered women like cattle. Right in front of me."

"He's gone now." Vadim stroked my hair, cradling me in his lap. "He'll never do it again."

"I'm a murderer, now." I sniffled. "I killed him."

"No, *I* did. And I'd do it again if I had to."

"But I ordered you to do it . . ."

"You did good." The circle of his arms tightened around me. "It was recklessly dangerous, although incredibly brave, to taunt him into attacking you. Had I known what you were up to, I would've never allowed it."

"It worked, though . . ."

He shifted me in his arms, lightly tracing the edge of a bruise on the side of my face.

"I'm glad the bastard got what he deserved. No one knows what happens to a demon if his woman is gone, but I've come way too close to finding it out, and I don't want to live through anything like that ever again. Immortal or not, I'm not sure I could go on without you."

"How have you been doing?" I asked softly, covering his hand with mine.

"Seeing you there . . . chained like that. It was like watching my own heart splayed on the ground and stomped upon." He let out a shuddering breath then drew me into his chest again. "I may have a hard time letting you out of my sight for a while," he warned, burying his face in my wet hair.

I knew what he meant. A few weeks ago, a statement like that would have raised all kinds of red flags for me. I'd been a ferociously independent person from the day I learned how to walk. Being this close to someone, feeling responsible for him, and caring about him so much still felt new and unusual for me.

My commitment to Vadim was real, though, and being near him was the only place I wanted to be.

"I may have a hard time leaving your side, too." I kissed his chest. "We'll take it one day at a time, baby. You and I."

Chapter 39

WHEN THE BATHWATER began to cool, Vadim wrapped me in a towel and took me to bed.

"We'll see how you're feeling tomorrow. I'd prefer not to take you to a local hospital here. I don't trust them. Natasha recommended a doctor in Minsk."

"I'm much better." I snuggled against him as he spooned me from behind. "Just a little tired now, and . . . um."

Lying next to him, under a pile of blankets, my shivering was all but gone. The warmth had soothed the pain, and the awareness of Vadim's strong, naked body at my back tingled along my skin.

"You need to rest." His voice behind me sounded firm, almost stern. Still, I knew he had noticed the shift in my emotions—his breathing changed, and I felt him grow hard against my backside.

"Or . . ." I took his hand off my waist and moved it higher, to my breast. "You can make me a little *more* tired." I pressed my hips back, into his growing erection. "So I'd fall asleep faster."

It was insane, feeling aroused after everything that had happened. However, the receding stress left an unusual lightness in my belly—jittery and unsettling. Despite the lingering pain in my body, or maybe because of it, I needed some physical contact, to help me shove aside the memories of the reason for the pain, which would take time to ease.

More than anything, though, I desperately wanted to have Vadim close to me—as close as was humanly possible, to make *him* my reality again.

"I want to dream of you when I sleep," I whispered. "Only you, none of what has happened."

He didn't reply but rocked his hips into me, grinding against me. His hand squeezed my breast as he rubbed the tip with his thumb, his other hand sliding under me and between my thighs.

"Very gently then," he groaned into the skin on the back of my neck.

"Okay," I breathed out as his fingers stroked along my folds.

"Let me do all the work." He nibbled at the side of my neck, rolling my nipple between his fingers at the same time. "Stay absolutely still."

"I won't move a muscle," I promised breathlessly, even as my thighs jerked under the skilful glide of his fingers over the most sensitive part of my body.

Heat spread through me, warming me from the inside in a pulsating flow, chasing the remnants of cold far away into the darkness where it belonged.

"Not your hand, baby," I said in a whisper. "I want you inside me. I need it to be real."

I had to feel him everywhere, in my body and in my mind. He needed to take over my senses, guard my memories, and banish my fears. I wanted him to fill me completely, so that there would be no more space left for anything scary from the outside.

"Just you," I begged.

Carefully, he wedged his knee between my legs, prompting me to open for him. Then I felt the throbbing heat of his tip at my opening.

I arched my back as he slid in, angling my hips to take more of him, greedy for every hard inch of his body.

With a low grunt, he moved back then plunged in again, sending a new wave of arousal through my insides. One hand on my breast, he worked me between my legs with the other, keeping up with the rhythm of his thrusts.

"Yes," I whimpered as the heat and pressure building up under his fingers collided with sweet, achy pleasure. Waves of ecstasy shuddered through my body while Vadim held me tight.

One hand pressed between my thighs to squeeze every last drop of my orgasm, he pumped faster, chasing his own release. With a long growl, he tensed for a moment, before his orgasm rippled through him, too.

Holding me in the circle of his arms, as the last tremors of our joined bodies subsided, he relaxed against my back for a moment then stirred again.

"How are you feeling? I didn't hurt you?"

Hearing the concerned note in his voice, I lowered my head, kissing his forearm across my chest.

"No, baby," I whispered. "You've made it all better."

True. The pain on the surface, as well as the one on the inside, eased under the rays of his love, making me feel like I floated on a fluffy, pink cloud, warm and comfy in his arms. And so very sleepy . . .

"Making love to you has an uncanny ability to turn the world the right way up again," Vadim murmured in my hair.

Love!

The sudden memory of Keller's cold, brutal words jolted me with panic, slicing through the feeling of happiness like a blade of a dagger in a hand of a maniac.

"Oh no, honey . . ." I turned around in his arms, then took his face between my hands. "You can't fall in love with me."

"I don't think I can stop that now." He smiled, golden streaks dancing amongst the warm green in his eyes. His eyelashes of rich, chocolate brown always seemed too long and too gorgeous for his fierce, angular face. "This feeling is like an avalanche. It keeps grow-ing bigger."

"No, please. They're planning to murder all of you. When you're one of the Forgiven, you become mortal, too."

"Who are *they*?" His voice hardened, as did his expression.

"The Priory. According to Keller, that is The Elder's plan—to wait until you all turn mortal." I shuddered. "Then exterminate you all at once."

"Do you trust this is true?"

"Keller was bragging to me, believing I wouldn't make it out of his hands alive . . ." Vadim's breath hitched at my words, and I stroked his shoulder. "What do *you* think? You've met The Elder—"

"Not lately. I haven't seen him since we started work on changing the rules. He's been dealing with us through delegates or via phone calls. If what you're saying is true . . ."

"How about the delegates? Have you noticed anything suspi-cious in their emotions towards you when you've met?"

"Some hostility, but no more than usual. Many members of the Priory have historically disliked us. They view our meetings as a nec-essary evil to endure in order to deal with us."

I squirmed under the blankets to stay awake. Even the sharp spike of alarm didn't seem to be able to put a stop to the bone-crush-ing tiredness that threatened to drag me under any minute.

"The Elder may keep some members in the dark about his plan for that purpose," I speculated. "He is aware that you can see emo-tions."

Vadim's jaw muscles flexed. "He knows all about us, but he seems to be keeping secrets of his own." He slid his gaze along my face, the sharp focus in his eyes melting. "You have to sleep now, Jade. Get well and restore your strength."

"I'm worried, Vadim, for *you*."

He ran his fingers through my drying hair.

"Sleep, my treasure. I'll think about what you've told me, meanwhile."

Chapter 40

"READY?" VADIM PAUSED at the door to the conference room at the hotel in Vegas and squeezed my hand.

I needed this encouragement, no matter how slight. There must be at least two hundred Incubi behind that door, almost all of them new to me. Meeting them felt like being introduced to Vadim's family. These were his people, his tribe.

"Just give me a second." With a free hand I smoothed out the wrinkles on the skirt of my dress, wishing I'd had more than ten minutes in the airport bathroom to freshen up. Apparently, Andras had called the meeting when Vadim and I were still in the air, leaving me no time to get ready.

"It will be fine," Vadim whispered, leaning into me as I drew in a slow breath in an attempt to calm my nerves. "They'll love you."

He nuzzled the side of my face. A gentle dusting of frost prickled my skin, taking away the excessive stress.

"Thank you." I smiled. "That works better than a glass of wine."

"Let's go." He pushed the door open.

The Incubi sat around a number of tables arranged into a large square in the middle of the room. These must have been mostly the mated ones, as many seemed to be accompanied by a woman sitting at their side. I recognized Andras and Natasha.

More demons occupied the chairs that lined the four walls in several rows along the perimeter of the room. They must be the unmated ones, as I didn't spot any females among them.

Everyone rose from their seats as we approached the table and inclined their heads in greeting as we sat down.

Vadim's position was directly opposite from Andras. This way, between the two of them, the Grand Masters would be able to keep an eye on the entire room.

"This is my Jade," Vadim introduced me, simple and to the point.

The demons around us bowed their heads to me once again.

"We've heard what happened, Jade," Natasha said in Russian to me. "I am so happy to see you well."

"Thank you." I fought the urge to touch the bruise on my face. Still angry purple, I knew even the generous amount of makeup I had put on it at the airport wouldn't cover it completely. The side of my face still throbbed, making me feel like the bruise was even more obvious than it probably was.

Vadim's hand covered mine in my lap, grounding me. "You all have heard what Jade found out about the Priory."

"That bastard Keller—" started a blond Incubus at the table.

I had got used to Incubi being generally larger than humans. This one, however, seemed to be bigger than an average demon. His hair was braided on the sides in a few plaits, with the rest of it streaming down his shoulders in golden curls, which brought Vikings to my mind.

"Ivarr," Andras spoke patiently to the blond giant. "Raise your hand if you want to speak. There's too many of us here today."

With an eye roll, Ivarr raised his arm.

"My point is . . ." He dropped his hand to the table as soon as all attention was on him. "Why would we go by what that stinking excuse of a human being said? He was a murderer after all, an abuser, and an abductor. It would be fair to believe he was a liar, too."

"We can't ignore what he said," Vadim argued calmly.

"Agreed." Andras inclined his head. "If the threat is real, the consequences would be too great to disregard. Besides, Keller's claim is in line with Raim's warning about the Priory. In any case, a further investigation is needed."

"At least we have been given an advance notice," another Incubus at the table added. "And can prepare accordingly."

Others voiced their agreement, and Andras raised his arm, calming the sudden commotion threatening to roll through the room.

"I insist we all stay in Vegas for now since our show running here is the main source of nourishment for the unmated Incubi. Those performing will stay at the hotel. The rest of us will remain in the area. I want everyone to keep an eye on each other."

"The chances of another summoning shouldn't be too high," Vadim speculated. "It seemed to be Keller's pet project. There is no proof of it having been sanctioned by the Priory. If that is the case, then with the death of Keller and his conjurer, it should be the end of it."

"What if word leaks that we are getting ready for their attack?" Ivarr spoke again. "The Priory may decide to launch it sooner rather than wait until every one of us has been Forgiven."

"Could they?" I whispered, leaning Vadim's way.

However, he seemed to be deeply in thought, and didn't respond right away.

The petite woman sitting next to me muttered quietly, "Maybe I should call Delilah, to get a general idea about the mood in the Priory."

"Who is Delilah?" I couldn't hold back the question, although she wasn't addressing me, or anyone else, for that matter.

"She is a friend, sort of." She shot a glance at Ivarr, who turned his attention to her at hearing Delilah's name. "She helped me after I got off the Base." The woman stretched her hand to me. "I'm Kitty, by the way."

"Kitty Jones?" I gasped. "You escaped from Keller's people, didn't you?"

"I'm famous!" She exhaled a soft laugh, squeezing my hand. "Yep, that was me. And Delilah helped me get back to my life afterwards. She has a strong dislike of demons, though."

"Is she a Priory monk, too?"

"No. Her father used to be, before he passed away. The organization doesn't allow female members. Delilah only volunteers her help when needed."

"Still too close for my comfort," Ivarr added, his expression guarded.

"Well, I wouldn't tell her what is happening," Kitty assured him. "I'd just have a general conversation with her and hopefully she'd say something about the Priory herself."

"Any word on Raim's whereabouts?" Vadim asked, bringing all our attention back to the main discussion.

"He hasn't been in touch since he left." Andras shook his head.

"Have you tried to find him?"

"The last time I saw Raim, he didn't seem to *want* to be found. If that's the case, he will make it difficult for any search party to locate him now."

"Sytrius could track him," Ivarr said with a confident half-grin on his face. "Just give him some time."

"We may not have that much time, especially if the Priory decides not to wait until all of us are Forgiven." Vadim's frown deepened. "They may start hunting us one by one now, those who are mortal already. It is important we have a talk with Raim. I believe he knows something, and I want to know what that is. How feasible would an effort to find Raim be?"

"He has quite a few properties all over the world. We know the location of some, but there may be more," Andras replied.

"Would Raim even want to help you?" I ventured to ask. "Provided you find him?"

"He wasn't happy with demon-human relationships from the start," an Incubus with flaxen-blond hair spoke up.

A dark-skinned woman at his side who was obviously pregnant, said, "Garrett is right. Raim fiercely opposed the new agreement right up until he left. Even as he seemed to go along with the release of the women once ordered to by the Priory, Raim still tried to do everything he could to keep Incubi and humans separated."

"If he knew about the Priory's secret plans of exterminating us," Vadim replied, "his motivation for opposing the changes might have been valid if somewhat misguided."

"What motivation?" Ivarr scoffed. "Concern for the rest of us?"

"If Raim really had any concerns about anyone else but himself . . ." Kitty spoke, her delicate features set in an expression of aversion, "wouldn't he have shared whatever information he had with the rest of us? I mean if he really wanted to help in the first place, why did he run away?"

"He does not sound like someone who would help in any way," Natasha agreed in strongly accented English. "Looking for him may be a waste of time and resources."

"It's not a matter of Raim's personal feelings," Vadim argued. "At the end of the day, he is one of us. Regardless of what he has allowed himself to become over time, the urge to protect must still be deeply rooted in him, just like it is in the rest of us. If we get a chance to talk to him, I suggest we call on that natural instinct in him."

"I don't believe there is much of that instinct left, but I'd gladly volunteer to beat it back into him when we find him," Ivarr muttered under his breath, and Kitty placed her slender hand on his bulging bicep in a placating gesture.

"Well, Sytrius will not be able to leave for any missions for the next little while. He has a family, and he should stay with them," Vadim said. "But we'll have to send several teams to check on Raim's known properties on this continent, Europe and Africa. I don't know if he has any in Asia."

"He had a villa in the Middle East somewhere," one of the single Incubi in the chairs by the wall offered, then added when all attention turned to him, "Turkey, I believe. At least he still had it in the nineteenth century, not sure if he still does, though."

"Right." Vadim nodded. "I suggest we select Incubi from the former retrieval teams for the search party. They are used to travelling and more familiar with the modern world than the rest."

"Looks like this is going to take some time." Andras rubbed his forehead.

"Raim can't disappear completely. He'd have to be showing up in public from time to time to feed," someone said.

"Unless he has acquired his own Sources," Kitty suggested quietly.

The idea of some private dungeon full of captive women sent a chill up my back, making me shudder.

"I still believe searching for him would be a wasted effort," Ivarr said as if to himself, but Vadim heard him.

He inhaled deeply before replying, "Well, for better or for worse, Raim has spent most of his existence looking after our interests. I hope he wouldn't wish us harm now."

"*Our* interests?" Ivarr glared at him. "Didn't the reason he held on to the position of Grand Master for this long have more to do with his insatiable hunger for power than with his desire to serve his kind?"

"Maybe." Vadim's tone remained even. "We could speculate all we want, but the only way to get a clear answer on Raim's motivation would be to ask him directly."

AFTER THE MEETING WAS over, the hotel staff brought in platters and drinks. With a brief apology, Vadim walked over to Andras. Pouring myself a glass of orange juice, I got up to stretch my legs.

Aside from the two couples I'd met, I hardly knew anyone here.

Zayne wasn't arriving in Vegas until the next day. He had been granted a one-day extension of his departure from Minsk, to sort things out with Tanya. As far as I knew, they had their movie date on Saturday, but there was a disagreement after that. Vadim got a message from Zayne after we had landed at the airport that he was coming to Vegas with Tanya and Sveta. It seemed they had been able to work things out between themselves.

I followed Vadim with my gaze as he moved through the room. Ivarr joined his conversation with Andras, all three gesturing energetically as the discussion seemed to teeter on the edge of an argument now.

"Ivarr is as passionate in life as he is in love," Kitty's voice sounded next to me, diverting my attention from my man to her.

"They all are." I smiled. "Aren't they?"

"True." Her warm expression grew pensive. "I'm really happy to see you here, Jade. The moment we got the news about you being taken . . . I couldn't rest until Zayne let us know you were okay."

"Thank you. I didn't know everyone knew about me."

"Of course we did. The Incubi world is rather small. What happens in the life of one of them often affects the existence of the rest. It may not look that way on the surface, but their relationships have been forged for centuries and are often indestructible." She leaned in closer. "I had no idea why Keller took me that day until Vadim's full report about what happened to you came in, including the plans Keller had for me. That explained a lot, but also made me realise that if I hadn't escaped that day, I might have been held captive in Kazakhstan all this time, too." She shuddered, rubbing her upper arms with her hands. "I'm so sorry you had to go through that."

"It could have been worse." I exhaled a long, heavy breath. Despite the horrors of those two days, I knew that the evil that man was capable of was much bigger. "I'm just glad it's ended."

"You are very brave." She nodded, gazing at me with awe and admiration, which made me smile again. "And smart."

"Come on." I slightly nudged her with my elbow. "Smart would've been to find a way to escape much sooner, like you did."

A young woman with a stylish chestnut bob approached us from the side.

"Oh." Kitty spun her way then back to me again. "This is Pat, my best friend. Jade." She gestured at me.

"Nice to meet you." I shook Pat's hand. "Are you . . . with someone, too?" Despite a certain number of unmated Incubi, I understood all women present were demons' partners.

Her chest rose with a sigh, and she quickly nodded.

"Pat is seeing Zander," Kitty answered for her, pointing at a pale, dark-haired Incubus who was talking to a small group of Incubi several feet away from us.

"*Seeing*? We've had two dates. Two!" Pat shook her head, biting her lip. "And now . . . all this mess . . ." Her voice broke, eyes glistening. "I haven't even had a chance to really get to know him. And now I'm afraid of having any feelings for him at all. But I can't stop liking him . . . A lot." She blinked rapidly, taking another deep breath. "What if something happens to him because of me and my feelings for him? This is so unfair . . . and . . ." She waved her hand in front of her face, struggling to compose herself.

As if sensing her distress, Zander, excused himself from his group and moved our way.

Kitty wrapped her arm around her friend's waist. "Pat, sweetie, nothing is going to happen to Zander or any of them. We will deal with whatever comes our way. All of us."

"I'm so sorry." Pat pressed both hands to her chest. "I didn't mean to get this upset."

"Patricia." Zander was at her side in an instant, a concerned expression on his face. "We should leave." He turned to Kitty. "I'll take her upstairs to my room to rest and will call for any updates later." He inclined his head my way. "Jade, I'm sorry I didn't introduce myself. Zander."

I shook his hand. "Nice to meet you."

"I'm so sorry," Pat repeated, leaning into him. "Jade, I hope to see you again," she said as Zander led her away and out of the room.

"Pat is visiting from Seattle," Kitty explained. "This is her second time here. She usually meets Zander in her dreams when they're apart."

"It must be hard." I meant the visiting in the dreams part. Vadim did it to me on the plane, during our flight here. I had a dream I was surfing, and he wanted to *see* what it was like. Personally, though, I preferred the reality of having him near, body and soul. The haze of dreams, no matter how vivid, seemed like a poor substitute.

"It's hard on all of us." Kitty misunderstood me, obviously referring to the current situation and the threat to the Incubi. "If there is anyone who can deal with danger, though, it would be our Incubi, wouldn't it?"

I nodded, loving the fierce optimism of this tiny woman.

"We're having a dinner at our place tomorrow night," she continued. "Pat is staying with us while she is visiting. Well, unless she is with Zander, of course. Andras and Natasha are coming, too. Sytrius and Alyssa . . . Oh, you have to meet their new baby. He is so adorable!" All worries melted from her face. "Little Nixi!"

"Nixi?" I smiled.

"Yes, his parents have shortened Phoenix to Nix, but he is too cute and cuddly even for that. Definitely Nixi. The very first cambion—human-Incubi baby. We all had been so worried about how he'd turn out, but he is simply precious. You'll see. Please come for dinner. Unless you need some time to settle in first?"

"Oh, it doesn't take me long to settle into a new place. I'll talk to Vadim, but I would love to come over."

"Great! We live, literally, just around the corner of where they've rented a house for you."

"Thank you. We'll see you then."

Just like that, I felt I'd become part of this wonderfully unique group of demons and people.

EPILOGUE

VADIM

"Wait for me." He stopped Jade from entering the rented house.

All the lights were off inside, but the two outdoor sconces at the entrance under the porch were on, allowing her to see well enough to unlock the front door.

"Isn't it a human tradition for the man to carry his woman into their first home?" He lifted her into his arms, not giving her a chance to answer.

She gasped then relaxed into him with a soft giggle. "That's for married couples, silly."

"We are more than married, my precious Jade." He kicked the door open then shoved at it with his elbow to close it after entering. "You're mine now, for eternity, which is a really long time, I'll have you know."

She giggled again—the sound peppered his skin with ripples of pleasure.

"This house seems way too big for just the two of us," she observed as he flicked the lights on in the foyer.

"Should we search for something smaller?" He marched into the living room, still carrying her.

"No, of course not. No point in wasting time and effort for that. Hopefully, this is all temporary anyway."

He knew she still harboured hope she'd go to her job in Moscow. Jade never mentioned it, but he saw the wistfulness when she talked about her work, and he hated the fact she had to give it up because the situation didn't allow them to move to Moscow at the moment.

"Wait here." He carefully placed her in one of the chairs around the large table in the dining area. "I'll get your dinner."

He went back to the porch to fetch their suitcases and the plastic bag with the restaurant take-out for Jade. That was all they had the time for after the meeting. Tomorrow he would make her a proper meal.

"We didn't get any sparkling water for you, baby," Jade lamented as he took the food from the plastic containers and arranged it on the plates for her—fish, salad, tiramisu for dessert.

"I'm not thirsty."

"I know you aren't. But that's not why you drink it." She shifted in her chair, closer to the table, and picked up a fork. "I'll make sure to get some for you when I go shopping tomorrow morning."

Although the house came fully furnished, they would still need to pick up some things for it. Cleaning supplies. More food for Jade. Sparkling water for him, apparently.

"You know," she bit into a slice of cucumber from her salad, "I haven't even seen the rest of the house yet, but it already feels like home."

"It does?" he asked, sitting down next to her, a glass of tap water in his hand.

He'd learned that people felt less uncomfortable when others at the table with them had something to occupy their hands and mouths, too. And he wanted Jade to be as comfortable as possible right now, despite the long journey and stress of the day.

"Yes. And you know why?" She put her fork down.

He didn't know the exact answer to her question, but he guessed it had something to do with that warm multi-coloured glow taking over all of her emotions whenever she gazed at him like that. Shimmering bright with all the colours of the rainbow, it ebbed and flowed, filling her whole.

"Because you're here, with me." She smiled at him. "I've travelled most of my life. Lived in an insane amount of houses, rooms, and apartments. Never minded any of them, but never felt any particular attachment to one, either." She reached for his hand, and he took hers—no gloves on either of them. "You are my home, Vadim, the only one I truly want."

That light that shone in her eyes—he could never have enough of it. He loved her tenacity, her zest for life, her resilience. The way she knew what she wanted and how she went for it, unapologetic for her desires.

He loved *her*.

Unable to comprehend the enormity of this feeling rolling over him in a swell that threatened to sweep him up whole, he reached for her, needing her close.

"I swear I'll feed you dinner tonight," he growled, hauling her into his lap. "Right after I kiss every single inch of you." He pressed his lips to her hair, her face, to the fragrant, delicate skin of her neck, taking in her scent, her warmth, the light of her love for him. "Jade. My treasure. My love."

The Cursed

Demons, book 4

"The Council is yours, Stolas." Raim rose from his seat in the meeting room. The old armchair groaned as if relieved to be free from his weight.

Raim was well aware that the demon had been using the human name Andras for several centuries now. However, he never addressed any Incubus by a human name. Ever. Lest they forget who they were and where they came from. And he was not about to make an exception for Stolas either.

"Lead it wisely," he added, not hiding a sarcastic smile.

He had no doubts Stolas would be selected as the new Grand Master. However, as intelligent and even inventive as the Incubus had proven to be in the past several months, Raim doubted he had the necessary ruthlessness and ingenuity to balance Incubi's interests with the Priory's demands.

For a moment there, Raim considered telling Stolas about the sarcophagus, the only *soros* stone urn that survived the journey to this world intact and was in possession of the Priory for the past six hundred years. Then decided against it.

The Elder would no doubt let the new Grand Master of the Western Council know about the source of human power over the Incubi the moment the demons tried to disobey any of the Priory's demands. So far, though, Stolas and The Elder seemed to get along splendidly.

A sting of resentment pierced through Raim. The Priory went against all *his* efforts to halt the integration of Incubi into the human society. Still, the centuries-old habit of looking after this ungrateful bunch of demons was hard to beat.

"Beware of the Priory," Raim couldn't hold back the warning before exiting the room. "They are the ones with the real power."

Not that it really mattered anymore. Nothing did. Incubi had doomed themselves the moment Sytry broke the rule of silence and spoke to that Source last year.

"Where are you going?" Stolas called behind him.

Raim didn't dignify him with an answer. Wasn't it enough that he was leaving the place he ruled most of his life on earth? Giving up everything he had built and failed to preserve?

Stolas can have it all. Raim owed him nothing more.

The white silk of his robe streamed in the air behind him as he swiftly walked along the corridor then up the stairs. Out of habit, he turned right at the top of the stairs, but stopped after taking just a couple of steps. There was nothing he needed from his room, not a thing he would miss if left behind.

Resolutely, he spun on his heels and headed to the exit instead.

The door at the Base had not been guarded for months now, and he walked out without having to say a word to anyone else.

Crossing the property towards a number of vehicles parked by the wall, he yanked free the jewelled clasp that held his robe closed at his shoulder and tossed it in the snow. The wind caught the silk, his robe flew open, and he let it slide off his shoulders and flatter to the ground, without slowing his pace.

Left dressed only in a pair of black pants now and a thin white tunic, Raim immediately felt the biting winter chill through just one layer of silk. The sensation felt invigorating as he climbed behind the wheel of a truck.

Fishing the keys out of the glove compartment, he started the engine and drove off the property where he had spent most of his time during the past several centuries.

Long ago, he had split the Incubi council into Western and Eastern and moved half of the Incubi here with him. Part of the reason for the move, possibly the only reason at all, was the desperate, stubborn hope that pushed him to search for her—the woman who didn't want to be found. That search ended two hundred years ago. Yet, he had remained on this continent.

His phone rang, and he yanked it out of his pant pocket. Without glancing on the screen to see who was calling, he rolled down the window and tossed the phone into the snowbank on the side of the road.

The Incubi had doomed themselves, rushing out there like a pack of eager puppies, wagging their tails, to claim the first female who would let them come close enough. Once tasted, the sweet energy of a human female was impossible to resist for his kind. It took over a demon's mind and soul like poison, eventually destroying them both.

He didn't need to stay and watch, as the Incubi whom he had tried so hard to protect would learn the true nature of a female heart. And they would fall, the way he had fallen.

Driving along the snowy road, Raim rubbed his forehead, wincing at the painful memories that tortured him every hour of every century. Yet, completely addicted to this poison, he made sure to feed consistently to remember everything.

"God did not curse me to endure the centuries of torment, Olyena. *You* did."

Want More Demons?

DOWNLOAD A FREE SHORT story, Zayne and Tanya, by subscribing to my newsletter, for news, updates, giveaways, and ARC of new releases.

http://bookhip.com/LJFDFS

If you already are a subscriber, keep an eye on my emails for this story, which is exclusive to my newsletter.

More by Marina Simcoe

Demons Series
Demon Mine
The Forgotten
Grand Master
The Cursed – 2020
The Last Unforgiven – 2020

Standalones Set in Demons Universe
The Real Thing
To Love A Monster

Science-Fiction Romance
Enduring (Valos of Sonhadra)
Experiment – 2019

About the Author

MARINA SIMCOE LIKES to write love stories with characters, who may or may not be entirely human, because she firmly believes that our contemporary world could always use a little bit of the extraordinary.

She has lots of fun exploring how her out-of-this-world characters with their own beliefs, values, and aspirations fit into our everyday life.

She lives in Canada with her very own sexy demon, their three little angels and a cat, who might be The Lucifer himself.

For more illustrations of all of her books please visit Marina Simcoe Author page on Facebook or www.marinasimcoe.com.

Please Stay in Touch

Newsletter signup
http://eepurl.com/c__RGn
Readers' Group
Marina's Reading Cave
www.facebook.com/groups/621598474945014/
www.instagram.com/marinasimcoeauthor
www.marinasimcoe.com
www.facebook.com/MarinaSimcoeAuthor/
www.amazon.com/author/marinasimcoe
www.bookbub.com/profile/marina-simcoe
www.goodreads.com/MarinaSimcoe

www.ingramcontent.com/pod-product-compliance
Lightning Source LLC
Chambersburg PA
CBHW021304190726
48288CB00003B/676